MW00860954

This Is a Love Story

ALSO BY JESSICA SOFFER

Tomorrow There Will Be Apricots

This Is a
Love Story

A NOVEL

Jessica Soffer

DUTTON

DUTTON

An imprint of Penguin Random House LLC
1745 Broadway, New York, NY 10019
penguinrandomhouse.com

Copyright © 2025 by Jessica Soffer
Penguin Random House values and supports copyright. Copyright fuels creativity,
encourages diverse voices, promotes free speech, and creates a vibrant culture.
Thank you for buying an authorized edition of this book and for complying with
copyright laws by not reproducing, scanning, or distributing any part of it in
any form without permission. You are supporting writers and allowing
Penguin Random House to continue to publish books for every reader.
Please note that no part of this book may be used or reproduced in any manner
for the purpose of training artificial intelligence technologies or systems.

DUTTON and the D colophon are registered trademarks of
Penguin Random House LLC.

LIBRARY OF CONGRESS CATALOGING-IN-PUBLICATION DATA

Names: Soffer, Jessica, author.
Title: This is a love story: a novel / Jessica Soffer.
Description: New York: Dutton, 2025.
Identifiers: LCCN 2024005223 (print) | LCCN 2024005224 (ebook) |
ISBN 9780593851265 (hardcover) | ISBN 9780593851272 (epub)
Subjects: LCSH: New York (N.Y.)—Fiction. | LCGFT: Romance fiction.
Classification: LCC PS3619.O37975 T45 2025 (print) | LCC PS3619.O37975
(ebook) | DDC 813/.6—dc23/eng/20240618
LC record available at https://lccn.loc.gov/2024005223
LC ebook record available at https://lccn.loc.gov/2024005224

International edition ISBN: 9798217046317

Printed in the United States of America
1st Printing

BOOK DESIGN BY PATRICE SHERIDAN

This is a work of fiction. Names, characters, places, and incidents either are the product of
the author's imagination or are used fictitiously, and any resemblance to actual persons,
living or dead, businesses, companies, events, or locales is entirely coincidental.

The authorized representative in the EU for product safety and compliance is
Penguin Random House Ireland, Morrison Chambers, 32 Nassau Street,
Dublin D02 YH68, Ireland. https://eu-contact.penguin.ie

For Alex, Ula, and Scout.
The greatest love stories of my life are ours.

1

CENTRAL PARK

Some people come to the Park because they want to fall in love for the first time, the twelfth time, the final time. Some have been used, widowed, or bored stiff. They have spent the past decade in deep introspection, falling in love with themselves—and no one else—first. Some come for a short respite—roughly twenty blocks west to east, east to west—from a spouse who will not help themselves or from no one home (she even took the dog; you can't imagine the sudden quiet). The Park is a beating heart, an adagio, a dreamy parenthesis.

Abe and Jane come after chemo and because they never know when it might be the last time. There are six bottles of pills, two notarized wills, and a nebulizer in a tote between them. Jane can walk only a few steps without needing to rest, but you couldn't tell that from the serene composure on her face. The Park is where the most important moments of their lives have taken place. The Park is their home away, homing device, pen pal, fifth season.

In the Park, romance is alive and well. Among the tulips, fritillaries, and anemones, juniors from Bronx Science make promises across the Whisper Bench—I want to exist in the same quantum state as you. An optometrist who has been married five times finds love again at the Rumi Festival in Shakespeare Garden. It feels like 20/10 eyesight. On Tuesday evenings from May to October, in Sheep Meadow, a small group gathers for Sensual Yoga (unauthorized; who's going to stop them?). They move their bodies in ways that make them weep or giddy or ashamed. At SummerStage, Bon Iver a capellas "Blood Bank." The Public Theater produces *Romeo and Juliet* for the sixty-second year. Everyone sweats. The cardiac surgeon writes a love letter to her husband on the same bench near the Center Fountain every Friday. She is in green scrubs and clogs. She couldn't save him, but in her letters, she imagines that she can and that they have shrimp lo mein on the couch again. Watching the kids push their model boats at Conservatory Water, the entertainment lawyer offers to try one more round because her husband wants nothing more than a gaggle of kids and she cannot bring herself to tell him the truth. Perhaps it's the body, she thinks, as referee. A group of divorcés—one a matchmaker with an acclaimed series on HBO, he signed an NDA, no one can know but this crew—gets their grooves back rollerblading at DiscOasis. Old love—we've been together since Eisenhower—recalls their vows, word for word, at the Inscope Arch. I promise to love you and your stamps forever. Margaux and Marc kiss every year for twenty-one years on the vernal equinox at Belvedere Castle. They have dedicated their lives to art and beauty. Belvedere meaning *good view.* Oh, the blooms. The housepainter, so far from home, watching for a sign in the clear blue sky on his twenty-fifth anniversary, forgets the heartache of time and distance for the brief moment that two red-tailed hawks glide by, dip, and land across from Trefoil Arch no more than ten feet away from him.

Every year, there are nearly 250 weddings at the Loeb Boathouse. There are nineteen other suggested venues on CentralParkWeddingLocations.com within the Park's 843 acres. There are hundreds of marriage proposals on Bow Bridge every year—we found each other on Facebook; we met last week; we have three kids and two dogs and a whole lot of chickens together. Most take place between Thanksgiving and Christmas, but there is an upward tick around Valentine's Day too. There are thousands of engagement shoots, mostly in June and October because, arguably, those are the Park's most standout times. The machinist wears all white. The personal assistant has been juicing for a week. In the Park, there is handholding, making out, blushing, the sharing of ham and cheese sandwiches, iced teas, double chocolate chip cookies, blazers, gloves, tissues, and headphones playing Billie Holiday. There is a lot of so-called quality time. There are at least a dozen domestic disputes reported to the Park precinct a week. Oh yes, sir, I really did want to wring his neck.

Some people come to the Park when the red-eared sliders are mating or when they're the best man at the *Swan Lake*–themed nuptials at Wollman and hoping the bride's aunt will be flying solo. They come to carve names into a tree—Lucy loves AF, Stella + Sass. They come to honor the one they will always love, especially on October 17 when it's as if the leaves are singing HALLELUJAH AMEN and they can throw them in the air and feel them on their body like whispers. They come for Jewish speed dating with their best friend and kiss the friend on the mouth on the way home just to see. No dice. LOL! They come by the busload in white sneakers on a Romancing the Apple tour. Some people come to train for marathons: they are running away from their problems; they are racing for their wife's cure. They come to learn holotropic breath-work in the Hallett Sanctuary as an antidote to trauma. It is my last resort. They come because there are long-stemmed red roses grow-ing in a location that won't be disclosed here. They have never been snipped. What kind of monster?

The assistant producer comes to the Park before filming. She is in the gray spandex she bought with the guy on the six-mile loop in mind. She wonders about his name: Brad, Jake? Or maybe he's Aus-tralian? Luke? Martha and Marilyn come after work; it is the only time they have to themselves before the kids demand a different dinner, no bath, twelve stories, told in corresponding voices, a lot of songs. I fucking hate Raffi! A feng shui consultant comes from West Virginia once, in the spring, to meet an old lover. He never shows. He shows; what a disappointment. Stephen and Mitch walk to and from work every day at eight and six, holding hands, plan-ning dinner. Caraway salmon with rye berry and beet salad. Elaine and Jack come with their two old Labs because their therapist said it was a good idea. It was! It was not! The sanitation worker comes to work; but he also comes for the gray catbirds' love songs, particularly in the morning in April near Shuman Track. They remind him of his first ex-wife, who sang in the shower first thing. Leena, the new vegan—she promised him she'd try—comes because there is no one waiting at home anymore. Some people come because, at home, the yelling has gotten worse. Some because, at home, they don't touch; they haven't in years. Some because the touching has become too much.

Some come only when the sun is out. Some come only in the dark.

For those who feel it, there is nothing like the warm embrace of the Park. North of the Lilac Walk, they're playing Chaka Khan, wearing short shorts, and grinding. Outside the Swedish Cottage, carnations are sold by the stem. See the nuzzling rollerbladers on Center Drive, the kids in nursery school at the Hans Christian Andersen statue, kissing each other's chins. There is a Oaxacan woman by the Mall who sells mangoes with chile and limon, cut into hearts, singing "Espérame en el Cielo" like she means it. The *Ancestor* sculpture at the Park's Fifth Avenue and Sixtieth Street entrance represents fertility and the masculine and feminine at once (though the sculptor's husband has faced allegations of sexual misconduct). There are Roy and Silo, the gay penguins at the zoo who attempted to mate for half a decade before giving up. It can be said: there is no greater ecstasy than reaching the pinnacle of Cat Hill on bike. No purer pleasure than holding hands, watching the ducks flap flap flap. Even as raging wars, another mass shooting, Me Too, hostages, hateful graffiti, youth cyberbullying give us no reason to

have faith in passion, the brown-belted bumbles are rapturous, pol-
linating beardtongue and American wild columbine. For some, the
Park's branches are arms stretched up and out, abating hate. It is
possible to see them as that. Perhaps, for some, to love the Park
makes seeing them as that essential.

2

ABE

Some days, you want to tell me everything that you remember.

You remember when we met. Tavern on the Green, July 1967. You were waitressing to pay for books at Cooper Union. I had just graduated from Wharton and was taking my father's clients to lunch. It was my era of "at least it'll make a good short story." They were Italian milliners on their first trip to America. It would.

You remember my pants were too short, my jacket was too big, but there was a leather notebook in my lap that heartened you immediately. You remember that every once in a while, I would jot down some words, urgently, furiously, as if they were house keys on the shore, at risk of being whisked out.

You remember when you brought us Bloody Marys and deviled eggs, I gestured to the blue paint on the latent part of your wrist and said, I bet you're very good. You remember recognition like a night-light. I remember I missed every word of that lunch. Sometimes, I think, the stories write themselves.

You remember mid-meal I found you—rushed, red wine down your front—by the kitchen and said, Excuse me. I had sweet eyes, you say. Like a horse by a fence.

You remember that I didn't speak. Instead, I reached for your hand and squeezed it. It was as if I was telling you something about safety, you say. Until then, you hadn't realized you'd felt unsafe.

Or something like that, you say. You can change the wording later.

You sit up taller in bed as if the remembering is an IV of something. Life or life twice.

Sure, I say. I nod. I do not tell you the truth: I haven't written in three years. It is not for lack of effort but focus, stamina, drive. I've been with you at all of your appointments. I go to the supermarket, pharmacy, acupuncturist in Springs. Sometimes, I come home, stare at the windshield, unable to mobilize my legs. I don't want to come in and you're not painting, clicking on a lamp for reading, making blueberry crumb pies in my wool socks.

Still, today is a good day. Your eyes are clear as a temple. The red asterisk of your mouth is far from slack. Your voice is whole as a bell. I can do better. Your voice is a match, lit.

I write that down.

Do you remember those awful shoes they made us wear at Tavern on the Green? you say. And the hats? It really was misogyny, wasn't it?

You shake your head but now you are smiling. When you are like this, it feels like hitching my wagon to your horse. I want to follow you raspberry picking, listen to you contemplate fish and sun and shadows in oil on driftwood. I try to attribute the clarity to something specific: a change in medication, sugar, sleep, the moon. I cannot.

I remember, from the day I met you, you lit up a room, put everyone at ease. I remember how you crouched down with the Italian guests so that when you repeated yourself—che cosa? che cosa? they kept saying—you could tell them the specials as though they were a secret gift.

I remember that whenever I saw you, it seemed, somehow, as if you'd just been swimming. I remember the plant life of your eyes, you smelled like spring, moved like a bird, but you were steadier and lighter than the rest of us. That has remained true, decades and decades later. I remember the gap between your teeth, the dimple under your nose, how your hair was lighter around your face. It might be overkill to call it a halo, a frame, an immutable, immaculate light. I remember I wanted to do everything over again when you were around—be bolder but also more still.

You remember falling leaves in Central Park, and as we walked, radio somewhere, gray clouds like ribbons in wind. I'd never noticed till you. I remember your back ten steps ahead of me. You were looking for acorns, rocks. You were planning to make sculptures with wax. I remember your deer bones, the way your steps were intentional, as if you were composing a song with your feet. What was that scent you wore? What happened to that polka-dot dress?

You remember sometimes, we'd stand under lamplight near Bank Rock Bridge or the Obelisk or we'd take the M7—down and then up—just to ride. You remember my hand on your knee, your hand on mine. You remember the Chinese restaurant that was next to a cleaner's, and on the other side, a church where we read each other's fortunes, though you don't remember any exactly. You remember the smell of soy sauce and old tea, white napkins knotted into swans, sauce always getting on my shirt.

I remember sitting across the table from you, how I felt flattered just being with you. I remember how people always gazed at you not just because of your beauty but because of the way you were quiet both before you spoke and after—and also because of what you said. I remember how light always found your cheekbones, butterflies flocked to your hair.

You remember, in the beginning, we walked everywhere together: the Park's Outer Loop, Upper Loop, from Columbus Circle to Harlem mostly parallel to Central Park West. You remember listening to the saxophonist under the trees, pignoli cookies from Ferrara, counting convertibles on Fifth. You remember pistachio ice cream and espressos, a black cat in a tree and a fire truck, a man who only walked backward—to and fro, singing Bob Marley, on the Seventy-Second Street Transverse. You remember I kept my hand on your back as if you were a stray egg—and that we never stopped talking, laughing, telling each other everything.

What exactly? you say.

When we met, you'd been seeing a Turk who wore turtlenecks, had lived at an ashram, collected art. Yours. You remember yoga in a temple, discovering the sutras, how you spoke them to yourself when you almost got mugged in the Park. You remember getting mugged, not in the Park. You remember even now: yama, niyama, asana, pranayama, pratyahara, dharana, dhyana, samadhi. You remember the painting wasn't going well. Your father kept calling and asking if you'd finally come to your senses yet. Yet?

I remember our first picnic in Central Park, somewhere north of Sheep Meadow. I remember we ate tuna sandwiches, dill pickles, Linzer tortes with raspberry jam. I remember you packed extra and gave it to two men with no shoes and a shopping cart filled with cans. I remember we lay on a blanket, our sweaters rolled up under our heads, and watched the sky. I remember how you made time expand.

I remember you turned to me and said, Isn't this something? Just being here? It is, I said. I remember, with you, the reel stopped running. Like: I am. You are. This is enough. Please stay.

You remember we were at the Sixty-Fifth Street entrance or by the carousel. You were peeling an orange or purple grapes with your teeth. You were in a green dress with long sleeves or short denim with rips, paint on your ankles. You remember it was your phase of flowers and bugs, mostly pastels. You could draw anything: a bird, a plane, the United States. You were learning hue, spheres, and hatching. You were so focused. I was in awe.

You remember I was writing short stories about a Mafia family in New Jersey. What did I think I was doing? I say. We both laugh.

You remember, in the beginning, how much we talked about art. How it felt. Wild in the head, calm in the body. Like having just sneezed or just yawned. I remember that before you, I'd never called it art to anyone. I admitted to loving it to you before anyone else. And though it was different for me, especially then—I had never imagined writing full time, it was a cherished hobby, a tic even—I knew that feeling of protection, satiety, you spoke of. It made me feel seen. You did.

I remember you'd ask me if I could see that blue bud, sparkle on pavement, schools of fish and coral in the clouds. (No.) I remember you imagined art out of everything: straws, water, mints. We'd sit on a bench and even if you didn't have paper, you'd make a crown out of twigs, twist leaves into perfect figurines. I remember you narrow-eyed, tight-jawed, always composing something in your mind.

You remember, from that time, nightmares, night sweats, waking up, calling out. You remember dreaming about your mother, the urge to show her a painted stone, city lights, a burn on your forearm from hot glue. When you woke, the longing for her was something physical. You lost her when you were twelve. Every day, you wore the gold bangles she had hidden on her upper arms when she came to Ellis Island from Baghdad. Your father was a geography professor but always getting lost. They met at a country club when your mother had just arrived. She cleaned the club kitchen at night. Ten months after she died, your father remarried a Croatian woman with parrot-colored hair and you went to boarding school. He couldn't be alone and you couldn't be alone with him. From then on, you took care of yourself.

3

You remember falling asleep in the studio, black paint under your nails, charcoal on your socks, your thumbs so dry they were like frost and cracking, the growl of the trucks, dirty East Fifth Street, men lined up outside the church. You remember pigeons that ate cigarettes, clapping for rats, purple light at dawn, and how it was the only time when you could hear the birds. You remember sitting in empty churches to watercolor. Something about the light in there, vastness, drama, the hollowness of sound. You remember you were smoking too much. The Turk was volatile. You remember being afraid a lot.

There are white pillows behind your back like graceless wings. On the little table next to your bed, a ginger tea bag, used tissues, lavender oil, a blurry photo Max took of a bench in Central Park—empty, in the pouring rain—in a wooden frame. There are unopened cards from Rio, Seattle, and Old Lyme from friends who are well and worried. Some artists, some from your book club, some wives of my friends. They adore you. Who doesn't? I keep meaning to read them to you. It is something, I think, how everyone believes they're your favorite. It has something to do with your attention to detail. Just being with you feels like being chosen, winning a prize.

I find your hand beneath the blankets. I want to say something about your fingers in mine as a chronicler of time, but it feels like committing you to something that I won't.

I remember, from that time, seeing other women—my mother was always setting me up with her hairdresser's daughter; she didn't know you yet—but really, truly, only that none of them was ever you. I remember going to you like there was a strong wind at my back. I remember the first time we slept together, you moved my face toward yours like it was a reading light and said, Here. I remember that whenever I left you it felt as if I'd moved away from a fire.

There must be a more subtle way to relay urgency. There must be a better word than love.

You remember that every time we were together, you talked more, breathed deeper, felt like your feet were wrapped in warm towels and held. There could be another metaphor here, you say. For protection, for coming back home when there was no home to begin with.

Or: it felt like putting a spoon into an old cup of coffee and stirring around and around?

I remember, in the beginning, writing poems about you and not sharing them. You were a moth, a petal, a sheet on a clothesline, a stack of old letters in the wind. You were everything, but how to say that? I remember, eventually, sharing them because you said, How else do we get better?

I remember how kind you were, but also how honest. I read like a fiend but had never studied craft. I was meant to work for my father. Textiles, like his father. And his. I remember, before you, not so much a feeling of destiny as of fate. And because my father believed that the best thing he could give us was stability, and because between my brother and me, I was better at numbers, and more reliable . . .

Oh, Abe, you say. That was such a tricky time for you. You didn't trust yourself.

I remember some days, we'd meet at the Ramble shelter in the Park and you'd watercolor; I'd write. I remember the first short story I was ever proud of I wrote as we were perched on a rock. You were making paper-clip flowers, our thighs touching, the sky flamingo pink, reflecting on the silver of my pen.

I remember that one, you say. It was about chess and a night mouse, wasn't it?

It was.

I remember that sometimes, I wouldn't hear from you for days. When I'd buzz your apartment, you'd come down, squinting, white paint in your hair and on your neck, hungry, thirsty, late for your shift. I was working, you'd say. I lost track of time.

In the beginning, it is not that I wrote for you but I had no idea how to make writing a life. Because of you, I found that the more I wrote, the more I wrote. And because a story runs on hope in the beginning, until it grows legs . . . and then it runs on those.

You cough. I lurch. The doctors say the coughing is a good thing: an expulsion. I try to think of it as a sign of life.

You put your hand to where your hair would be. You rub your elbow, squint your eyes, as though you are wishing for something or wishing something away. Me too. Sometimes, it's as if you're blurred. Or maybe: underwater. You move as if in slow motion to rub your nose. It's the medicine. It's everything.

You reach for your legs. They ache in the evenings.

Shall I shut the windows? I say. Turn on a light?

You shake your head. Outside, there is a salt breeze that we dreamed about affording since my first book sold and the Roman collector with a glass eye purchased the giant steel sunflower you welded on our fire escape. In those days, we never would have imagined dying here. When we moved, this place felt like more life.

Do you want to keep on? I say. You nod, close your eyes.

You remember the first time you invited me up. You hadn't noticed how bad it had gotten till I was there: the unpaid bills, laundry, anti-war sign so big that you couldn't see out your window. You remember I took your laundry to my mother's and your bills and paid them. You remember I opened the window, put the sign on the street.

You remember I brought you matzo ball soup and a silver ashtray. You remember tulips in the Park, pennies at Bethesda. You remember getting yelled at for feeding apples to the horses on Seventy-Ninth and how we did it anyway and then raced down Fifth. You remember the time we got caught, no pants, by a policeman not far from Bow Bridge. We were sure no one was around. You remember tiramisu and the opera. Creativity begets creativity is something you liked to say. Which opera was it? We can't remember.

You remember when you showed me what you'd been working on, it turned out my favorite painting was also yours. Yellow shoes were in it but that's all you remember. It was so long ago now. You sold it to a man who lived in Canada. I remember he was in gas.

4

You remember meeting my family. You remember feeling, because of them, that it was as if I'd been taking a vitamin since birth that you never knew existed. As if you were deficient in something that I got.

You remember our first Hanukkah—challah, kugel, brisket, sufganiyot. You remember my brother, David. How the good thing about being an outsider is you can spot another outsider from a mile away. You sat together at every brunch, every dinner, every nosh from then until now. We used to call you two Javid Dane.

You remember my father, showing up late, kind but kind of evacuated, reading in the living room as everyone gathered in the kitchen and helped. You remember making eyes at me: that that wouldn't be me. Until then, I hadn't ever placed fault. It wouldn't, I said with my eyes. You were a beacon, a gut check, a litmus test, even then.

You remember how my mother always kept a hand on yours. You remember the first gift she gave you: a blue cashmere shawl. It was so delicate, so mighty. Every woman needs one, she'd said. How could you be anything but grateful? You wore it thin.

And though fussing isn't the same as mothering and no mother could make you miss your own mother less . . .

You remember sandwiches on stoops with David. He was living downtown then too. You went on walks when everyone else was sleeping, played pranks on each other, exchanged rare art books you'd found used.

When was it exactly that he told you he was gay? It was well before he told any of us, certainly. In retrospect, it makes perfect sense.

You close your eyes. You ask me for your rose water. It reminds you of your mother, whose own mother used it on her. I mist your face. Some days, you sweat only on your upper lip, cold everywhere else. They say it's normal. I've stopped asking what's normal, what's not.

I look around. There is a series of your petite watercolors, six, on the wall, gray, blue, violet. Maybe sea, maybe sky. On the shelves: my books, translated into dozens of languages.

Art built this house, I think. Art and your vim.

You remember we were walking by the Ladies Pavilion in the Park when you said that you could not be with someone who would not put their art first.

And I knew then: I would do it—not for you but because of you. Because you, despite everything you'd been through, were the wisest person I'd ever met.

You gave me one year.

For you, art was simple. A one-to-one. For me, there were more variables. I'm not equating loss to freedom, believe me. I know what you'd been through. I am not making excuses either. What I am trying to say is that it was a different time. Is it inane to say that I wanted to please my parents? Is it macho to say that I wanted to take care of you? I'd always felt: I'd write when I could.

You shiver. I cover your legs with a blanket. You made it. You made them all. I sometimes wonder how you knew so much even then. You learned everything from your mother in such a short time. She was one of eleven. Her name, Lulu, meant *pearl* in Arabic.

I long to meet her even now. But it's more than that: I long to give her to you.

You close your eyes. Soon, the room pulls taut with quiet. I put my hand on your chest. I'm not checking so much as reminding myself.

How many times have we done this over the years? I begin to do the math. At first, it's comforting. Soon, the numbers fall down the well.

Go on, you say. Go on, Abe.

I remember when I wasn't with you, I felt it in my jaw. I remember everything I wrote made me think of you and the other way around.

I remember that—for me—that, as they say, was that. And if life is a series of befores and afters . . .

I want to ask you then—forgive me—what it was about me that you loved. For some time, I wasn't the artist you wanted me to be. I was predictable, neither dark nor stormy. Perhaps it was my mother and brother?

Jane? You do not answer.

Then I remember a sound you only ever made—and you made it since the beginning—when I gathered you to my chest. A singy exhale, as if you were laughing but also crying but also writing a poem with your breath. Whewooooooooo. And then we were still, you and me, me and you, cloaked and kept, heart to heart, cheek to chest, belly to belly. Maybe for you, I think, joy in security, security in consistency, consistency in love.

That's something.

Some nights, I sleep beside you in a chair or on a stack of pillows or I rest my head on the wall and sleep like that. I like to count the number of times you shift in your sleep, as if that could do it. Or as if sudden dancing could stop the illness in your bones. As if you could break it, shatter it, with unbridled movement, like a horse, like the wind.

Some nights, I like to count the beautiful things you've made around us—delicate vases, a drawing of us scrawled in wild inky strokes, a string-and-wax sculpture that sparkles in sun, more. It is not just how talented you are. It is that you make things that feel personal—olive branches, love letters, life rafts tossed in. Some nights, I like to remember deep into the darkness. I write it down or don't. Some nights, I can't.

A doe walks by the window. Who would believe that she stops and sniffs your pansies, stuffs her head under a thicket of gold ones so it sits like a crown between her ears?

5

The next morning, as I sleep in the chair next to you, you reach for my hand. Abe? you say. For a moment, I forget the last year. For a moment, we are just waking up together. Life to live. Errands to run. And yet, here we are. Medicine to give. Bedpan. Juice. Isn't it something, I think, how sleep can betray even reason, even time.

And yet, your eyebrows and lashes—who knows how they've clung on?—haven't changed since you were twenty-three. It isn't poetic to say horselike, and yet.

Today you are wearing pink-and-white-striped pajamas, a bib on your chest. I will not remember you this way. As if it is a choice. As if you can avoid closing your eyes and fending off a cliff or a body if that is what appears, if that is fate.

Before Bernie, the nurse, comes, you say you want us to do more remembering. You once said that the nurses break a certain seal on the house.

You remember introducing me to Bea, whom you'd met at Cooper Union, who started with the bottlecap forms way back then. You remember meeting my friends from camp, from Wharton: Lee Cohen, Jacob Rosen, Matthew Goldman. A doctor, an accountant, and a lawyer walk into a bar. Every one of them, you said, so adult, and already in the suburbs. Didn't that seem a waste to me? It did and also it did not.

Is it any surprise that they loved you more than me? Is it any surprise that they told me not to lose you, whatever I did?

I remember how many weddings we went to, how you slipped your foot into a high heel, dabbed lipstick on your bottom lip, braided your hair down the side. How fully formed you were even then. Like concrete, cast. I remember how you sucked on lemon wedges, touched everyone on the arm, danced with people much older than us. I remember how you made them feel younger but it wasn't just that. It was as if you gave everyone rhythm. Even me. I remember from across a crowded room, you called my name: as if you threw it into the air for me to catch. I remember how you always reminded me to bring a notebook. And you always brought a pen in your pocketbook for us to share.

In those years, we told each other everything, except whenever I talked about work, you covered your ears. Abe, it is time, you said. If you really want to be an artist, you have to act like one.

It was our fundamental rift, wasn't it? Where we came from, and therefore where we felt compelled to end up. I know, I'd tell you. And I did. Still, I had responsibilities that you did not, though I didn't know how to put them to good use. You, on the other hand, used your grief like momentum. It carried you, compelled you.

I just asked you to wait. I begged you.

You remember it was 1970 when I told you I'd bought a brownstone near the Park. I'd borrowed money from my parents. I remember not telling you that—the part about my parents. I gave you a set of keys. We stood in the foyer, sipping champagne. You remember herringbone floors, stained-glass windows, the "maid's quarters" with beautiful north light. I told you it could be your studio, if you wanted.

You remember fighting it at first—it wasn't money from art—but taking the keys anyway. You had been fired from another restaurant job. You were painting pearls and also finches. I remember how you made beaks so small and quick they were like heartbeats. You remember feeling, for the first time, that they might be something. They might be really something. You just needed more time in your head. Restaurants were demanding, demeaning places. I bought you an easel, a terra-cotta planter for your brushes.

In the meantime, I signed up for a class.

You remember trying to make a deal with me: you'd move in when I quit, when I really, really quit. Move in now, I said, and if things were the same in eighteen months . . .

It didn't feel like lying. It felt like hope that things might sort.

I remember our love making me feel lighter. You remember it making you feel more solid. You suggest a metaphor here. Feet in the sand as the tide goes out? Yes, you say. I write it down but there is no rhyme or reason to this work.

You get tired. Today you are happy. It was a good day. You close your eyes. It does not feel like surrender. It isn't mine to give up.

Remember, Jane, that time we rented a tandem bicycle? I ask just to keep you with me. It was years later. Remember how fast we went down that hill in the Park near Ninety-Third? You nod, but so often, you just do.

I'm not really asking you these things. You couldn't answer anyhow. But it's habit: the expectation of your response. Like catching an apple that you've batted my way. The satisfaction of that. The sacred code.

Sometimes, when your eyes are closed, I cover my face. Sometimes, my greatest accomplishment in a day is to not wish desperately to go first.

6

CENTRAL PARK

The Park is open 365 days of the year from six a.m. to one a.m.
though there are no gates or locks, nothing to keep anyone out if
there is a passionate desire to get in. At certain times of year, activity
is prohibited on Pilgrim Hill due to significant dog-related damage,
too much humping and romping—especially with the greyhounds
and French bulldogs. Especially the males. The Great Lawn does
close for the season—and is padlocked. It makes Park fondling
harder in the winter months. It is harder, anyway, standing up, no
warm surface to lie upon.

The Park was designed in 1858 according to the Greensward Plan,
inspired by the English countryside and developed by Calvert Vaux
and Frederick Law Olmsted, who married the widow of his brother,
John. There is a book about their romance, having much to do with
the Park. There was a fierce design competition, with thirty-two

other competitors—all of whom were tasked with including three battlefields, a winter skating ground, a drive, a parade ground, a grand fountain, a flower garden, an observatory, a music hall, and four roads traversing the Park—and a budget of no more than 1.5 million dollars. Olmstead was the only one who did it, which likely had everything to do with the inspiration and muse of Mary, the wife.

The Park is half a mile wide and two and a half miles long. There are nine bodies of water, including the Gill, the Loch, the Pool, and the Lake, all of which look natural but are actually human-made. There are five waterfalls, each one fed from the municipal water system via one forty-eight-inch pipe at the Pool grotto near 100th Street. There are more than eighteen thousand trees that cool and clean the air, including one of the country's largest and last remaining stands of American elms. It is a habitat for wildlife and provides a stopover on the Atlantic Flyway for more than two hundred species of birds. There are also coyotes, most common during mating season, January through March. See the bite marks on the vet tech's hand? He was trying to impress the woman he'd just met on AnimalLoversAndLoversInGeneral.com: @PussyLady123. You should stick to domestics, she said as they took a cab out of the Park to urgent care. Their first and last date. It could have gone either way.

In the Park, there are more than ten thousand benches. The North Meadow Butterfly Gardens provide a habitat for more than fifty species of butterflies that pass through. The rocks in the Park were formed through volcanic activity around 500 million years ago. Summit Rock is the highest natural elevation, and the second highest is Belvedere Castle, a site the National Weather Service has used to record temperatures and wind speeds since 1919.

Any true New Yorker knows that every Park lamppost, or "luminaire," as they're called, has an inconspicuous metal plate with four numbers: the first two or three indicate the street closest by; the last one conveys which side of the Park you're in—even numbers mean east and odd mean west. This way, you're never lost. When Max was eleven, he ran away. He planned to stay with Samantha B., the prettiest girl in school—though she hadn't invited him. Just before the Sixty-Fifth Street exit, he changed his mind. The luminaires guided him home.

On the middle school history teachers' first Park date, they compete with trivia. Did you know that a part of the Park used to be a village of more than fifty homes called Seneca Village, before the city claimed eminent domain and razed it to make way for the Park in 1857 and all traces of the settlement were lost to history?

Did you know that in 1847, the Roman Catholic Sisters of Charity founded the Academy of Mount St. Vincent, the first institution for higher learning for women in New York, in what later became the northeast area of the Park? A fire destroyed the structure in 1881. Composting happens there now.

There is what happens annually in the Park, and what happens every year.

On New Year's Eve, there is a NYRR Midnight Run. Everyone kisses at the end. Winter viruses be damned. On the day before

Halloween, a pumpkin flotilla—happy faces, scary faces, hearts for faces—makes its way down the Harlem Meer. There are parents dressed as Barbie and Ken, Bert and Ernie, Meat and Cheese.

The Italian Garden in the Conservatory Garden has a small, discrete meadow perfect for a picnic for two. (It was also a setting for *Stuart Little*, the story, not the movie.) On Valentine's Day, couples abound. Barolo and tiramisu recommended. Was Jaclyn surprised when her ex-husband brought her here? He wasn't an ex then. Still, everything he did was set up by an assistant, the blonde or the redhead. What do you get when you google most romantic spots for lunch in NYC?

In the fall, there are marionette performances at Swedish Cottage—two monkeys live happily ever after. The Breast Cancer Walk begins at Naumburg Bandshell. She died at forty-one. I'm racing for her cure. Arguably, there are more fallen leaves per capita than any other place in the entire city. Why does it always smell like a fireplace? No one knows.

In the winter, there is sledding down Cedar Hill; Olmsted and Vaux's "Winter Drive" of pines, spruces, and firs from Seventy-Second to 102nd Streets are at their most fragrant. The Arthur Ross Pinetum now features seventeen species of pine. Every December, the smell lights the way.

In the spring, there is weekly bird-watching with Birding Bob, as well as catch-and-release fishing at the Harlem Meer (largemouth bass, pumpkinseed sunfish, carp, chain pickerel, bluegill sunfish). There are fishing poles available to borrow at the Charles A. Dana

Discovery Center, along with instructions and bait (corn kernels). The history teachers go. They break up. There is too much competition between them. Not enough sport.

In the summer, there is pickleball at Wollman Rink, swimming at Lasker Rink, a French festival for Bastille Day, Shakespeare in the Park—always a love story—as well as penguin and sea lion feedings at the zoo. We come here for the animals, but also for the breeze.

At SummerStage, there are eighty free and benefit concerts annually. The last big concert at Sheep Meadow was James Taylor's in 1979. He played to 250,000 fans. That was also the night that Bea got pregnant, after the show. Her career was just getting started. She didn't keep it. She never told Jane. Max was five then. This is her only regret: not the abortion; that was right. The not telling.

In the Park, the greatest number of injuries are due to cycling accidents, some fatal. At the southern end of West Drive, bikers often clock in above thirty-two miles per hour. In one weekend alone, there were 103 cyclist speeding tickets. Slow down! The Park is for everyone! Do you hear?

When the oncologist gets hit by the courier on his way east, she falls in love. It is absurd. She is a feminist, a scientist, single—thank God—and far too old for this shit. Still, there is something about the burl of the man, lifting her as if she's a mermaid or maybe a broken kite. He places her on a bench, and as she looks at the cherry blossoms above her head, pink, innocent, she is reminded of her very own biker, decades and decades ago. Back then, she believed that love was enough—if only you could protect it from machismo and volatility, expectations and despondency, diseases of all kinds. She was younger then, sillier, but brighter too. That was before. It was all possible then. She only had to believe.

7

ABE

The next day, you are exhausted. You remember with your eyes closed, white lips, the blankets pulled up to your chin. Your voice is like flashes in the radio, flares sent up. Soon, David calls and I put him on speakerphone so he can read you some new Sedaris that he's sure will make you laugh. He's in California—orange trees and pomegranates and a much younger partner, whom we love. They send olive oil, dates, and cookbooks for vegetarians. You've done their portraits more than once. Their favorite is presidential, over the top, framed in heavy gold, their bulldog, Toothy, between them, and they have it, so proudly, in their living room. Front and center. They say they're with us, they love you. We hang up.

You've gotten a second wind. You start up again. You want to remember.

You remember the brownstone: mahogany panels, the hexagonal room at the top where we put citrus trees that we bused down from

Harlem, and how they grew up against the glass in winter like modern dancers onstage. You remember how the northern light made your work better, the brass stove, pink marble in the bathroom, bookshelves stacked with art. You remember I got you boxes from the liquor store for your art supplies. You remember asking about every detail of my class. Every Tuesday, you packed me dinner.

You remember that when Dr. Ira Schulz of San Fernando bought a painting for two thousand dollars—the violet one with flecks of gray—you took us to Barney Greengrass. You remember how you'd never felt someone else's pride like that. I leaned across the table and got cream cheese on my shirt. That never stopped, you say. The cream cheese? I ask. I just want to hear your laugh.

You remember keeping the windows open in January, the Guggenheim, two pots of coffee before lunch so you could paint (you were working the night shift then). You remember finding inspiration in everything. A penny, a raisin, a tooth, a book, a building, a crocheted lobster, a crow in the snow. You remember how many times you tried to draw your mother. You remember trying to remember her: it felt like playing a piano with no keys.

I feed you soup. I tell you we can stop. No, you say, and then something that sounds like "this is for us," but I'm not sure.

I want you to know that it never felt like I was supporting you. Like you were living in my house or I was taking care of us both—even if it was a different time and I was raised differently. Instead, you bought me books, bound my journals with pebbled blue leather, brought in greens from the Park and put them about the house in vases you'd painted. You came to bed late and held my back and said, What a day. What a day. What a day.

After a while, Bernie comes. She pads up the stairs in her socks, swabs your face with a warm cloth, makes a pot of cerasee tea. I go down to the kitchen, pretend to be having breakfast. My pajamas are inside out. This is not the first time. When was the last time I trimmed my nose hairs? Took out a fresh pair of slacks?

Bernie asks me if she can make me some toast, when was the last time I've eaten? Okay, fine; toast, good. But also: I want someone to hold my hand.

Instead, I keep on.

I remember you wore robes made of silk and my tall navy socks; you kept a pen in the bun in your hair. You remember how on Sunday evenings, my mother came over to do laundry, to see your work, to drop off a roasted chicken with garlic and lemon. We ate it with green beans and cucumbers and, sometimes, applesauce. Inspiration, you realized, could be born from ease. I was working on a collection of stories about boats and bridges, missed opportunities and fate. You were working with twine and ribbon. Sometimes, you would help Bea with her bottlecaps. She has such specific vision, you'd say. I'm all over the place. But it was never a question of wanting to give up.

What I appreciated about working for my father was how it clarified time for me. There were no fourth drafts.

You remember that when I asked you to marry me, we were on that stone bench that overlooks Conservatory Water, eating blackberry ice cream with peanuts. A publisher had just taken on my poetry and first novel and I brought you the letter with my grandmother's diamond ring.

You remember our wedding. Your feet pinched, champagne with raspberries, being introduced to most of the guests by my mother. You remember sable and Brie, pink satin, the smell of lilies, and how I kept finding you, making you feel on-kilter. You were the only one who knew about my news.

You remember Turkey, Greece—that was a surprise to everyone but we did it—tomatoes, black rice. You remember white houses and water the color of flags. You remember ruins of stairs with no end, cats flicking their tails that smelled like the sun.

You remember when I told my parents about the book deal, you were with me. The first thing my father said was, Okay, but . . . And I promised him I wouldn't quit; I wouldn't let him down. I promised you too. Different but not mutually exclusive.

You ask to take a break. You lie down but the words keep coming. Forgive me that I do not tell you to stop.

You want to tell the story of Max.

8

You remember that we weren't planning it. You never thought you'd be a mother. You remember that you never thought you wouldn't necessarily and thinking that perhaps there are two kinds of women and maybe you were the second kind.

You remember, too, an inkling your whole life that pregnancy wouldn't be possible. Your mother died from cervical cancer. She'd always said you were a miracle in more ways than one. You never got to ask her: Which?

Sometimes, I wonder about your fervor for art. Was it a response to that, her loss, both? I'm not saying that every woman should want to be a mother, believe me. I do not know what I'm saying anymore.

You remember you knew, in the beginning, because you'd reach for inspiration—you were working with feathers—and come up with nothing. It wasn't as if the well was empty, you say. It was as if the well was altogether gone.

You remember it probably wasn't the best time. When is? You still smoked; you were painting nudes and using lots of chemicals with the feathers. My poetry collection had just come out, the novel soon, good reviews et cetera—I played it down, it didn't feel earned, you worked so much harder than me. I was still working for my father. David had moved, was an architect. Furthermore, my publisher couldn't offer me an advance.

Once I asked you, it was in the middle of an argument: How would we survive? You said that you thought that we had different understandings of survival.

You were not wrong.

You remember finding out about the pregnancy on a rainy afternoon and saying out loud, to yourself, standing up, I'm having a baby I'm having a baby I'm having a baby, to make it seem real. You remember thinking it was the most natural thing in the world and also the most far-fetched and maybe that wasn't normal. You remember you'd just mastered stretching your own canvases and you'd have to quit.

The rest can be filled in later. Or not. Soon, you're asleep. Or maybe you've just turned off your lights.

We lost the baby early. We got in the tub together.

9

You remember, after that, suddenly a baby was all you wanted. You remember making love like a chore. You remember closing your eyes and knowing that there was something unhealthy down deep. What if this was, actually, the beginning of something? Or just not meant to be?

Or maybe: rot under the boards.

You remember I slept on the couch and everything I said felt like an insult. You were grateful for the hours I was at work. It never used to be like that.

Let's skip that part, too, you say. You can add in what you need later. What do we need? In story, you can drop a few lines down.

You remember, in the end, it happened when we least expected it.

You remember, in the beginning, being pregnant like you were apart. You were algae, swaying. Or maybe the baby was? And you were the salt?

You remember making a mural in the nursery with frogs and sheep and roses, dragging home an abandoned dresser with no knobs from Seventieth and Columbus. Painting it white with yellow stars, feeling that you should rest but also fearing being too delicate. As if pregnancy was a fine balance and also somehow up to you.

You remember you could eat nothing but grapefruit. My mother had them shipped to us from Florida. She peeled them for you as you sat on the lip of the tub. You remember your stomach turned at milk, rice, chicken, zucchini, oats, chocolate, plums, dill, pepper, any kind of sauce, bread, cheese, tea, tonic water, salt. When you retched, my mother rubbed your back and you thanked her. She wasn't your mother even if—and also, and so.

You remember I wrote you haikus about your belly, your feet.

I remember feeling like we could do anything, if we did it together. I remember knowing, believing, that you would be patient, intentional, kind. I remember thinking that a child wouldn't take anything away from us other than maybe sleep and maybe time.

You remember feeling, discovering—maybe it was the pregnancy, maybe it was having no mother—that everyone really has a child alone. You don't want to seem ungrateful. It is just the truth, and also biology.

You remember eighteen hours of agony. You remember when he came out, it felt like fleeing. He was gone in a hurry, had left the oven on, and there was fire ravaging inside of you. You were the house. You remember shutting your eyes, covering your ears, wishing to be walking near the Park again, to be alone with a grapefruit and a spoon, or reading on a bench with nowhere to be.

That must have been so awful, I say. I apologize. It is hard to say anything else to the person you love the most.

You remember knowing immediately that it wasn't supposed to be like this. His cries were like sewing needles, you say, striking you all over your face. You remember the smell of wet basement, how everything felt damp and thick. You threw up twice into your lap. They gave him to me first. You were in a ball on your side.

You remember and you start to sway side to side, to cover your chest. You remember that when we took him home, it didn't get better. He wouldn't latch. The harder you tried, the louder he cried. And you cried. Some days, if I wasn't home, you would put him in his crib, go into the bathroom, and shut the door. You'd rock yourself on the cold tiles, beg for help and also for forgiveness, and also, sometimes, that it would just stop. You ask me if I knew that. In a way, I say. But also not.

You remember promising to do anything to go back to the way things were. Sometimes, it felt as if the world was spinning and it wasn't that you were dizzy so much as something had come loose and you were unraveling in circles, in chunks.

You remember that for weeks, you had nightmares. You remember falling asleep, standing up, waking with a gasp, your hand at your throat. You remember digging your fingernails into your palms, gritting your teeth whenever you heard a bird, brakes, a door open. You remember taking sips of cough medicine, getting so tired and also so wired. You were always hungry and also nauseated, so exhausted but you couldn't sleep. You remember you missed your mother so much that it felt as if your chest was going to split open.

My mother would come over, cook and clean, and promise you it would get easier.

You remember you couldn't ask her if she was sure. She wasn't yours. You weren't hers.

Oh, Jane, I say. I am so sorry.

Then you don't want to remember this part. You skip around.

I remember—I hate to say it—that it was then that I was really trying to make a name for myself in the writing world. My second novel—it was part of a collection of three—was done; the third one nearly. I had an editor who believed in me; he wanted to take me out to dinners with people who could change things. I wanted to go.

At the same time, my father was wanting to sell me the company. Time, he felt, was of the essence. I did feel I owed him something. Money but not just that. I also felt I owed it to us but that was beside the point. Either way, I wasn't there with you as often as I should have been. I take full responsibility. More than that, I wish I could take it back.

I will not say: I didn't know. But I just didn't. That, too, is entirely on me.

You shake your head. It was an impossible time, you say. Impossible.

You remember I asked my mother to spend most days with you. She made babka, scrubbed the toilet, sang "You Are My Sunshine" to Max. It came easily to her. You remember some days she put you in the tub and washed your face with a cloth bubbling with soap. You'll be okay, she said and said and said.

You remember that when my mother wasn't there, you panicked. You remember how hard it was to look Max in the eyes. Not because you were scared of him but because of what he might see in you.

You remember that every night, between bottles, I'd try to hold you. As if putting you back together was something physical and also up to me. You remember jumping at my touch. You remember there was no music in the house for months, just the sound of dishes and the tub running and also crying. No art. You remember the neat stacks of laundry that my mother did, stew cooling on the counter, your bowl uneaten and with a shiny film across it, spoon on the floor. You remember closing the curtains, though I opened them every morning. You remember how bright everything felt at every time of day except the dead of night, and also how loud.

I remember it was different for me. I somehow knew it was just a phase, gleaned solace from tasks: changing diapers, making bottles, doing dishes, cleaning up. But solace wasn't what I needed. Just you, shining your light.

I remember Max falling asleep in my arms. Warm body, sweet smell. I remember believing that timing was everything. It would all fall into place.

You remember that it felt as if you never really knew where I was—working, writing, whatever—and were surprised by how little you cared. The only person you needed was my mother even if the only person who could save you was you.

I remember that when I was home, it wasn't that I was angry at you, but I was surprised. Well, and maybe angry. Max was getting bigger. He had your cheeks, my eyes.

You remember the face I made every time I found you in the bathroom, alone. How hideous of me.

I'm so sorry, I say. You squeeze my hand.

You remember that when Max was four months, I got you a hotel room for one night. Rest, I said. We'll be fine here. I knew we would. And maybe I needed it too.

At first, you fought it, couldn't go. What about Max? If you got lost? Fell? You went. You remember the room was white with dark, thick shades that kept everything out and a large tub, silver drain. You remember the maid's name was Nancy, she brought you grilled cheese, let you stay in bed as she cleaned around you.

You remember that time, you didn't stay for a night, but for six. There were other times. You stayed for three days, or seventeen. You don't remember what you did, all those hours without Max, without me, not working. You ask me if I remember. I wasn't there. Sleep? Weep? You don't know. I don't know either. You didn't stop me, you say. No, I say.

In the meantime, I remember, I worked in the office. I wrote. I made crispy egg sandwiches with tomato and dill. I told my mother you were meeting a gallerist and she pretended to believe me. She made large batches of lemony stew for my father, and for me. She took turns eating with each one of us because my father could do without babies. She read my manuscripts and loved them. I felt good about them too.

I remember that Max wasn't an easy child, but in certain ways it was easier without you. I never felt underwater with him. You like to say that is because of who I am but I don't know. What I want to say now is that I know how lucky I am, and have been. Without your mother, you were a bird without your flock. How hard it must have been to do anything. Make art, fall in love, have a child of your own.

You remember that every time you'd come home from the hotel after being gone, you'd get up before the sun. There was so much hope, so much promise before anyone was up. You remember thinking, today is the day. Happiness is going to start here again. You remember hearing Max and everything deflating. You remember thinking: that moment hadn't been the beginning of happiness after all. It had been happiness itself, arriving just before it was gone.

You remember you weren't there when Max had his first bite of food, sat up for the first time, really laughed. His first word was *please* because he'd heard you begging it for so long. But the way he said it, it sounded like *peace*.

You remember you didn't see any friends for months. Bea came over more than once and you wouldn't go to the door. You remember you were embarrassed, too tired, didn't know which way was up. You remember how you braced yourself whenever you heard a bird, brakes, a door open. You remember that everything felt like, like what?

Glass.

And you just had nothing to say.

I remember that being a father didn't feel the way I had imagined it would. I don't know if that is because of Max or because of you. Nothing was as we thought it would be. But I did love when he laughed at my funny faces, watching him sleep. In a way, I loved that part the most.

You remember being a mother didn't feel the way you had imagined. What had you imagined? Connectedness, at the very least. Hope. Instead, as soon as he could, he called you Jane. Nane, in the beginning. Never Mama. Or Mom. You remember how it felt like a line drawn. Not from him to you. But in between, as though with a key, jagged, corroded, divisive.

You remember that it was the longest time in your life without art. Making it or looking at it, or thinking about it even. You had nothing left.

It would have been different now, I say. There is language for the kind of pain you endured. You should have been medicated earlier, you say. Maybe that wouldn't have fixed everything but it might have changed the course. I say that perhaps it was my fault. I should have been less focused on writing, the business. I should have been more take-charge. I didn't want you to feel judged. I didn't want you to feel worse. My focus was elsewhere. I didn't know what I was doing, only that I didn't want to lose you.

That's fair, you say. What can we do?

You remember that something about my books coming out less than a year later, one and then the other—from the perspective of a suburb, lonely, pristine, two families always trying to one-up—and doing well, enabled you to get back to your art. Max was one then. Maybe I would have given up otherwise, you say. But *you* did it.

You remember when you threw yourself into clay and then collage and then woodwork. You remember how it felt: spiritual and also like being lifted by a wave. You remember feeling larger and stranger in there without us. You remember a series of wildflowers you did from newspaper, yellow velvet, and scratchy twine. You even got them to sway. You remember putting them on the windowsill for people to notice as they walked by. You remember listening to what they said, feeling it enter you like sugar, or maybe light. You remember imagining, sometimes, a big sunny studio in France that overlooked a garden where you could work all day and night, if you wanted, whatever you wanted, whenever. You imagined showing your work. The loop of creativity possible without Max. Without me, even. The potency of that, in comparison.

You remember that we were okay but we weren't great. We had dinner and sometimes held hands in our sleep. You remember when I began teaching at the college in the evenings. It felt like purpose and creativity, both. In the meantime, I really was getting closer to quitting my father's business as you wanted, but that was the least of it.

You remember, some days, telling yourself, this is who you are now: a bad mother in a loving marriage who will one day be all right again. Who will right things again. You often wondered when too late might be. And what.

You remember the way whenever you held Max, he kept his head up. He looked at you as if you were a stranger. And in a way, you him. You remember thinking of how beautiful he was, but sort of objectively. Everything objectively. You couldn't muster another way.

You remember knowing that a tone is always set in the beginning. You and Max. It is like art. First impressions are it.

You remember when the gallerist in Milan called.

You remember that first time, you left us for a month. You called only when you knew Max would be sleeping and you focused so intensely on how I was doing, and what.

Today, you ask me if I begrudge you that time away. No, I say immediately. And then, Perhaps I would have. But we had my mother. My books did better than anyone thought they would. I was distracted too. The students were inspiring. Their drive. It was easier for me, I say. Simpler. Max was. But art was too. We worked differently. You are a sailboat, reliant on the wind. I am a truck. I wrote no matter the weather, no matter the mood. Until now.

Not that it wasn't hard some days, and awful others. It was. But, for so long, I could compartmentalize. You could not. Bless you for that.

You remember once—Max was in playgroup in the Park near the North Meadow—asking some other mothers if they all had wanted to be mothers and if they thought their babies knew that and they said, Of course. Their faces were doing something proud and beaming that yours never did, you thought. You couldn't make it do even when you tried.

I ask you if this is too much. No, you say. It's critical.

You remember how fast Max could run, how good he was at building things, cutting things, remembering things. You remember he wrote his name before any other kid, tied his shoes, swam to the deep end, locked a door. You remember when you knew how formidable he'd be. You were watching him at Heckscher Playground at the south end of the Park. The kids gathered around him, kneeled. He was telling them what to do without words. And they did it. You remember feeling both embarrassed and proud, wondering if any of him was yours. And knowing that if so: it would be despite you.

Then I mean to tell you something about your clarity of vision, your wherewithal. How he inherited that. But I say it wrong. It comes out as something about stubbornness instead. I am sorry.

He could be so cutting to me, you say and shake your head as if lightening the load. Charming but also, so cutting.

I remember he was good at math, uninterested in nature, food. I remember he reminded me of my father. His masculinity. I remember being aware of how powerful he was. He could look at a person and dismantle them. He could talk anyone around in circles.

Perhaps, I think, a father's blessing is not taking things as personally.

But what does a father need a blessing for? Really?

Max was a part of me but also apart from me. I lost less sleep. I never heard him coughing when you did. I didn't long for an apology. I bore the brunt of less frustration. It isn't because of me. It is the feeling that you'd never get back what you gave, physically, physiologically. A father, by definition, has less to recoup.

You remember when you started painting about it. You remember, at first, the guilt of using him. You already had so much momentum, maybe you didn't have to. But you did. Sometimes, you don't get to choose. It came pouring out of you, you say. You remember stepping back, knowing it was something. You sold three pieces without telling me. It was more money than you'd ever had. You remember being afraid of my response. It felt like celebrating failure.

You remember my response. It is not something I'm proud of. I wonder about not including this. The difference between dialogue and conversation is that one you can take back.

10

It is the middle of the night, and I am sleeping in the chair. You wake me up by whistling. Abe. Honey.

I'm up. I'm so glad.

You remember when the blaming started. You remember it wasn't just Max. You remember the feeling—like we'd gone flat, distant, murky, like water left in a glass for too many nights in a row. Max was maybe four.

You remember thinking I'd grown out of the things you loved, and wishing I'd grown into them instead. When was it that I'd stopped smoking altogether? You'd started again. And when did I start chewing like that? And though by then I'd published the series, the poetry, and I'd been teaching graduates for a few years, I was still

making most of our money from the business, which was taking longer to sell than I thought it would. Was always splitting my
time. I took my writing for granted, you said. The benefit of being
a man. The hubris. I could just do it. Or not do it.

You remember, after that, months of not yelling so much as everything felt as if it could shatter in an instant. You remember Max
faulting you for the pasta, the shirt, the light, the dark. In the evenings, you and I ate without looking at each other or sharing. You
had learned to give him so much space, you barely interacted. You
and I went to sleep at different times. There were miles between us
in bed. No sex for how long? And you couldn't rest. You remember
going back into your studio, closing the door at midnight. Locking
it. It felt like water sealing overhead.

You remember, sometimes, trying to imagine what we would have
done without my mother. She kept the house together. She and Max
had secret handshakes. They laughed as she gave him a bath. Sometimes, often, it felt as if she was the only reason we were all still . . .

Your voice trails off.

You remember going to California to see my brother, staying with
him, waking up early to have espresso together on his porch—and
imagining staying. You remember that David still hadn't told me,
or my parents, about his sexuality. And how it felt like another stack
against me. That David trusted you first. I was his brother, after all.
And yet.

You remember it was the only time we really yelled. You remember when I told you that you loved your work first, me second, Max third, and maybe that was the problem. It also wasn't true. Back then, I think I thought it was an uncomplicated choice and a simple hierarchy. Forgive me, Jane. I was so wrong.

This part is awful. Maybe unnecessary? It feels like a tangent, and yet.

You remember wanting me to stay at work longer, go away for a weekend, read in the other room even if it meant just you and Max. You remember I was already gone a lot.

You remember thinking that maybe too much had happened, then suddenly not enough. Does that make sense? You're really asking now. I tell you that it does.

It is the middle of the night. We don't have to do this. It is the opposite of letting go. It feels so long ago now, so insignificant.

It is a testament, you say. I tell you it's a relic. I tell you that is a good thing. It feels as if it's spoken in another language.

Alice. I can barely recall her. It all feels remote. Untranslated. Keep it so.

You fall asleep immediately.

Here I am. I am thinking about arc. This part, Alice, isn't the twist and turn. The wrench or the climax, the part when the reader thinks they've got your number and you rehook them because you can.

This was just a moment. I never should have done it or brought it up. This is a love story. Joy doesn't read flat on the page. I'll take happiness, our happiness, even when it writes white.

11

CENTRAL PARK

In the Park, there are more than two hundred unhoused couples and quite a few throuples, though they're harder to enumerate. Some got together at the Ravine, in the Robert Bendheim Playground restroom, the Ramble, in the rain under a tender canopy of trees. On Valentine's Day, Jesus and Betty, Hope and Tinks, have a double date at the south corner of Great Hill. They listen to the Lovebird Trio from afar, eyes closed. They imagine themselves in fresh clothes, shaven, spritzed with something citrusy. Some sleep together on leaves, on hoodies, on a fresh pack of women's products. They stargaze. They hold their lockets, love notes, loved ones, close. Luna found a wedding ring in a puddle and kept it. Peter found one and turned it in. The Hero family snacks on chocolate kisses, discarded or dropped. I bet it was that class of second graders! I bet it was Santa! I bet it was God! He listened! They read to each other from the pamphlets left over from the Rumi Fest. *Lovers find secret places inside this violent world where they make transactions with beauty.* The old-timers know the Central Park Five never did it. Some of them were within earshot. They can never forget the sound. What's the word for the opposite of love? It isn't hate. It is far crueler than that.

According to law, there may be no solicitation, public nudity, or sex in the Park. Weddings without authorization are prohibited—as are parties of twenty or more without registration, though there is a weekly Sex and Love Addicts Anonymous meeting at Center Fountain that gets packed. No one may graffiti I LOVE YOU, ALAINA or JONATHAN HAS NO DICK (or anything) on the USS *Maine* National Monument. They may not pull a Cusack and play Peter Gabriel at an unreasonable decibel level, though Tinks did try. There are hefty fines for excessive noise, especially if you're without an address. They are enforced. Toplessness is discouraged, as are open containers of Cristal and sharing a tuna sandwich within nose-shot. Romance is subjective. Public lewdness in the first, second, and third degrees will be punishable to the most extreme extent of the law.

In the Park, cars, cabs, and for-hire vehicles are forbidden; tandem bikes and horse-drawn carriages are okay. Crime is 64 percent lower than the national average; there have been four reported rapes this year. The Park is the only place in the city where the red-eared sliders mate in eyeshot, Treble NYC croons "Empire State of Mind," a miniseries captures fifty-two couples, each from a different U.S. state or territory, as they marry in a mass wedding at Bethesda Fountain. Tulip or daffodil dedications to a loved one can be purchased through the Conservancy. Abe has spent ten thousand dollars over the last few years—and has requested purple and white tulips specifically. One can donate a bench too: SHNOOGS, HOW LUCKY ARE WE. HAPPY 30 YEARS, DYL AND AMES; WANT TO RUN LOVERS' LANE? ROBIN + SAL, MARRIED AUGUST 12, 2011; LADY-BIRDS: 2003–THE END OF TIME.

Some people come to the Park to make something: a prom corsage, a graffiti ghazal on the sunlit grass near Bow Bridge, an enormous Cupid's bow and arrow of rose petals—it is the only way I'll get her back!—a sex hex (robin's nest, cough drop wrapper, two drops of rose oil, hawk feathers, and a song). Some people come to destroy something—drop a ring down the grates, chuck old T-shirts into the Lake. The Park has such romantic gravitas. Love born here. Love died.

Some people come to the Park and leave behind verbal abuse, someone satiated, two rabbits mating in a cage. We thought they were both male. Some leave an unsent breakup email in their drafts. He's taking me to Harry Styles this weekend; I'll do it right after. Some leave on the coffee pot. Some leave on the camera, just to see. I fucking knew it! The opera singer / mom leaves her wedding band in a drawer in case Mr. Nice Tush is also on the Upper Loop at this time of day. I'd like to sing to that tush directly. Alice leaves behind the notebook her husband picked up for her at the supermarket because she's afraid of what it might be like to try to write a gushing sentence about him. He'll want to see. And who wants to write about painless love anyway? Wasn't it Abe who always said that happiness writes white?

On the Outer Loop, running south, the runners speed up, slow down. They make eye contact. They are hot, slicked, breathing heavy, hearts boom boom, endorphins out of their ears. At home, the bad news is blaring. The kids need another snack. No more sugar! There is a pile of dishes that is starting to stink and the only underwear left in the drawer is unflattering, NSFW. Here, sprinting, flying, it is not that the runners feel sexier than anywhere. They just don't feel flattened out. They check their watches. Ten more minutes. Nine. Eight. Don't stop. Do not stop.

12

ALICE

Meet him after class. Wait until the room has emptied out. It smells like erasers and sweat, wool and wood polish. Pretend to be organizing your notes, collecting a pen off the floor, clasping and re-clasping an earring. Remember that line he wrote in his first novel about women's ears: like stray treasures, crinkled and pink.

Stand close when he's looking down. Speak more quietly because your mother says that men, like kittens, respond to whispers. Tell him you need help with narrative arc. Somehow, whenever you write, time stands still. Look for cues. He is putting books into his briefcase. He is checking his watch. There are no cues yet. Take note.

Okay, he says. Come on up.

Carry your coat to his office. Don't put it on. Walk in front of him
when he holds out his arm. Ladies first. Be aware of the defining
angles of your back, your neck. He's behind you. Wear the Chanel
No. 5 that your mother left on your nightstand. Every woman
needs this, she'd said as she turned the bottle to face out. You knew
she was talking about men.

Steady your breath as he unlocks the door, goes in, dumps his stuff
on the desk. Wait for him to get organized, settled. You want him
to feel not rushed.

Try not to obsess—it will only jack up your speaking voice, run
you around in circles. Still, he is the reason you are here. Mostly,
he is the reason you write. There were other schools that you could
have gone to. There are other writers you love. But him. When you
read his work, again and again, you felt like a character in it. Like
he writes from his heart to yours directly. In a way, you have been
writing back to him since his first book came out, five or six years
ago—you were working next door to the bookstore—when you
were just getting into literature, and it was just beginning to save
your life. In a way, it is as though he understands you better than
anyone. And you him. And the suburbs. And your mother.

Think, for a moment, about cinema and drama. How nothing, in
real life, has ever measured up. It is never as good as you imagined
it. Until him. Breathe out. Look up and then down again with just
your eyes. It is all too much pressure and also just enough.

Then start by saying something sincere about his body of work. You've read everything—the novels, stories in magazines, the small book of poetry. You loved that too. Tell him—and be conversational—that he's changed your mind about moths, semi-colons, even Scarsdale, where you're from. Also, about getting old. He laughs with his mouth closed, without looking up (also better than you imagined). You didn't mean to joke. But okay.

Maybe the flattery is too much.

Change tack then. Tell him about O'Connor. Or maybe Carver. Tell him the other work you have enjoyed so far, that you've sped through, that has made sense to you in terms of plot. Thank him for that. He's opened up a whole world of fiction, and you want him to know, you say. This class is so important to you. Still, he hasn't looked your way.

Realize that it wasn't the right time for any of it. A lost opportunity. Keep the faith.

Notice that he's flipping through someone else's story. He lands on a middle page and smiles. Good, he whispers. Cameron's? Terry's? Ignore the urge to tell him that they're not serious. They're taking this class for credit. You've been writing your whole life. Wonder if he knows that. Wonder how to get it across without being sentimental. Your mother has told you not to be too much.

I have some specific questions, you say. Pull up a chair not across from but next to him. Cross your legs. You are a forearm's distance apart. Joke: Sorry! Is this too close? Make sure your laugh isn't spitty at all. Hold your voice up from the bottom. It makes you sound more adult.

He pushes up his sleeves. He's old enough to be your father, but his hair is thick, his face unlined, clear eyes; his arms are strong from something outside. Woodworking? Jogging in the Park? He leans against the wall. He's in a cotton sweater that does something nice to his shoulders. In the beginning, there is potential for magic in everything. The way he wears his sweater feels like a gift. He smells like oranges but also, leather. He turns on a light on his desk. The thing about his eyes, you think. They must have been the same when he was three. Goodness but also mischief. The color of a squirrel's back.

Catalog the items on his desk: one deer antler, two stained mugs, a stack of anthologies, a pair of knit gloves, an expensive pen, envelopes with frayed tops, a dead pink flower, a toy car and a toy dinosaur, a wooden block with the letter *M*, a photo of his wife—must be, blurry in a gold frame. She's in white and the floors are painted white, she's got a gap between her teeth and a dimple, and behind her, there's a large plant in a terra-cotta pot.

There is what you've liked about him for years: he writes about women with kindness and reverence; at readings, he wears suspenders, chews gum, laughs at his own jokes.

There is what you like that you're just finding out. Everything else.

Ask yourself if you feel guilty. Ask yourself why you always put the cart before the horse.

So, he says. As far as your work, I'm not sure the issue is arc. Ask him what the issue is. Surely, he says, you're not writing the story you want to write.

Wonder if this is your in. Or maybe a suggestion? Or maybe too much can actually be too much. Stop staring at his face.

13

In the next class, he asks everyone to write a confession. He says, and there's that smile again, I'm going to write something about my son. Hands over eyes. Everyone laughs. And go.

Avoid the urge to write about him. Instead, write about how you've fallen in love with the city. Write about the comfort of garbage trucks, the guy who has honeybees on his roof across the way, coins of old gum, kebabs, the poetry bookstore with all the cats. Write about the pasta place where you and Margaux go and sit under the Christmas lights and drink red wine on Tuesdays. Write about the hawk that has three different lovers in Central Park. Write about buying blueberries on Columbus, jazz on the C train, and the flowers that grow up out of the sidewalk cracks. It's the city that's the spell.

That's not exactly a confession, he says when you read it out loud. It feels more like a review. But I like it.

Say thank you. Do not beam. Try not to take it more personally than is right.

The next class, he asks everyone to write about love. Do yourself a favor. Don't. Instead, write about your high school boyfriend, Andrew. Write about how kind he was, how he wrote you a song in G-flat, how he tasted like milk, his forearms (nothing much), the leaf wallpaper in his hallway, his parents' club on the hill, and the way he hummed in his sleep. Write about how sometimes, you had the urge to punch him in the face. Finish it with a thing about love but not in love, et cetera.

Where is Andrew now? he asks.

Wall Street, you say.

He nods knowingly, but you're not sure what he knows. He scratches his beard.

What do you think? he asks the class. No one says anything.

Finally, he says, You're still writing around it. You're circling.

I know, you whisper.

In your apartment, when your roommate is doing an extra shift at the tavern, turn your lamp down low, put on jazz, light a candle that smells like leather. Cover your bed with books that you know he likes and you like too, mostly. Some you don't understand.

Spend hours, afternoons, evenings, writing about him. Little anec-
dotes, things you've gathered. You've heard he has a wife and his
son is young. You've heard he lives near the Park. You've heard that
he doesn't sleep around, but once, you saw him with a TA from a
couple of years before. She was very beautiful, red-haired. They
were laughing in the lobby and she was in a blue dress that lit up
her whole face. It felt as if they were either in love and everyone
knew it or they weren't and didn't care what anyone thought. Recognize the inconsolable feeling. It makes you feel so alive you're
almost dead. It's not that you have violence in you. It has something
to do with your father, maybe. And your mother. That you've
avoided stepping on ants your whole life, and just once, you'd like
someone to step over you. You don't like to think about it head-on.
You don't want to go sour in your heart.

When Margaux asks about the class, lie. Tell her that you're writing
about your mother. Realize you haven't mentioned him to anyone.
Maybe there's nothing to tell. Maybe you don't want to jinx it.
Maybe you worry that once you tell anyone anything, you'll have
to tell them everything.

What even is everything? Margaux looks confused.

A couple of weeks later, after work, go to office hours. The sun is
long gone and there he is, reading in the dark, his feet, socked, on
an ottoman. He has a child's backpack on one shoulder, but he's not
going anywhere. He looks relaxed but also poised. Wait for him to
make eye contact. You're wearing a camel coat with a tie that
cinches your waist. Be a silhouette in the door. Be a prism. Cough
once.

Hi, he says. What's up? Resist the urge for small talk. Your mother says it betrays agita. Instead, tell him you have a confession. Tell me, he says. And something about how he says it, you almost do. You almost tear up. Don't.

I'm working on the thing I'm meant to, you say. His eyebrows ascend. Be prudent with your words.

How does that feel? he asks.

Touch your chest once. Think about all the pages you have of him. Don't tell him specifically about having written about him, sitting just like that, there. Instead, wonder out loud about the difference between déjà vu and projection. Also, inevitability. Wonder if writing makes you ever so slightly prophetic.

Now you're getting it, he says. And then drops the bag, looks around fretfully. Do you know the time? He picks it up again, curses, tells you that he doesn't know when he became a person who is always late.

Another day, ask him to help you with your opening paragraph. He's in his office. He sits up in his chair. Want to come in? he asks. Go in. He offers you an apple from a paper bag. It's from an orchard, you can tell. Imagine him at an orchard. Plaid scarf. Leather boots. Wife? Stop imagining.

He asks you to tell him about yourself. Tell him about Scarsdale. Tell him about your mother. Tell him about your first job as a camp counselor, second in a dermatologist's office next to a bookstore, third selling watches for your mother's jeweler, after college. Well, you say, she sold him all her things when my father left. He owed her. Then tell him about your ex-stepdad, the one who brought all his books and then took all his books and still sends you ghost stories and Dickens and sometimes earrings—aquamarines, peridots, opals—on your birthdays.

Is that right? he says.

Ask him what he wrote at your age. Crap. Ask him if he studied fiction. No, he says. Business. I'm self-taught, which is a slog, and I do not recommend. Take my word for it.

You're not sure what he's referring to exactly but it seems as if the door is shut, if not locked.

Ask him what he's working on now. He dangles a manuscript between two fingers. It's a big one, he says. Hopefully, the one. He seems proud.

You want to be in it. How can you be in it?

Ask him how often he does this. What? he says. Care about my students? Always. For you, with him, hope is always on the brink and so very very very personal.

Don't overstay. Instead, make up something about a museum. Meeting a guy friend there. Too much. He tells you he's happy for ya. But you misunderstand.

You're happy? you say, taking it as an insult, thinking about his wife.

He laughs, maybe blushes, balks. Happy for you, he says. He means about the writing. Oh.

And, he says, smiling. Happiness is fleeting anyway, isn't it?

Whew.

Count the months till the end of the semester, when you must have one full piece of work. A short story with a beginning, middle, and end. He once said that beauty is not enough. Something must happen. It must be intentional.

In the next class, he has everyone write down a dream with as much detail as they can muster. You write about the one you have again and again where you're on a boat; no waves, everything is very still and peaceful. You're trying desperately to get off. You're dying for something different. When you finally manage, you realize you've not been on a boat really but there's been a blue membrane over everything, like dried glue. It was a trick of the eye or the mind or whatever. That's when things go wild: the waves, the dips and doozies. There is more to life than floating, you think. There are patterns, drama, art. You want to start over. Or start again. You long for life, stirred. You write about all that.

He doesn't read yours aloud.

Go to his office before the next class. Explain the dream piece, but before you can finish, he cuts you off. You're still avoiding it, he says. He mimes stirring something tiny with his pointer finger in the air. Around and around.

Finally, use him. Use everything. For the next class, write a scene full of tension. It's about someone who might be you. She is a writer. She is alone on a front porch around the holidays. In the meantime, everyone is inside. She is unhappy in her relationship. It has gone flat. But it is more than that. She is looking for something.

A man comes out and everything changes. He is mysterious: darkened with smoke and work and cold tides. The conclusiveness of his shoulders as if they are demanding her smaller. Tension and yet no one moves. Something about slow dancing and potential for magic in everything. That charged and melted feeling. Angst and conflict. Everything cinematic. Like clouds that don't cloud the sky.

And still, nobody moves.

In the piece, in the end, not much happens. The woman's boyfriend is drunk somewhere. The man is married. After a while, he gestures to inside. He says, Me too, or maybe, Me either. But something has happened. The moment shimmers. Time lengthens. In story, it can do that. He said so. It is a question of weights and measures. And how some moments matter more.

In class, he asks you to read it out loud. Stand up. Your heart is pounding. Go slow. Once, your voice cracks. You're not going to cry exactly, but it's hard to speak. When you're finished, you keep your eyes closed.

Now we're talking, he says quietly and claps once. Atta girl. Open your eyes. Take him in. Let him do the same for you.

Now we're talking, he says again. But, for the next draft, he says, work on the male character. I don't believe him.

Feel like he's somehow letting everyone in on your secret. Which makes you wonder if there was no secret at all.

Go up to his office. Feel ready to explain. He beckons you in with his arm. He's balancing a stack of books with the other. There is a mug of coffee steaming on his desk. His phone rings. The books drop to the floor.

Excuse me, he says, holding up a finger, looking at the mess. And then, Hi there.

Go in. Start to pick up everything. Hear that her voice is soft and gentle. The ups and downs of her tone. A hummingbird nose-deep on a purple lupine or maybe bees in the sun. Watch him listen, nod. He tells her he'll be home just after class. They can deal with it then.

When he gets off, he looks at the ceiling as if for weather or maybe just breath. He looks at you as if you've woken him up from a deep sleep. It is then that you feel you have no place here. Stop with the books. You were just getting somewhere. It is possible to back up without moving. Do.

Or maybe go to him. Don't move too quickly. He's a broken bird. Be soft and strong. Do the opposite of shrink. Put your hand on his shoulder. You're not trying anything exactly. In some ways, it just feels like the right thing to do. When you touch him, his arm twitches once. It settles. Let him look at you then. Hold your face just so. In the beginning, it's as if you've shattered. All the pieces are shiny and new. You are a white blouse. Empathy. Youthfulness. A long neck. Cold fingers on his shoulder. The faintest smell of rose and jasmine. Not yet the sum of your parts. Be a sudden gift.

After a while, you could take your hand off. Don't. Leave it on longer than expected, than you mean to. Something takes over. He doesn't move away.

For a moment, you think about your story. Consider the trigger. The moment that changes everything. Is this it? Consider how nonaction can be action too. He is still looking at your face. In the beginning, everything is only the slightest bit distorted. Like a face flattered in a car window.

Has anyone ever looked at you like that?

I'm sorry, you say without thinking about it. It is instinct: second nature because of your mother, or maybe because you're not a man. It is then that you see something pass over him. It is lightning quick. Like a shadow from outside but sort of the opposite. A spark. You would have missed it if you weren't poised. And hoping.

Let go only when you see a balloon out the window, floating up. He sees it too. He moves back and everything drops. As if you've been holding something with your eyes between you two.

Hope, he says, cracking the silence like a wake. He points at the balloon. Hope personified, he says. You know what I mean?

Nod.

That day, as he teaches, he looks at you again and again and again. He's downtrodden, clearly. He's rallying. You can support him just by being there. By being you. Once, you make a comment about rhythm. How sometimes short sentences can make a story hustle and pant. He smiles and nods, hands clap. That's it, he says.

There is seeing and then there is being seen.

14

After that, meet him again in his office. This time it's about language.

Authorial distance.

Release of information.

Realize what an interesting thing it is: how so often it feels like it isn't about you. Some days, he says your name loudly, claps when you walk in the door though you've done nothing to deserve it. Some days, it's like you're a candle in the corner. You've done nothing different. It's him.

Don't ask him about his wife or the confession he wrote about his child or the letter *M*, though you would die to know.

One time, you find him staring out the window. When you look, all you see is the usual stuff. Water towers. Gray buildings. Clouds like wisps. You don't want to startle him. Whisper his first and last name. Apologize immediately. When he comes to, he shakes his head as if to rid it of something, as if he's choking or he's got bad news wrapped around his throat. You apologize. You have nothing to be sorry about, he says. Stuff on my plate. Green beans, borscht, et cetera.

It makes you touch your heart. He puts down his work and claps his hands. Well, he says. But he doesn't finish. He asks if you want to do a writing exercise together. You do.

When he writes, notice how his face changes. It goes soft, as if it's been covered with petals. You can tell he is in it. Sometimes, his mouth changes and you're not sure if he is smiling or grimacing. He chews his pen.

Shit, he says out of nowhere. He looks around the room as if it might explain.

I've got to pick up my son, he says. To be continued.

The words repeat in your ear for a week. To be continued. To be continued. To be continued.

His son.

You gather your things together and you imagine gathering things together. You know?

In your room, you read his short story about the affair again. That part when nothing and everything happens. Two people are standing on a dune, their faces flattered by ocean light. They've been brought together by circumstance but also sadness. He is a widower. She is a math teacher who cannot bring herself to eat. That isn't you, of course. Remind yourself that he wrote it before before before. And yet.

Your father sends you a letter. It arrives tea-stained on the envelope and inside. He asks about school, about your mother. All he says about himself is that he's doing fine. The weather in Colorado is always good. Last time, he was in Wyoming. The time before that, Texas. The time before that, you didn't know for two years. He remembers none of your birthdays, or graduations. Sometimes, he includes a check for a hundred dollars. Your mother would kill you if you cashed it. You don't. Write him back. Tell him that you're in school again and you love what you're learning. You have a professor who's changing everything for you.

It is the first time in years you don't wallow in the mess of your family for days.

In the meantime, learn more about eyeliner from a lady at Bloomingdale's named Linda, who also waitresses at a place that serves horsemeat where she dates the owner, who is married. Go bra shopping with Margaux and settle on black lace with a tiny satin bow. Margaux knows that you know that she knows, but you both just do a lot of smirking. Margaux has a line of boys and men interested in her because she's got gray eyes that she opens and closes as if they've got better things to do. She dances to music in her head and everyone stares, wondering which song. She is going to run the world.

It feels important to say: it is not that you haven't been approached by men. You have. It is just that you have always imagined being with someone older, wiser, long dinners, skillful sex. Gravitas. You've imagined a short story, no surprise. Maybe this one. And perhaps that's your main problem: the imagining. It gets in the way. It has always made real life pale, pallid, pathetic, in comparison.

Until now.

One day, in his office, sit in a leather chair across from him, doing a prompt. Be suddenly aware of your elbows, fingers, knees. You can hear the ebb of his breath. Every once in a while, he looks at the ceiling. The answers are there. That day, his is about fishermen in Nova Scotia. Yours is about a restaurant downtown. It's not very good. When you talk through it, he says that what's critical is that everything must further plot or character or both. He tells the story of an entire family in five hundred words. His capacity for language. And yet, he's never not generous. That is very astute, he says of your line about antique linen napkins. It makes you imagine his hands holding the sides of your face.

You want to ask him what this is. Instead, you imagine what the *M* on the wooden block stands for. Michael, Mickey, Micah, Matthew, Malcolm, mine. Yours.

You remember how once, after a breakup, you asked your mother why it was over. We'd stopped making memories, she'd said. After that, every time things were going south, you'd just ask: Memories or not? That's how you'd know what to expect, when the money would stop coming in and you would have to clean the house yourselves.

And then you moved out.

What you're trying to say is that with him, everything—even as it happens—you know you'll never forget. What you're most attracted to is everything. You don't know what you wish for except more of this. Even on the days he doesn't look your way until you go to him. You know that when he does, there will be the feeling.

Memories, never not.

Soon, you see him constantly. He is in a button-down or a brown cashmere sweater with patches. He is drinking coffee with milk or he is eating challah toast. His beard is unruly or neatly kept. He stands up when you walk in or he has his head in his hands and exhales sharply before he half smiles at you. He has a stack of mail or a stack of papers. He notices your necklace or he apologizes for not being himself. A lot a lot a lot lately, he says.

You can tell. Also, you want to ask him what that means exactly.

Sorry, you say instead. Do not pry.

One day, bump into him on the bus near school. He's in a long coat with a high collar, dark with dark checks. He says he doesn't usually come this way. He needed to get some air. It's complicated. Is this an opening? Listen with your whole face. Don't ask about her. Take some lint off his shoulder instead. It's not her hair. There, you say as you drop it on the bus floor. It flies away.

As you walk into the building, suggest that you help him in his office. You'll organize his books. It might be helpful to . . . Before you can finish, he says he'd like that. Some days, it's not that you want him as much as you'd like to tuck him in for a nap.

In the books, look for notes. There are none from his wife. None from any lover. One from Frank. Wilkinson? you think. His editor at *The New Yorker*? It says, I think you'll love this one. I did. But that's it.

Buy him a book of poetry that he doesn't have. Watch him open it with gentle hands. Wow, he says. I haven't gotten a gift in a long time. Let it be a sign. Wish you'd written something inside. How dumb.

Dust. Open the windows. Bring him one of those candles your mother loves and light it with a lighter that you bought specifically for this. You're really something, he says when he comes in. Thank you.

You can choose to take that as a compliment. You wanted him to say that. You can choose to think he read your mind too.

You've watched the way he puts on a coat and stuffs gloves into his pocket. Some days, he offers you half his blueberry muffin. Once, he'd just gone for a run and changed, and you watched him roll his sweaty clothes into a ball. Sometimes, you can tell he's a father just by the way he takes care.

Sometimes, you can't imagine him with a baby exactly but instead, driving, his son in the passenger seat. Maybe they're going to pick up juice, or go to a carnival, or to visit the mansion where a poet once lived. They're just being quiet, listening to music, trees flying by, heat on, all the support everyone needs. Wouldn't that be nice. To be his. Or his.

What do you know?

Recall a book review in which they say he has an uncanny insight into the psyche of women. He feels how women feel and how they are. He depicts them fully realized, complex and beautiful. In his books, there are old women, a shopkeeper, a neighbor, a hairdresser, a pregnant woman, daughters, and also someone who may be his wife. Every one is cared for like a plant. That was the thing you noticed most. It makes you wonder about his mother. What kind of woman.

Sometimes, you want to sit for him and let him write your story as if it were a portrait. As if depicting you would fully realize you. As his muse, you'd finally know.

When he asks how the porch story is going, lie. Make him think that's the only one. Is it true that he feels flattered by it? Or did you make that up too?

One day, he asks you if you'd like to go for a walk in the Park.

Meet him under the bridge next to Bethesda Fountain. Meet him in the scarf that your mother says brings out the color in your face. Meet him in eyeliner and pretend you've just been at a matinee with friends. Meet him when the sky is violet pink. Be flattered when he says you look nice. Notice he has an armful of short stories, drafts, yours in there somewhere, and a navy cap, pulled down hard to his brows. Wonder if you're meant to relieve him of the stories. Say phew under your breath when he stuffs them into his bag, puts his hand on the small of your back, and you walk. Be a delicate fruit or blossom. Be ladylike in your neck.

As you walk, he asks you question after question. Talk of books and your mother and her boyfriends and your roommate who is from Russia and puts fresh cherries in her tea and leaves the cups to mold. Look at him when he talks about the fellow writers he happens to like and those he doesn't, how he always writes in blue ink, is superstitious, how he's worked for his family's business for longer than is good for his writing and other things. But it all works out. It was the only way we could make it work, he says.

You and your wife? you say. But he doesn't respond. He's still talking. Maybe you're not meant to say *wife*.

Act amazed at everything. You're not acting, but there is a special thing you can do with your eyes. Do it.

Stay with him until dark. Wonder where else he has to be. Or not. Wonder about that too.

End up at the Boathouse. Red and tinsel and eggnog and Burl Ives. Stand outside. The windows are golden and warm as toast. Let them cast light on your face. Let him face you. You are both leaning. There is so much leaning, in the beginning. There's even a porch.

Do not think of his wife. Do not think of the graduate school bills in your room, unopened, or what your mother would say (What an odd choice, Alice), or how you're craving egg salad. Instead, think about how, in the beginning, you get to be seen. You get to show how brave, how complex, how uniquely yourself you are constantly. You want him to say, Oh my gosh, you're so. Show your empathy. Show the way you hold your heart when you laugh.

There is something, you say. That you've been thinking about lately.

Oh yeah? he says.

Nod.

Do you remember, you say, that part in *West* when Middy ends up in the Tetons?

He nods slowly, wistfully. His face opens to you like a fan.

He writes a letter home to his daughter, you say. He explains everything. Remember that?

God, he says, as though it was his own life, lifetimes ago. What made you think that? It was such a weird book. I haven't thought about it in some time.

His face scrunches up like a paper plate. You want to pat it flat with your hands. You want to touch him. Don't.

Instead, tell him how it cleared up so much for you. Mean it. It did.

He raises his eyebrows. You want to touch them too. So much of what he does, who he is, feels like an invitation. Say yes.

My father's out west, too, you say. Then, for a moment, you imagine telling him everything. And also: not having to but feeling connected nonetheless. You've never felt anything like this before. Try not to reveal that on your face.

And the poetry? he says, covering his eyes. You read the poetry too?

Get closer then. Get brave. Wrap your hands around his. Be gentle and firm. Coax him. Uncover his eyes.

I did, you say. I read everything I could. Your work has meant so much to me.

Stand there a while. You and him. Him and you. It feels like you've unlocked some metal latch, some mental latch. His jaw loosens. His head cocks. Someone watching, you think, might think you are posing for a photograph. You and him. Him and you. You are the only two.

Put his hands against his own chest then. Beats like coconuts in a pot of boiling water. Yours too.

That line about language, you say. How it enters us like stars as we sleep. Open mouths.

Yes? he says.

It changed my whole life, you say. Made me feel like someone knew what I needed.

No, he says. Stop that.

He doesn't mean it. And he knows you won't.

We are illuminated, you say. By words, polished by memory, over and over and over. Language enters us like cold water, like a stream.

You know it by heart.

His heart darts then, from one eye to the other, his mouth, his forehead. It is not unlike a small animal, you think, seeking shelter. You're sure: you've answered a question he didn't know he'd asked. What you want him to see and what he sees align. There's power in it, and powerlessness too.

Walk to the East Side entrance, touching sometimes, sometimes not. Feel like you'd follow him anywhere, for any amount of time. And from then on, you will only ever write in blue pen.

Do you have to go? he asks. You're standing under a lamppost. Take it as a compliment. String and restring the words. Consider subtext. In real life, there is just conversation. Tell him yes. But wait. There is a pause. Wait and weight. He is looking at your profile. Let him. Stop feeling the cold wind. Atmosphere, unlike weather, is a literary device. It holds when you want it to. The trees make a sound as if they're about to say something. It begins to snow.

You're so, he says. But he doesn't finish. Close your eyes. See the moment replicating itself in words.

For the first time in such a long time, a moment isn't its measly self. It isn't dulled with routine, or boredom or immaturity. It isn't too much or too little. It is just. You're so.

15

After that, the default resets. You forget what it's like to not be re-minded of him in everything. A walk, the weather, putting on socks. Imagine him always. He is pulling you out of cold water, a dense couch, the snow. You are in nothing but socks or suds or old silk, and he lifts you. You are a quilt across his arms. He is thinking about you or he isn't. He sleeps on his side or he doesn't. You have no dream that is neither about him nor not.

You write down everything.

Your mother calls. After a while, she asks what's making you so happy. She can tell from your voice. Just tell her: I've met someone. Feel adult for keeping this secret. Him. This.

Make a list of all the things you want to share with him. The swingers in your hometown; that you once saw your father holding hands with the pharmacist, a man; Jean Sibelius's *13 Pieces*, op. 76, no. 3; Carillon; the full-page doodles you do with lipstick and Q-tip and water; that you've never been to Europe but you have a box where you keep images of Italy, where you'd most like to go. There are citrus trees, cats in windows, and water electrified by blue.

When you're getting dressed, imagine he's watching you. Showering. Eating cucumbers. Falling asleep. At a bookstore, he's watching as you run your finger across the paperbacks on a low shelf and your hair is wild and wavy from rain. It makes everything lift.

When you're out to dinner with Margaux, imagine he's at the table across the way and he can't stop looking at you. You're in a green velvet dress with a low neckline and blush and lipstick. You're in good underwear and Chanel No. 5 and your bed is made. You have Borges and your journal on your nightstand and the heat is turned off. Just in case.

Instead, he is very busy. You haven't really seen him since the Park. Some days, wonder if you made it all up. You try not to spiral, but what can you do with this imagination of yours. There is no end to the devastation you can conjure. Cities burned.

Buy new shoes that make your feet look delicate. Cut out ice cream and then eat pintfuls of mint chocolate chip in your bed. Spend hours in the poetry section of used bookstores, stealing lines that you could use. Everything coalesces around the idea of you and him, him and you. Sonnets, Coltrane, lines about forests and waves.

For weeks, linger at the library, at the café with baklava, at the bench with the A + R + C inscription. What else? The material flies but it's more than that. You fly too. One night, you stay up till dawn. Pink rounds the corner. The sky unblanks. The pages too. You've filled a notebook, tried the story three ways. In most ways, it works, you think. You know the ending. It's the middle that's tripping you up.

Your mother is in town. You're not entirely sure why. She wants to meet in the Park. Suggest Bergdorf's instead. Some places are sacred. She wants to talk to you about someone new she's dating. Realize only one person can be the giddiest, and dating someone new, in a way. And that, for now, that person is not you. She says you need new stockings, and blush. It's dire, she says so loudly that everyone turns around to look.

Weeks later, be surprised when he asks you to meet him during the holiday break at Grand Central during the evening rush. He says he wants to give you something. Some things come out of nowhere except in story. In real life, anticipation in your throat like smoldering. You cannot really sleep. It's as if you are skimming over dreams, over life, meals, walking, everything. You almost get hit by two different cabs.

Meet at the timetables. He's in that coat you want to wrap around yourself but only because it's his. You didn't put on lipstick. You're convinced it's bad luck based on history with him.

Hi, he says.

Hi, you say.

I'm sorry I've been so unavailable.

Tell him it's all right. You don't know whether to touch him or not. He is carrying a tall paper bag. He puts it down on the ground, pulls out a stack of antique napkins, done up with a blue bow.

I wanted to give you this, he says. I never forget a good line.

He repeats yours. You die.

But don't. Instead, thank him. Kiss him once on the cheek. You pull away but hold on to his sleeve. Look at him. You want to kiss him again. Don't. You want to ask him what this means. Don't. You want to ask him when he knew. You always did. He has to go in a moment anyway.

Pretend to look at the schedule up high. Wassaic. Poughkeepsie. New Canaan. New Haven. Danbury. Over the loudspeaker, a missing child has been found and is with Security. Graze his hand with yours. He is looking at the schedule too. But he closes his eyes, nods. It is almost imperceptible, but you know what to look for. There is a cast across his face like warm evening light. It is not just the atmosphere.

Some secrets are feelings; they are passed like gifts.

After that, carry this moment like a penny in your pocket. Over break, meet your mother for lunch. Tell her it's serious but that's all you'll say. And not just because she's been broken up with and can't handle anything. But because.

At a party, some friends ask what's gotten into you. Where have you even been for the last five months? Reveal it to just one—lots of I shouldn't say! I shouldn't say!—but avoid details. She tells everyone. You knew she would. They look at you differently. Anyone who's read anything worth anything knows who he is. His book is in the window of the bookstore. His *New Yorker* story about Upstate New York, the teacher dying of a heart attack, everyone breaking down, is in last month's issue with the picture of the scarlet flowers and hummingbirds on the front.

Don't expect to hear from him. You don't know what he's going through exactly—it feels like exhaustion but also disappointment—but it is a lot. You're sure now: it's about his wife. And you respect his needs.

On the first day back, wear the charcoal dress that your mother says makes you look long. Wash your hair. Don't pick. Have read all the Butler, Mahfouz, Pynchon, Amis, and King. Be prepared to tell him what you really think because whenever someone does that in class, he leans back in his chair, grins, and claps once before responding. Cheers on that thought, he says and upends it. Every time. Isn't he something.

Instead, be surprised that he's freshly shaven. It makes him look older and more tired. He is wearing a green parka and jeans with two swaths of light blue paint. You've never seen him like this. The first class is a one-hour free write. No instruction. He is writing too. He calls on three people to read aloud, not you. But the way he listens to them: it softens you. His eyes do that thing. Sometimes, it feels as if he's grateful for everything. Not just you. Isn't that enough?

After class, you have to wait your turn to see him, and when you get to his desk, he asks if you can pick this up another day. He apologizes as he rubs his eyes. You say, Can I just tell you one thing? And then, don't. And he doesn't ask. That was a stupid thing to do.

He's not wearing a ring. You can't remember if he ever did. This feels like the biggest mistake of your life. Observation, he said in the first class, is the writer's most effective tool.

Your hands are empty at your sides.

A month goes by. In class, he calls on you but he drops his eyes or he doesn't. Either way, it doesn't feel particular. You search for clues again. There must be something. Anything can be something, but you're not an idiot. Sometimes nothing isn't something. He is maybe avoiding you in his office. You look for him everywhere: the lobby, the coffee shop, the bus. Your roommate asks you who's died, if you left your sense of humor in Scarsdale. You spend hours in the library, hoping he'll come in. He doesn't. You wonder how he spends his days.

You sleep with a guy named Colton, who is getting his MA in comparative lit, and when it's done, he says, Maybe you can look over one of my papers sometime? My professors say I'm not thinking creatively enough. You're not even offended because you weren't thinking about him when it was happening, not even for a second. What do you care?

You haven't had a full meal in weeks. Just cornflakes, coffee, and kiwi. You've been listening to an album called *Adagios for Rain*.

On the first spring day, he's walking toward you on Amsterdam with a big bouquet of lilacs. Despite all your scheming to cross his path outside of class, he just shows up. This is what life does.

See how he moves faster when he sees you, waves big waves. Something good has happened, clearly. Do not ask him what. It has to do with his wife, you think. He's wondering, he says, if you'd like to walk with him. He has some time. It is then that you tell him about the books you read over break. He's impressed, says as much. When you tell him about Chekhov, he says he agrees, actually, and that he hadn't quite thought of that before. You laugh out loud. You realize how quickly you're talking, the balloon feeling in your chest. You realize that your cheeks are on fire and you think, if this walk ever ends, you'll die. You're not being dramatic: it is what it feels like.

And yours? you ask. You make a silent wish for some kind of revelation. High highs, low lows, he says. But when the writing goes well . . .

So, not his wife. He trails off. He is smiling with his whole head.

It could be worse. It could be better.

When you end up in a not-so-good neighborhood on Amsterdam, you realize it's not his size that makes you think he can protect you but something to do with the way he walks and talks. His voice is a straight shot. He takes long steps with a long back. His beard is full again. He's wearing a gray wool hat above his ears.

After a while, you get a coffee, share a bagel with vegetable cream cheese. There's a tiny bit on his lip, which he wipes away with your napkin. The flowers are beside him as you two sit on a stoop on Eighty-Ninth Street. They're not for you. You imagine what your mother would say. Is this ridiculous? It is just that she doesn't understand. You aren't hurting anyone.

What do you feel? he says, pointing at a blimp in the sky. About when the writing coalesces?

Utter euphoria, you say with a little too much fervor, a little too much sex. But the truth is, you do.

I'm glad, he says. Like nothing else matters, right?

Don't say: But you always would matter to me. Do not even think it.

When he talks about the difference between sentimental and emo-
tional, you want to change everything you've ever written, every
way you've ever behaved. With him and everyone.

There is this character that he's written. She's a young girl, brave,
funny. When you read her, you remember feeling as heartened as
you ever had. In a book, or otherwise. You wanted to be her, to be
around her, to have a child like her one day. Lucy. She's the catalyst
for a lot of action in his second novel. Sometimes, you find yourself
wanting to ask him: Am I brave like Lucy? Can I be? As if it would
be the only way to know. As if his telling you would change things.
You.

One day, in his office, you're about to tell him there's not much left
for you to do with his books. It must be getting obvious, and you
don't want to seem ungrateful. Instead, he comes in from his sem-
inar, and you can tell it's been a hard one. His hands are in fists and
he's just standing at the door as if he's afraid of stepping on a nest.
You want to tell him that you'd like to fix anything he ever needed
fixed but then you think of being sentimental. Can I bring you a
coffee? you ask instead. He nods. Sometimes, you think you know
what he needs better than he does.

Do not imagine his wife.

When you're happy, imagine holding his hand and he kisses your
neck just once, loud. You're at a café and both drinking tea, facing
out toward the street. He orders three pastries, none sweet. When
you're sad, imagine he wraps his arms around you from behind and

sways you. There are half-drunk glasses of wine and pasta on a counter, you're not sure whose. And you sway. Imagine that with him, sadness loosens like a marble that's been stuck.

Imagine he's a very good dancer, he's an excellent cook. After dinner—a whole fish, tomatoes, onions, lemons—he reads out loud that thing you wrote about the mountains you went to once with your father when you were five. He is blown away and he tells you. Imagine he's a capable driver; he laughs loudly with small children, his; he loves to swim.

16

There is only one-third of the semester left. He's on sabbatical next semester, and even if he weren't, there's no promise of anything. You have this nagging out-of-sight, out-of-mind feeling that sometimes makes you want to take the whole thing back. You're still unsure of the circumstance-to-coercion ratio. You can't force him to do anything, but sometimes you wonder if he would have sought you out. If he'd make any effort to find you if you disappeared. The thought makes you equal parts embarrassed and sad. Longing starts in your belly, ends up in your face.

So you plan it. The scenario that seems most probable, or convenient, or maybe inevitable. You've been imagining it for weeks. There is no other way for this to go.

Invite him to your apartment. Your roommate's working an extra shift. Tell him that you want to thank him properly for the class.

It's not a lie. You do. Your characters have gotten so much stronger. Your sense of arc more deliberate. You understand momentum differently. Like, come on. You have no idea if he'll say yes. There have been moments, and yet. You have no idea what's going to happen.

If there's anything worse than waiting in your apartment, alone, the place clean, a candle lit, greens on the table, good underwear, you haven't felt it yet.

Twenty minutes late, he knocks three times. Open the door. For a moment, he seems smaller than usual. Maybe it's your fault. This place, or something about the cheapness of these walls. Either way, it's like he's taken off his sunglasses, and without them, he's lost something. The word that comes to mind is *clout*. You're just nervous. Move back.

He comes inside, stops at the table, looks around, gathers details like scattered coins. He goes to your books, bends down, pulls out dog-eared copies, nods or laughs. It is his pacing, too, you realize, that is attractive. Your mother is always in a rush. It makes her seem mundane. You are endeared to him, but it is more than that. His confidence. You wonder about it. Is it the writing? Or age? Being married?

He goes into the kitchen. He asks you about your coffee maker, your roommate's Georgia O'Keeffe poster, the empty wooden bowl on the table that you got at a flea market and felt added some drama. He is a good person, you think. Engaged, concerned.

After a while—maybe you should have planned something—you sit next to each other on the couch. You think about offering him some wine, but you aren't great at opening bottles. And you're sure what he drinks at home is better. But there is something you can offer him. There is a reason he's here.

Face him. Start as you planned it. Start by telling him how much writing has always meant to you but how now it's different. There is a framework now. Tools. Use intentional words when you speak: consideration, amplitude, approbative. Tell him again about what his work has meant to you. How it is in you. Like stars. Go more slowly for this part. Drag it out. Be specific. This is when things shift. You watch him soften and lift, in a way. He looks at you. Turns his body toward yours. His eyes are like stones in a glass. He reaches for your face, puts his whole palm against your cheek, and you lean your body's weight. That is when you realize that you cannot feel your feet. There is eye contact. Then there is this.

Scoot closer then. His face flicks with expectation; it feels like he has been on the brink of kissing you for so long. Count backward from ten. Your heads are angled slightly back. Bows. Arrows. Drawn. For a moment, he wraps his hands around your ribs. You want to tell him that he can crack you open, if he wants. Do anything, if he wants. You trust him that much. Or maybe it would be worth it that much.

He holds your chin as if to prevent it from sinking. There is something sharpened here. A knife inserted and turned up. You have no idea if you have pinkies or pinky toes. This is the face you tell no one else. There is protection from speed, from sound. Everything feels sudden and finite. Like jumping into water. Or like straight hair, just combed.

Soon, he puts his face into your neck. Soon, you cannot catch your breath or do you even have it? Is this the thing of getting older? you wonder. Or being a father? The lovingness of it. The care. When he kisses you, there is kindness and adeptness. And rhythm. His hands are everywhere; his arms are walls behind you. He is more capable than you imagined. Stronger. You imagine yourself falling. It won't hurt. Or maybe it will. You don't care.

You have no idea how long this goes on for. It has never felt like this. He kisses you harder, then more softly. He moves you to where he wants you. On your back. Neck flat. You are a doll with heart. You are his. And sometimes, it is as if he is boring through a casing, a wooden hull. There is something inside you he wants. Something that he knows is there. No one knew. Until now.

And you wonder then: What is the difference between a snapshot and a memory? A thing that happened and a scene? Maybe something about arrangement? Something about breath? Because it's perfect, this moment. You want it to stop but also no. Whisper, Yes. Hear yourself feel. Make cups with your palms to feel it. What? There is a word.

For a moment, you almost laugh. You almost cry. Here: the words, even the words, cannot keep up. You hear yourself say, Please. The things you don't know how to ask for. His hands are warm. You are a door that stops swinging between them. Also: you are a spark.

And though shit will hit the fan eventually, has to, first: there is this. Whatever the word is for that. The not-words. And the world slips down or it feels like that. It cleaves into before and after this.

Wait, he says. Wait. One word, twice.

Just like that, everything drops. The trajectory scatters out from the top like dimes. He moves away, eyes closed. He stands up. He shakes out his face as though clearing it of something awful. His hands are in fists. You shudder.

I can't, he says. Or something like that. And you think—this is what you actually think: You can do better than that. Do better. You are thinking about the words.

You hold your actual heart then. He puts his face in his hands. Life bobs. Maybe you were just floating on rhythm all along. Or tides. He never even took off his clothes.

I'm so sorry, he whispers. I let myself get carried away.

He puts his hand on top of your head. You are a small dog. Woof. Look up at him. Your urge is to beg. Don't. His face has shut like a book. He puts on his scarf, hat, everything. You don't dare move.

Inevitability isn't the same as predictability. You didn't imagine this particular thing. Watch him leave. Cover your body with your arms. Still, you can't get up. You're not sure if your legs will even work. Is this even your skin?

Watch him close the door gently. Is he afraid of breaking it or you again? You have no idea.

17

After that, there is the time in his office that you close the door behind you. You just want to ask him about—what exactly? Everything. He opens the door back up. Stands against it. I can't, he says. It is not who I want to be. He is shaking his head, looking at the floor. He doesn't move aside. What else can you do? You just go, mouthing: It is. It is.

There is the time you see him in the rain, blocks from school, and he hugs you. A short one. You're going to be okay, he says. You're just getting started.

He pulls away and sort of lets his tongue hang out in exhaustion or maybe for air.

There is the other time. I wanted to ask you, you say when everyone has left the room. It's the final day.

When you said, You're so . . . Do you remember that?

I do, he says. His eyes won't connect with yours.

What did you mean? you ask.

It's just a turn of phrase, he says.

And that is that.

One time, not long after, you are in the Halls of Gems and Minerals at the Museum of Natural History and you're sure you see his wife. But you can't be sure. You've only ever glimpsed her in a photo. At the museum, you follow her around and around. You are intimidated by the way she walks, captivated by her long neck. *Secure* is the word that comes to mind. Like if she was on a deserted island, she'd be fine. You are maybe too obvious, and after a while, the maybe-wife says, Hello. You cannot say hello back. You run. On a deserted island, you would not be all right. You've got no idea how to make a fire from sticks.

For the rest of your life, you never finish another short story. You drop out of the program the following semester not because of him so much as because you've realized your heart isn't in writing, even if it felt like it might have been.

You go to graduation anyway, for obvious reasons. You see him and he stands a person away from you in a crowd and wishes you well. He actually says, I wish you well. You feel like you might throw up.

Afterward, you meet your mother for lunch. She asks if you are using the blush she bought for you.

It's not working, she says. You touch your face.

You do not work in writing or in publishing. For a while, you do billing for your ex-stepfather because it's simple and you can stay in the city and do the reverse commute. Margaux has graduated, is working for an artist named Haldi. It's abusive, the way you see it. He barely pays her, demands she go to Paris with him but makes her sleep on a cot, asks her for feedback and steals all her ideas. Margaux says it's part of the process. And she's always taking you to fabulous parties and you can distract yourself with champagne and bubble skirts.

You hear that his wife is an artist. You see a photo of her in an art magazine that you buy with the express purpose. Margaux's got her finger on the pulse. It was her at the museum. Sometimes, you wonder what you would have said to her. Nothing is what. You don't want to hurt him. Maybe because some part of you still believes that he'll come back around. And also: she is not a woman who would stand for it. And if you want her to be an important figure in your life—and there's a perverted way that you do—forget it. Forget it.

You join a book club just to make yourself read. You skate over all the words. Everything is icy. You have to read the same lines again and again and again. And what does it matter? There's no one to talk to, really. Not really.

Years later, you take a poetry class at a community college. There are moments when you remember the ecstasy and agony of writing. But then you try to write and fall flat on your face. Overall, your judgment is underwater too. Anything that anyone writes seems great to you—maybe because you're not writing yourself. Furthermore, you don't trust your professor. He's no expert. Or maybe you're just used to something else.

Just before your twenty-seventh birthday, you meet Fred through friends. He is more handsome than he is smart—you can tell that immediately—tall, thick eyebrows, lean swimmer muscles, good in suits. He smells like white soap, has no pores, no cracks for unwellness to slip through. An expensive watch doesn't clash with him. He is a success story without even. And though you sometimes think about juxtaposition and irony, it's rare these days. Unless you've been drinking wine.

Fred is kind. He doesn't read anything but the *Journal*. He likes films about history. He golfs. He comes from a good family, not super wealthy, the town over from yours. His father is a therapist. You wonder about being his patient. You wonder if you can get the answers anyhow.

Soon, you invent less. There is less cause. Comfort is intimacy. Intimacy is comfort. It doesn't feel like giving up, and yet. It feels like an unscrewing of something.

And to say that your mother is over the moon. Fred likes her too. Sometimes, he says things like, I don't know why you give her such a hard time. She won't be around forever.

You have to forgive him. And her. What choice do you have?

You haven't heard from your father in five years. Fred says, We have each other now. He isn't wrong.

Fred loves you each day. That is the truth. Never once is it dependent on the moon. Or tides. Or anyone else. There is no one else. He is supportive. You have your moments, but mostly they're because of you. Because of what you lost. In some ways, because of your mother. And father.

After a couple of years, he urges you to go back to school for special education because you talk about kids a lot and you're so good with them. You love school. You love the kids. They are all good inside. You realize you didn't really enjoy the drama so much as you fell into it. You blame the writing for a lot of that.

Until you get pregnant with your first child, you work at a school in Yonkers. Your coworkers are great. So is the administration. Sometimes, the kids ask you to tell them stories and you do. Everyone says what a knack you have for it. You should write a children's book but you don't. You could though.

Two years later, you have twin boys—Ethan and Noah—and they are insane until they are five, and then they are good, kind kids.

Noah doesn't have a creative bone in his body, but you can imagine Ethan as an architect. He started moving around the furniture when he was six. Let's have it like this, he said. It is a thing you say to each other for years about furniture, food, an outfit, vacation plans, and hopes. Let's have it like this. Let's have it like this. You love to take them to the Park not because it reminds you of Abe exactly but because you are comforted by the memory of being at the start of something, once. An uncracked spine.

When the boys are eight, you have a daughter, unplanned. As it turns out, she is a child with autism, and you give up your job to take care of her full time. She is brilliant. She is simply brilliant. She wants you to write a children's book too.

And him? You google him maybe once a year. On Sundays, you read the *Book Review*. Fred has switched newspapers. He's gotten much more liberal over the years. Probably because of your daughter. Never once does he ask about Abe—not only because he doesn't know about him, he doesn't, but because that is not the kind of relationship you have. You do puzzles together. He washes; you dry.

From what you've gathered, Abe has stopped teaching, which is a shame. He's written for all the important places, and more novels, and a second trilogy became a television series that has gotten much recognition and praise. He won that writing award that makes all the difference, and frankly, you're not surprised. Objectively speaking.

Of course, you wonder how he feels about it all. Writing never seemed to torment him as it did so many writers. Life did. But maybe that sorted too. No way to know.

One day, Margaux—never had kids, husband's an architect, both big deals now—emails you a piece from the Style section. It is about them. They are white-haired, aged. But they look as if they have a special, superhuman kind of strength and grace. Something about their necks and mouths. The way they stand with their arms down, leaning on nothing, unawkward with their hands. They are in their kitchen, which is painted dark green, and there are copper pots hanging from the ceiling that they must use. They have brown rugs, a wooden bowl full of pomegranates. She is in a mint-colored necklace, a gap between her teeth, a dimple. He is wearing his wool hat and looks distinguished. Is that the word? Your judgment doesn't hold up in this way anymore.

You wonder if anyone ever saw you together. If any of your moments outlasted themselves.

Sometimes, when you can't sleep, you imagine writing him a letter. You want to tell him he couldn't have managed a child with special needs. It takes so much out of you. Not that it's not worth it. But you want him to know all that you have done. What you have been through. You feel it's important that he knows.

Instead, you flip over and put your hand on Fred's cheek. This is a good man, you say in your own head. And he is. This is enough. You think about all those times that life didn't measure up until it did, with him. And you try to do the math of making this moment measure up. But to what now? The equation gets twisted around. You have a full and meaningful life. What does that equal exactly?

After that, there are two possibilities for how it goes.

One, you never reach out. Some nights, you dream that you end up together, but you're both young, the same age, and the world isn't the real world. It's good to you in ways that life never ever is. There is an unnatural sense of ease.

The other option is that you reach out.

You don't.

If you ever take out a journal to start writing, you end up writing about him. Maybe his is the only story you ever knew. Maybe his tire tracks run so deep that any time you try to run in any other direction, you can't find a trail. You're not even sure you loved him. You don't know the word for it. It has something to do with fiction. Or loving a ghost. And you don't blame him for anything. You're just very, very tired.

The only time you ever communicated again was during your final semester. He was on sabbatical. You'd switched your concentration; your paths never crossed. But you left him a copy of the story of you and him in his mailbox in a yellow envelope, typed, no name. You had finished it while you were still in his class, but you couldn't share it. Not then. In the end, you were proud of it. It had arc.

The school forwarded the same envelope with all the pages to your home address that summer. It arrived when you were dripping from the pool, no shoes on. You stood next to the mailbox. A whole-body beating heart. When you opened it, you shouldn't have been surprised. You scoured, checked twice: there was not a word on a single page except the final one. No coffee stains or stray feathers either. Nothing. Just a tiny slit in the paragraph about the woman in a blurry photograph. The one in which she is wearing white and there is a gap between her teeth and a large potted plant behind her. It means nothing. It probably caught on something. Like, what did he care? Let it rip. On the last page, in red ink: We try to avoid drama for drama's sake. The content of a romance novel is actually romantic even if the writing is mediocre.

And so you wonder, which came first? Character or the invention of character? What would watching the snowfall look like without the words? Without the writing and all the sunlight it casts? Which is to say: impossible to know what you truly loved in him, if anything. If it was him or him or him or him or him or him or him or.

18

CENTRAL PARK

Some Park-goers are hopeless romantics, abstinent, transitioning. A Colombian nanny has millions of followers for her XXL nail-tapping ASMR content, the ex-NFL superstar for his thirteen engagements, the freshman for her underground erotic sonnets. A jeweler and his wife are celebrated for the longest marriage in city history. They will be wheeled in, despite the heat, and photographed by the Boathouse in their original wedding clothes. The economist is into electrostimulation. The lady who lunches: klismaphilia. The gym teacher just wants home-cooked meals every evening and sex twice a week; missionary is great. The sommelier from Per Se is entering at Columbus Circle in underwear that isn't his. The Ayurvedic healer has yoni eggs shoved high up as she sloshes through the sleet. The accountant has just gotten his first wax for a younger lover. The poet in grad school is closed for business. No *ands, ifs,* or *buts.* She's twenty-three but has known since the first time. The gymnast on her way to the University of Michigan has just lost her virginity. Can you tell? Can you see it in my face? Jaclyn rarely comes this far uptown, but it's more convenient for her mother, who says that there is nothing a brisk winter walk amid nature can't fix. The last time Jaclyn came to the Park, she walked the Bridle Path; it was a different season; she was falling in love with Max.

Some Park-goers are on the apps, in the films, filmers themselves. Some write love letters; some do it for a living. There are nuns and repeat offenders. There are sex therapists and love guides who rely on ayahuasca for recovery from sexual abuse. Check out my feature in Goop! There are those who have been traumatized and come to heal alone on the rocks when they're warm. I feel safer here than I do at home. David brings his young lover and bumps into an ex-young lover and they all go for primavera and bruschetta at Sambuca. There is a divorced couple—they met at a NESCAC and married immediately after graduation—on far ends of the Park—southwest, mideast—with new partners, but they are texting each other. The kids would never believe it. They've moved out; the dust has settled; don't they deserve a second chance?

Every Monday, Wednesday, and Friday there is a Mommy and Me class in the Park near Safari Playground. It has the highest coupling success rate of all the classes in all the boroughs. Single mommies (I'd prefer to do it myself; he left me; she died) languish in the support of other mommies. Being here feels like being held up. Married mommies wonder if they're in flux, confused, or just learning their true selves, finally. They are in dresses, incorrectly buttoned, pads, sweaters with lacy milk stains down the front. They schlep diaper bags full of quartered grapes and sunscreen. One forgot the sunscreen. One forgot a diaper. One forgot her words. Here, use mine! Some long to go back to careers in marketing, tech, retail. Some always wanted to be a mommy, but this is hard. Some want another three, ideally all girls, and soon. They sing "Five Little Hearts" and "Peekaboo, I Love You" and can't stop staring at one another. Motherhood makes you more beautiful. This love makes you raw. This is just a phase. I'll never go back. In the Park, mommies discover that kinship can also be wildly intimate. They didn't know. They know now.

Dolly and Diller are fourteen-year-old bassets who have been walking the Lower Loop since they came to the city from Honey Brook, Pennsylvania, at ten weeks. They twist up their leashes so they can walk with their heads pressing into each other, velour ears, watery eyes, leather snouts. They make their way down past the Dairy Visitor Center and the Chess & Checkers House. They always pee at the same time, often near the Balto statue at East Drive and Sixty-Seventh, north of the zoo. They've never liked huskies; their pheromones are bitter. When their walker takes them off leash, they roll around in the fallen oak and maple leaves, green and brown, crunchy and crisp, arms around each other like pieces of a puzzle, united at long last. They have one million followers on Instagram, have been photographed for the Valentine's Day issue of the *Times*, can slurp spaghetti like the Disney cartoon. Two days after Dolly dies, Diller's heart gives out. He had been in great shape. We can't believe it. The vet diagnoses him with takotsubo syndrome, after the fact. Also known as dying of a broken heart. Their ashes are scattered near Heckscher Ballfields, together, of course, where they loved to watch the games and howl at the catchers' gray mitts; they look like a husky's face.

After leaving the Park, the interior designer yells at her spouse over nothing: recycling, tea bags, something she didn't say but wanted to. The immigration attorney loses it over a pair of shoes. Do you know what I see every day? And I have to come home to this? People look in the mirror, feel undesirable, undesiring. I used to be attractive. They are wan, lethargic, bloated from the holidays, long nights out, in, a broken heart. Some are spinning from so much time spent watching reruns. What did we even do all day? Some are still organizing drawers of socks.

In the Park, the couple will not fight in public, so they talk about their kids instead. The gynecologist's third wife stops obsessing over when he'll text back. Reception is spotty near the North Meadow anyway. There is nothing to do, I guess, but notice the baby bunnies, and breathe. The caretaker, Bernie, and her husband can't help but sway to the tuba played by the man in a leopard costume. The husband hates Bernie's hours and what the work requires of her (everything), but here they are. They stand apart, then they stand together. Soon, they hold hands and wave. The weatherwoman, who usually adheres to a list of indisputables, is heartened by the guy with freckles on the bench. He's sharing a mixed-berry muffin with his corgi and trying the water fountain to refill his bottle, but it's frozen; nothing comes out. He seems like a good guy. Maybe I don't hate freckles after all.

19

MAX

Max promised himself he'd never get married. He believes that motion is a virtue, the world could do with less compassion, and monogamy is for the witless. At twenty-three, he had all his shirts embroidered with AYCGAW (Anything You Can Get Away With) on the cuffs. He threw them out at thirty when he became obsessed with not trying too hard, but the notion stuck. He had sex for the first time at fourteen in his parents' bed not because he wanted to mess with them but because his bed was just too small. He sold his first Picasso his first year out of college. A Magritte sculpture the next year. Both to the wives of billionaires: a Russian oligarch, a Texan Jew in oil, respectively. Both good in bed.

Max likes to say, I run this city (Manhattan), wink, smirk, and then pretend he's joking. But there is a lot that he is offered, given, can dispose of, because of who he is. He didn't inherit any of it. His father is a professor and a writer; his mother is an artist. With success, to a degree, in his opinion, but not the kind you can sail away on. They have been together for nearly five decades—an unshakable unit, double helix, a hot-air balloon, up, up, and away. Max has feelings about that, too, that you can probably surmise.

Max has been with a lot of women. To count them would be to throw darts at a moving target. Would be gauche. There have been dancers, Romanians, preschool teachers, baristas, lawyers, plastic surgeons, landscapers, cleaning staff, and one politician who would probably surprise you. Has he ever been stopped in his tracks? No. In love? He did say *I love you* once. He was broken up with a week later for good reason. It was a last-ditch effort. Sometimes, Max convinces himself to do traditional, everyday things. It never works.

The only woman he's ever known worth giving up gluten or caviar for, not that anyone asked, is his father's mother, his grandmother, Bubbe. She's been gone almost ten years now and it's not that it still hurts exactly—no tears—but often, Max has to snuff out the urge to call her and tell her something of note. Max, she often said in response, be good. Be good, Max! He was so often not good: scheming, philandering, not calling his parents. Still, Bubbe adored him, made him apricot-and-raspberry rugelach every week until the end. It must have been all that caring she did for him as a child, Max thinks. He heard somewhere that it is affection and not biology that bonds, though they had both. Max and Bubbe. Bubbe and Max.

Max's own mother, beloved, industrious, never not steeped in all-consuming creative thought, had major postpartum depression after Max was born, and then was knee-deep in her art—a jerked response. And then she got hit with cancer so big, so deep, that Max mostly remembers her ushered from the front door to the bed, the bed to the front door, coated and hatted, by his father. Come, honey. Let's get you comfortable. Let's get you into a cab. Max is okay. Bubbe is here.

They were never a family per se. They were a triangle broken into lines. The one from him to his mother especially dashed. The one to his father intact, but faint.

A really nice thing Max can say about his mother is that she would die for her art. A really nice thing he can say about his father is how much he loves her.

Be good. Be good, Max!

The first time Max sees Jaclyn, they are at an art opening on Twenty-Second Street and Jaclyn is wearing a silk dress with a black sweater around her shoulders, drinking sparkling water in the middle of the room. She is taking in a painting of a blue pig, looking genuinely interested. Max asks around—who is she?—and only then does he go up to her, prepped. He introduces himself, kisses her on both cheeks, then steps back as if suddenly stunned by the shock of being close to her. As if she's an ember, an October rose. He asks her if she is a model. Typically, a woman this attractive who isn't a model will be offended. Jaclyn's face doesn't flinch or crumble like a sandcastle at noon. Instead, she answers him with four words and excuses herself politely.

Something about her self-sufficiency reminds him of his grandmother, whom he'd like to tell as much.

For weeks, for Max, Jaclyn is a curiosity or perhaps a bar, raised. He sleeps with other women. Some he just takes to dinner and then he goes, alone, for ice cream and a film. But the more time that goes by, the more he finds himself genuinely wondering about Jaclyn: what she thought about the blue pig, her feet, her ice-cream order, favorite film.

In the meantime, Max's mother is very sick. Max should go out to Orient to see her, but the effort feels daunting. In healthy times, he'd go every couple of months, stay for an hour or two. Abstractly, they'd talk about art, a new way to brew coffee, a silly amount he'd made on a deal. Some relationship of his had always just ended—if you could call them that. Max is never looking for feedback and his mother never offers it. Max can't remember a time when he took her advice. There was a precedent set up when he was very young. Her with kid gloves. Him with arms crossed.

Max's father calls as Max is getting in the shower. Max sends it to voicemail. It is not that he does not love his mother. It is that when he thinks of her, really thinks of her, he sees her nightgowned back in bed, curtains drawn, a slightly sweaty, sweet smell emanating, and it coaxes in him a feeling of dread more than nostalgia. They have had their moments, but mostly when they least expected it.

When his mother mistakenly spilled flour on the floor and they made shapes—a pirate, a duck, a lamppost—until his father walked in, primed for damage control.

Everything okay? he'd said, arms out.

Her current sickness leaves him with an exhausted feeling that he cannot shake. When he thinks of her, he longs to fold into himself like a cot. And sleep.

Max is busy. People expect a certain energy from him, a certain vim.

Soon, Max sees Jaclyn at his local coffee shop. He steps in and pays for her matcha. She is reading the label of a bag of nuts and looks up only to thank him. Max knows that he is at the end of a long line of people who have bought her drinks. Still. There is a draw to her, the strength of her stance, the subtle moves of her mouth. Sit with me, he says, putting a hand to the small of her back. Jaclyn picks up her matcha and protests his offer without words. It is then he realizes that there is not a lick of makeup on her face though it looks somehow lit from behind. Her eyes are tidepools. It occurs to him that she looks healthy. As if illness were a baseline, a dead giveaway.

Let me walk you wherever you're going, Max says. They walk five blocks south. Never once—in language or physical movement— does Jaclyn scurry to appease him. She speaks so softly that he nearly trips over her feet to hear. Her words are like putting down bills to pay. The intention of it. All this: Max likes.

Hey, Bubbe. Guess what.

In the meantime, Max is getting serious about hot yoga. There is a particular studio on Kenmare where no one bothers him. He turns off his phone, closes his eyes, grunts as he moves his body into positions he's only witnessed in bed. And on-screen. It is where he does his best thinking, at yoga, the sweat purging information inaccessible to him otherwise. Lately, he thinks of Jaclyn. He imagines walking through a small white gallery with her, biking behind her on a windy autumn road. Is it the thrill of the chase that's digging its claws into him? he wonders. Or is it her? He's never been clear on that with any woman. He's only ever been disappointed when he's caught up in the race.

He remembers to call his father back but doesn't. The day gets busy. Then he forgets.

Max sees Jaclyn at Gutai, Frieze, PPOW. He sees her at a mini Christo retrospective in the Park. He's at the Met Gala after-party with a woman who owns a vegan ice-cream cone company and used to be in Cirque du Soleil when he spots Jaclyn in a fern-green gown. Her hair is shiny, cascading down her back, the color of patent leather, in a bow. He follows her into the bathroom. She laughs, pushes him out. After that, he cannot find her again. But she's stuck into him like burrs.

In the meantime, Max's father calls again. His mother is really very sick, for crying out loud. First, when Max was small—just after the postpartum lifted—then again five years ago, but that wasn't the worst time. Sick and then sicker and then less sick and then really sick again. They are out in Orient full time now, God knows why. Why they ever sold their place in Manhattan, Max has no idea. It makes it impossible to see them. The trip is lengthy, to the literal end of the world. Max apologizes to his father. It's the time of year. He asks him if he has everything he needs. His father just says Max's name once—Max—as if he's driving a heavy shovel into frozen ground. Max's relationship with his father is friendly, finite. They can play cards or browse a used bookstore like the best of them. But they rarely do. Years ago, everyone had to take sides. Including Bubbe. Who took his.

One day, during yoga, Max has to shut his eyes against an image. It is his mother's body, as if photographed, floating in a tub of water, all sinew and length. Her mouth is loose but with residual shape, like a ribbon untied. There is something dead about her but she is not. Her eyes blink against him. Max stands up quickly, the floor creaking, the yogic silence of the room breaking wide open. There is a queasiness in his throat and it feels like having walked in on his parents, naked.

Cut it out, he whispers to no one. The whole class goes, Shush.

Be good. Be good, Max!

Max goes to Singapore, Rome, and Nashville. He sees Jaclyn at the Union Square Greenmarket eating a pretzel. He sees her walking out of Brunello on Madison with two bags, heading toward the Park.

Once, he stops. The other time, she is too fast. There is no progress made. He continues to move through his life like an arrow, shot. Lingering is for the indolent. He gets lymphatic drainage massages, drinks celery juice, has suits custom fit to his body. He is studying Buddhism and his guru tells him to get a dog. He gets a money plant instead.

His father calls. His mother's new medication isn't doing what they'd hoped.

I'll come when I can, he says.

He is not trying to be mean; he just knows they have it taken care of. They always have. Her cancer is an intimacy between his parents, a sacred pact.

Max invests in a new building in Tribeca, and a juice bar on Little West Twelfth. He goes for acupuncture, the kind where they stimulate the needles. He nearly flies off the table. He grits his teeth. He works late and drinks a bottle of Rothschild 1937 with a woman he's slept with a few times. She has a young child. You can tell from her hips and the way she checks her phone.

Max sees Jaclyn getting her hair done in the window on East Sixty-Seventh. There is a brush rolled up in the front part of her head that makes her look royal. Max isn't above groveling. With him, it is more sport, less desperation. He gives her a calla lily he plucks from the arrangement in front, and Jaclyn acquiesces to a date with him only when he offers to talk to a Miami client about Lili Reynaud-Dewar: the multidisciplinary French artist, focused on intimacy and, also, the female body. Jaclyn's been championing her work on Instagram. Max has noticed.

A few nights later, Max takes Jaclyn to Keens. When her filet arrives, barely cooked, Max flags down the waiter to send it back. No, she says. She eats the entire thing, pooling blood, with a fork and knife as if she had been trained by the queen of England. His mother has eschewed red meat since her first cancer diagnosis. He is not making a connection here, or even an opposition. It is just that he isn't used to being surprised.

After dinner, Max and Jaclyn walk through the Park. The moon has everything lit up like candle wax and she leans into him, whispers something about how beautiful. It reminds her of a painting. It occurs to Max to say something about his mother, who has often painted the night—not for a reaction but out of genuine impulse—but he holds his tongue. He knows how romance works and, for him, that is not it.

Max sells two Reynaud-Dewars. Jaclyn doesn't call to thank him, but she does let him take her to the orchid show at the Brooklyn Botanical. Does it sometimes feel like she is humoring him? It does. Does he care? Not exactly. The humidity, the pressing heat of the greenhouse, brings out the smell of her hair: rose, desert. Being up close to her feels like being near an owl. Max is suddenly tired. He hasn't been sleeping well. There is a loose feeling in his chest as if a knot has been snipped from its sides. He leans into Jaclyn, to her sacred smell. She leans too.

Bubbe. I just wanted to tell you.

His father emails. They are going to be at Sloan Kettering later in the week for his mother's treatment if he'd like to offer some support. His father gets terse and clipped when he's an intermediary between Max and his mother. It's habit from Max's childhood, when Max was always on the other side of impatience and his mother just couldn't.

Max can't remember a time when they felt like a team. Which came first, Max wonders: cracking a mirror, spilling glue, screaming, or passing through his parents like wind through a chime? For how long was she sick the first time? A decade? Two years. It was a house littered with eggshells.

For a moment, Max considers meeting them at the hospital. It is always hours in the waiting room—his father pacing, his mother dozing on and off. People look at Max with pity. The devoted son. Then he starts with the phone calls. They look at him with disdain. Come on, Max.

Max emails back that he has a meeting, which isn't untrue. He signs the email: xx.

Does he think it will be harder to bed Jaclyn than it is? He does.

They've just been to a tulle show at the Frick. There they are, in his apartment, drinking Japanese whiskey. She's taken off her jacket. Her shoulders glisten like sugar, cooked. She is leaning against his kitchen counter and the strap of her dress falls to her elbow. He doesn't go for it. He lets things simmer. The scorch of her gaze when they are out is replaced by near glassiness with trust here. That was easy. Never not, in a way. Jaclyn is a white leopard in a crocheted dress until the dress pools on the floor like spilled milk. Her breath reminds him of summers, sun on sand. She makes not a sound, eyes closed tight to keep it all out. She is focused on something inside herself rather than out. He is competing with a world otherworldly, he thinks, which is nothing he can't handle.

Max has an inkling. He will not shut his eyes.

Weeks go by. Max believes devotedly in not putting all his eggs in one basket. Still, he is reminded of Jaclyn especially at dusk, and when he hears the horn in the Park played by a guy with no legs, and at the beginning of yoga when he is meant to set an intention. Sometimes, a thought of her devolves into a thought of his mother, and so Max reaches out to a married woman named Caroline with kids not much younger than Max. Her husband is always away. He owns two airlines and a soccer team. He bought a Hockney from Max last month.

His mother's oldest friend, Bea, calls. She makes kooky bottlecap art, unprestigious.

Would you like me to go with you? she asks.

I've been busy, he says.

With what? Bea says, and Max pretends it's hard to hear her.

Once, when Max was eight, Bea smacked him on the chest. He had said something about all the other mothers at school being at pickup or maybe a soccer game.

Your mother isn't like all the other mothers, she said. You'll be glad one day.

Which?

Jaclyn goes to London for a month.

While she's gone, Max has a recurring dream. He and Jaclyn are on a motorcycle, doing hairpin turns along some cliffs in Big Sur or maybe Greece. She's on the back and when he turns around—he's heard a sound—he discovers she's fallen off. He can't find her anywhere. He searches in the rocks, along the road, but then gets distracted by a hotel bar with a tall cracked mirror. But it is actually Tavern on the Green. His mother is in the reflection, young, focused. And then she's not. When Max wakes, there's a hollow feeling in his throat that makes him cough.

When Jaclyn comes back, Max does not tell her the dream, but he feels it in every interaction they have like a third wheel or a storm, looming.

On a busy Monday, his father calls the office, passes the phone. There is a loud bang and then some crinkling. Hi, his mother says. Her voice is cracked down the middle. The radiation does this. After

the niceties, Max tells her that he'll come out to Orient in a week.
She hasn't asked.

For a moment, Max almost hangs up. Then it occurs to him that
he should give her something.

I'm seeing someone, he says.

The line is silent.

Jane? Max says again to his mother.

Oh, she says, clearing her throat. I thought you were talking to
someone else.

Max takes Jaclyn to the opera. Sometimes, he wants to parade her
around like a pet peacock. Other times, he wants to shrink her into
a corner or a velvet box so that he can look at her. Just him. Just her.
Are his feelings for her bigger than they've been for other women?
They are softer. Or he is. She does not cry at the opera as other
women do, but she closes her eyes to feel it. He has done this, too,
himself, at times. He keeps wondering when she'll splinter into
storm—and what he'll do. His capacity for hysteria has always
been nil.

On a Saturday afternoon, Jaclyn suggests they meet at the Reservoir. She is in a leather jacket and jeans, a gray scarf. They walk
along the Bridle Path. Her legs are long and she doesn't struggle
to keep up. At first, she asks him about his parents, but she already

knows who they are. She loves his mother's work, his father's two trilogies, and the miniseries they made of *Dahlia Diane*. She asks him about his childhood and he says what he always says, I was an impossible kid. I nearly killed off my mother. Usually, it feels light and airy. And true. Today, it does not. Jaclyn looks shocked, hurt even. I can't imagine anything being too much for your mother, she says. Max almost takes it to heart.

I think she might be on her last legs, he says as if to rectify things, ingratiate himself. It is so unlike him to be this vulnerable. Immediately, he wants to take it back. Jaclyn has stopped walking. She faces him, goes for his hand.

I'm so sorry, she says.

No, Max says.

What he wouldn't give for a do-over. His right nipple. Twenty-six years of his life.

Jaclyn bobs her head down. Max takes a deep breath. He brushes some hair out of her face and kisses her on the mouth. The kiss goes on long enough for Max to recalibrate, for the moment to reabsorb. In the meantime, he allows Jaclyn to confuse passion with passion. He can do this for her. For him.

When they back up, Jaclyn's eyes are slick. Her face is softened. He takes her hand and they fall back into stride again.

Let's talk about you, he says, and imagines patting himself on his own back.

Jaclyn tells Max that she is one of four girls, grew up on the Jersey shore. Her father has two restaurants and a bar. She got married young to the son of a Russian tycoon whom you've probably heard of. That explains it, Max says. He is impressed when she's not offended. Maybe he wants to offend her. It is his nature to trigger. It is what he knows how to do.

When they part at the Central Park South exit: If you ever want to talk about her, she says.

Max is flushed with sudden warmth. Disarming and sort of sickening too. It shoots from his belly to his throat, nearly knocks him back.

That is kind, Max hears himself saying. They are not words he would actually say. And yet. There they are. And there she is. Jaclyn, her face a dumpling of concern. Max nearly reaches for it. He nearly holds her cheek, and thanks her. Thank you.

I'm okay, he says instead, trying to feel his feet. I'm fine.

Max bumps into his old friend Todd at Holiday Bar. They don't see each other often but they go back. Todd is a banker, happily-ish married, two little girls, West Village town house. He likes to get the dirt on bachelor life, and Max likes to dish it. This time, Max mentions Jaclyn. You like her, Todd says. Max shrugs. Is there dignity in your loneliness? Todd asks. Am I lonely? Max says. Love, he feels, should be about adding to a whole. Not adding to a hole, you know? He's not trying to be funny. So you're a hole, Todd says. How is your mom?

Max doesn't invite Jaclyn to the Biennial—which, this year, is elaborately relocated to Sheep Meadow due to museum renovations. He is sure she'll be there anyway and he hates redundancy. His mother has a piece in it and has made the nonsensical decision to go with his father. The two of them. They hire a driver in and out. Max shows up late. The sun is setting, orange glow, and there is an intricate lighting system set up, as well as white cranes draped in fabric to designate the space. It is art in itself but it doesn't matter. Max isn't paying attention. Instead, he is searching for Jaclyn. He does a loop. After a while, a cocktail, lots of handshaking and air-kisses—where is she?—he finds his parents, perched on a pair of wooden chairs with white ribbon wrapped around the back, leaning into each other. As they do.

Hello, parents, Max says, four kisses. There is a security guard posted next to them and Max's first thought is they're making sure someone can carry her out, if need be. They are in brown and black, their boots and scarves and belts nearly identical. His mother looks all right—though too much lipstick. Max slings an arm around each of them. He is briefly alarmed by how small they seem, short, bony—squirrels—but what can he do? He flags down a waiter, another cocktail down the hatch. Still no Jaclyn. Max looks at the crowd, the place crawling with people who have given him money.

And because he doesn't know what else to say: Let's do this, he says.

His parents look at him with confusion. Oh, Max, his mother says.

Well, his father says and claps once. But he doesn't finish his thought.

Where is Jaclyn? Max thinks. He yearns.

Sometimes, Max wonders if it is because of who Jaclyn is or because Max can't be sure of who she is that he keeps on with her. She is so much shadow, or maybe so much light, that he's unsure of the actual thing of her. And what is the connection, really? Some people are bound by mind, body, or heart. Never Max. For Max, with any relationship, even with this one, it feels like eating glazy fruit tarts and forgetting to wash his hands. The whole thing sticky, if not truly connected. Is that enough? Is that this?

The next night, Max and Jaclyn are at dinner at il Buco outside in wool coats. It is late. The moon is passing over and under the clouds like cards, shuffling. The streetlights are out for whatever reason and it feels like a different city with light only from apartments. A couple walks by with a baby in a stroller, covered in blankets. Max watches Jaclyn's face for clues. Jaclyn smiles at the mother but doesn't peer into the carriage.

Yes? Max says when they pass. Yes what? Jaclyn says. You want one, he says.

Doesn't matter, she says. I can't. Her face shuts like an elevator door. Max doesn't ask anything else. He is flooded with relief. For some ungodly reason, the image of his mother's funeral occurs. There are thousands of people, bleary with grief, a gospel choir, a female rabbi, candles flickering in the wind. And there is Jaclyn. He is with her. She holds his hand and nothing else.

Can Max imagine Jaclyn as a mother? He can. Does he feel like he's getting away with something? He does.

Be good, Max. Be good!

The next week, Max is meant to pick up Todd for dinner and off they go, but when he gets there, the babysitter has canceled. Todd's wife is already at girls' night and cannot be bothered. Todd asks if it's all right if they just hang out at home. Max likes Todd's two girls—can never remember whether or not they're twins. But they're good, curtsy when he comes in and then watch their iPads with silent, animal intensity. He and Todd drink beer at the counter, eat hummus, order pizza. After dinner, the girls beg Max to read them a book on the couch. They pick it. It's about speaking of the things you fear so they don't overtake you.

And you're afraid of what? Max asks them, one, then the other.

One says the hiccups. The other says boobs.

Boobs? Max says. She nods.

Yes, he says. Better to be a man. Less boobs.

You're demented, Todd yells from the kitchen, cleaning up.

Max bows. Thank you! he yells back.

When Jaclyn orgasms, it's slow. She meanders down an ice floe. Then, a sudden exhale, eyes open, brows furrowed. She sits up, stands up, quickly. It always feels to Max like she's a tiny bit disappointed. Like she didn't mean to do it. It makes Max want to try again. With her, it feels constantly like he's underperforming. It has never been like this with anyone. She is a drawer that won't open. A bird that won't fly. He is clapping his head off.

She stays over. First thing the next morning, before toothpaste, sex, or coffee, Jaclyn turns to him, pulls the sheets to her chin.

I was in a car crash when I was married, she says. It damaged my uterus.

That's awful, he says, meaning it. For the last twelve hours, he would have done anything to please her. Now it feels as if he's sweating in wool pants.

His mother. Cervical cancer, hysterectomy, IIA2, IIIC2, IVB, leaking, lining, tubes.

Sometimes, he feels like the only one who's whole.

Max goes to hot yoga once a day, sometimes twice. His twists have gotten deeper. He can bind behind his back now, rest his hands on the ground behind his head in standing forward fold. The sweat pours off him. Memories stream as if he's being turned upside down and shaken. The bags under the eyes of his chemistry teacher, a painting of a broken chair that hung in his father's office, a woman he used to date who sent her sheets to be dry-cleaned in France, Jaume Plensa, banana cream pie, his mother's paint-splattered jeans—out of nowhere, she is running to a sink to retch—a water tower on West Seventy-First. Jaclyn occurs to him, too, but mostly just her face. Thank God.

Max remembers the sound of his mother throwing up in his youth, clear as day. The walls were thick but it didn't matter. Sometimes, he'd put a pillow over his head and hum "You Are My Sunshine" at the top of his lungs.

Jaclyn's boss, Margaux, takes Jaclyn to Vietnam for a month. Jaclyn often talks about Margaux's amazing marriage with Marc. He's an architect. They're so aligned. Seek art in everything et cetera. Okkkkkayyyyyy. The night before, Jaclyn and Max sleep together. She has to leave before sunrise for the airport. Max thinks she'll email. She doesn't. Or text. Finally, he calls her. Margaux picks up and promises to relay the message.

The famous Max, she says. I know your father. Friend of a friend.

Either Margaux doesn't relay the message or the message doesn't matter. Max doesn't think to tell his father about what she said.

As Max is searching for a particular set of cuff links, he finds an old birthday note—Happy 15th!—from Bubbe with a check for one hundred dollars, uncashed, and a red glitter car on the front. Inside, among birthday wishes, in her old-lady Jewish scrawl: Kindness begets kindness. Love, Bubbe. Max doesn't know why he saved this one in particular—it feels atypical—though he did many others. He never cashed any of her checks—knowing he would one day be rich.

For years, Max all but moved in with Bubbe. He would do his homework at her kitchen table, eat all her crackers and cheeses. Already then, his grandfather was on the decline, in the front room with all his things. A nurse came most days. They were never close, Max and his grandfather. He wasn't a man people were close to, not even his own sons. He was a man who took everything too seriously. Himself and everyone around him.

Alone in his closet, Max apologizes to Bubbe. I'm not not being kind, he says. And then, though no one is listening, and Bubbe's been gone long enough that he cannot hear her back, he whispers, Sorry, to no one. Maybe.

Finally, on an unusually warm day, Max sees Jaclyn. It is a surprise. At first, he walks right by her, doesn't even notice her. He's thinking about something else, a deal, an endless negotiation. Jaclyn is outside Mah-Ze-Dahr on a bench, cross-legged, eating a croissant. Is that a cinnamon roll? Is she in sweatpants? This is so unlike her, Max thinks. He's never seen her dressed down. He should stop. He should touch her and make sure it is, in fact, her. He should ask her:

What the hell? Where has she been? Instead, he puts his head down, speeds. Her complete obliviousness of herself, of him, her focus on the pastry. It makes his forearms itchy, and his back. He jogs to his meeting and tries to shake the memory off his mind like flies.

Max goes to yoga. He buys expensive rare books and a pair of handmade brown suede boots with fine laces from the place he loves in Portugal. He bumps into Margaux at Gramercy Tavern. She's at a meeting too. All leather and cashmere and silver.

Were you in publishing before art? Max asks her, but what he means is, Where the fuck is Jaclyn?

No, she says. I knew your father when I was studying art. Through a friend.

Days later, he is meeting a client at Buvette. There is Jaclyn on a different bench, same sweatpants. Max stands in the crosswalk, watching her talk to herself. He watches her lips move. Her face looks chalked over. She puts her hand on her belly and only then does he realize who she is talking to. His heart falls out from between his legs.

And he wonders, has she ever talked this much? It looks as if she is telling a story.

It is not a day for a down coat, but she is in one. Max will call her. He will call his mother too. The cars are beeping. He texts his client to meet at a bar down the street instead. There, he drinks and drinks and drinks.

A particular memory recurs during yoga. A few years ago, when his mother had relapsed, though Max didn't know it at the time, Max walked into their town house. He found her there, eating soup and crying over it. She'd spoon some to her mouth and it would bubble out, thin and wobbly. She was a child, an invalid. Some was on her apron, orange-stained like vomit. Her shoulders were shaking as though someone was moving them from behind. Max backed out, shut the door without being seen. The responsibility of approaching her, dealing, was oppressive to him—and outside their scope. Max cannot remember his mother feeding him soup as though landing an airplane in his mouth. It never happened. At a certain point, his mother must have just given up.

He wonders if it got easier after that.

20

Once, Max dated a therapist. The relationship was okay. Went on for a year. It ended with her screaming at him on the corner of Sixth Avenue and Bleecker. One day, you're going to have to attach to someone, she said. It isn't healthy, the way you behave. Childhood aside.

Will I? he said. He was really asking. And also, isn't it? I feel fine.

Jaclyn's left a bobby pin at his apartment, which his housekeeper has ceremoniously placed on the kitchen counter. It is the only item other than a politely folded dish towel she'll allow. She is making a point. Is it that Jaclyn is special or just another hair to vacuum off the rug? He wants to ask, but her English isn't great.

Max's mother is on morphine. His father preps him though they've been through this before. The first time, his mother wouldn't stop singing Hanukkah songs and making peanut butter and jelly sandwiches. He remembers how his father kept retoasting them the whole week long, eating them in triangles, his mouth twisty and dried out. This time, on the phone, she launches into a dreamy meditation on the sky and the color blue. Max is reading emails as she does.

It is a feeling, she says. Do you feel it?

What? he says.

Connection, she says.

It is not that he doesn't want to hear what she has to say. He is just not sure that she'll remember it. He writes Love instead of Sincerely to a client by mistake and presses send and then it's too late.

Where is Jaclyn?

Max calls his mother back. His father is elated to pass him through.

I do feel it, he says.

Feel what? she says.

They are both quiet for a good long time.

When Max wakes up, the phone is in his hand, dead.

Jaclyn calls on a Saturday. She apologizes in a voice that doesn't seem to him like hers. His first instinct is not to take care of her but to ask her, What the fuck? He does not. Instead, he invites her over. She shows up an hour late. He had wanted them to catch LaToya Ruby Frazier's opening at the Brooklyn Museum for an activity, some distraction from whatever's eating Gilbert Grape—but that's out of the question now. He's had two bourbons and is hopped up. Hungry but also not in the mood to actually eat. She rings the doorbell. She's in jeans and a worn white T-shirt, no bra. She sits down on the couch and pats the seat beside her. He starts to kiss her, not because he wants to, but in an attempt to change the mood. She shrugs him away.

He knows what's coming. There is only one thing to do.

I have to tell you something, she says.

You're pregnant, he says.

I'm pregnant, she says. Only just.

It is different with her here. It feels like blame thrown in his face like pie even though she hasn't, at all. Max wants to open a window. Instead, he draws up into himself, a couple of inches taller, insides stretched like a rubber band. There is nothing to lean on even though he's sitting down, so he holds on to a pillow.

You said, he begins to say.

I know, she says. I can't keep it. Most likely, it won't even be viable.

So you're just telling me, he says.

Yes, she says.

Max's mother would love a grandchild. He is surprised that the first thing he thinks of is that.

Max has another bourbon. Then, another. Jaclyn stares out the window, then at him, then out the window again. Is it possible, he thinks, that she looks extra beautiful tonight? Glowy? He cannot be sure that it is not context rather than fact—or if it even works like that. Eventually, Max orders in sushi because what does he know? Jaclyn just eats the rice, but she eats the rice. He asks her if she wants to stay over and she nods. They lie in bed, holding hands, looking at the ceiling. With his other hand, using his pointer, he writes *PLEASE* again and again in the sheets until he knows she's asleep. He thinks of an artist he knows who makes videos of himself dancing the spelling of words. You have to follow his feet to make sense of the thing. Max remembers one: *Never Finished, Only Abandoned*. It's da Vinci.

Once, when he was small, Max fell asleep on the floor next to his mother. He woke to her in the dead of night, whispering over him. Maybe she was singing. Either way, he'd never seen her face so full of love, compassion, need.

He'd make a horrible father, he thinks. He has so much to work through.

A few days later, Jaclyn texts, asking if he'll go with her to the appointment. THE appointment. What is he supposed to say?

This is attachment, he thinks. Isn't it?

The room in the doctor's office is small and dark. Max leans against the wall near the door. Jaclyn's socked feet are on the table. Her toes curled under like snails. On top, a cardigan unbuttoned, her bra white and lacy and demure. The technician turns off the light, presses a button. Jaclyn closes her eyes and breathes deeply. The screen lights up. There is a loud thump and then the room fills with bright dark swimming light. The technician runs the wand back and forth over Jaclyn's taut belly. It's like that film room at MoMA where everyone is hushed and not really sure why. Jaclyn holds up her head with one hand. She is silent but she moves her face this way and that, as if inspecting a tricky entrance.

What are we looking for? Max whispers.

The technician looks toward Jaclyn for the okay. Jaclyn nods.

We are looking for the diaphragm to move in and out, she says. That means the function of breath is developing.

I'm sorry, the technician says.

Same, Max says. And he is.

Jaclyn's eyes are shut to him. Please, she whispers, repeatedly. Like someone keeps punching her in the gut.

Outside, Max and Jaclyn stand in the blinding sun. It feels as if they've just landed from outer space because of the light, but not only. There is a kebab cart and Max's stomach growls. He looks at Jaclyn, who is wan, on a boat, headed downstream.

He should just tell her how he feels. The truth is exposing and soft. He does not tell her. He cannot.

After, Max goes for ice cream. As a child, he used to go with his father. Even in winter. It was better, always better, to be out.

In yoga, the teacher asks them to let their bodies respond to a wish. What does Max wish for? His right knee gives out. He spends the rest of the class wincing, but he will not give up.

In the hall in the home in Orient, there is a black-and-white photo of Max and his mother. It is large, often tilted, framed in silver with large sloppy watermarks. In it, Max and his mother are at a playground in Central Park. There is a large slide in the background and other children, though they're blurry. Max's mother's face is square to the camera. Objectively, she is a beauty, though clearly exhausted. She is holding Max over her shoulder. All you can see is his small back, cloaked in a plaid wool coat, a bear hat, pulled down low. His mother's eyes are glassy with cold or maybe fear or who knows. How could he know? He's never been a parent.

Max sends Jaclyn flowers with a note: Anything you need. But what he means is not that. And they both know it.

Max asks Todd if they can have another dinner with the girls. They greet him at the door and say, Very nice to meet you, and then scurry off like twin princess mice. They watch the iPad during Chinese food. But then something switches like a light and they go nuts, crying, screaming, shrieking. A doll narrowly misses smacking Max in his skull and he excuses himself. And Todd says, If you're smart, you'll make your exit before it gets ugly.

Nothing feels better than night air.

Fuck.

That.

One day, during yoga, there is a couple behind him in their fifties maybe. Experts at the sport. During Savasana, as he leaves, he notices they are holding hands. Cute, he says out loud. But what he means is, Fuck that. His knee is tissue, cord, body, torched by flames.

He sends Jaclyn flowers again. He isn't sure if he's meant to ask if she'd like company. He is sure she has friends to help with everything. She has Margaux.

Max sleeps with his assistant, who then resigns. He hires a gay guy with whom he will not sleep. Simple.

He takes pills before yoga. His twists have gotten better. They shoot the endorphins right to the sky. One day, the teacher comes to Max, crouches down, all shiny dancer muscles and spandex. He pretzels Max's back and arms in such a way that deepens the twist exponentially. Max sees the tears on the mat before he feels them on his face. Fuck, he whispers.

Good, the teacher says.

No, Max whispers.

Yes, the teacher says and pushes him deeper, harder, more.

His father calls. Max sends it to voicemail.

He sleeps with everyone. A waitress, an intern, a dentist. A red-headed yogi comes back to his apartment. They drink two bottles of wine. He's over it but he keeps on. When he's on top, she says no and he says yes and she says, Jesus. She leaves right after, her yoga mat unrolled and trailing like a broken tongue as she races out the door.

That was bad, he says out loud, but he's very drunk and it sounds like, Yes, I bet.

Max looks different in the mirror.

He imagines conversations with Jaclyn.

I'm so sorry.

I have feelings for you.

Which? Jaclyn asks.

Max's knee gives out on the street. He has to take a cab three blocks.

His father doesn't usually ask, but then one day, he does.

Come be with your mother, he says. The firmness is freeing.

Max cancels all his meetings, his brunch. He gets his car out of the lot. The new convertible smell never gets old. He takes some calls as he speeds past Ronkonkoma, Medford, Manorville. He listens to Radiohead with the windows down. He makes great time. He stops at Starbucks only to pee and get a flat white. He gets to Orient in time for lunch. He planned that accordingly. Lunch takes time.

Max brings Balthazar—lentil salad, goat cheese sandwiches, serrano ham, orange croissants. His mother loves a sticky bun, so he's brought three. He doesn't know whether or not she's eating, but there are days when his father eats triple when she's not doing well—taking on the calories as if it is possible to pass them along through devotion. His father is standing at the front door, waiting. He hugs Max tight.

Good to see you, Maxie.

You too, Pop. And Max means it. For a moment, he wants to tell his father about Jaclyn.

Wash your hands first, his father says.

It strikes Max as odd that this is where his parents chose to end up. So removed from everything: culture, art, spice stores. They were such New Yorkers: their shoes and bags and memberships and ability to walk great distances in all weather reflected that. They knew every stop on the subway, the best place to get Pakistani food. They gave out fifty holiday presents every year to people within a ten-block radius. They shopped for groceries in small batches and carried their wallets in inside pockets. They only bought coats with inside pockets.

To Max, this place always felt like a summer house. He's never spent more than a night. His room isn't exactly his room. It's a guest room to which his mother added finishing touches that she thought he'd like: lime-wash walls she did herself, the whale vertebrae they found on the beach a decade ago, a large-scale photograph Max took of a wave. His mother painted driftwood and assembled a frame for it. Max could sell it now. Not as his—that wouldn't matter—but as a piece unto itself. It would sell if he was selling it.

As Max walks up the stairs, the fucking knee, he thinks of Jaclyn. Appointment aside, lately, he's been wondering about the distinction between love and habit. She's been in his life for quite some time now. More than most. A constant despite work and weather. It's only natural, he thinks. Right? Perhaps he is not endeared to her so much as hung up on the disappointment of the thing. Burrs, stuck in. Not her but it. He wants to call the therapist and go, See? Right? But the therapist would know immediately. She'd say something like, Okay, Max. And how does it feel? And Max would have to be honest. It hurts.

Max opens the door to his mother's room, which was once a reading room with a blue velvet sofa, cabinets, and heavy stacks of books teetering like tall, clothbound sculptures. Now the sofa is gone. So are the stacks. The room has the largest windows in the house, views of water on three sides. One window is cracked open. The curtains sway. He has seen his mother prone many times over the years, but it would be impossible for anyone to call her weak. Sometimes, he thinks her cancer is the only way she can recover from her day-to-day. She has so much force, most of the time, although not in relation to him. She swims in the dead of winter. As a child, he would wake to her working with clay. Later, he'd come home at four a.m., drunk, disoriented, and there she'd be, braiding wool. The most oriented of all: her.

There is a *Vogue* article in which they call her fearless. She is known to the world as an artistic octopus, capable of any medium. Her silver hair has been written about. And her jewelry—which she's promised to donate to whichever second-grade class at PS 84 is around when she passes. She's been volunteering there since forever.

Max's mother slurs her words in her sleep—something about purple and beads and birds. Her face is puffed as if she's underwater or upside down. There is a bergamot candle, lit, meant to harmonize the smells of sickness: medicine, detergent, sweat. It does not. Max doesn't like to touch her when she's unwell. As a child, he never liked his feet sandy—even worse wet and covered in sand. All he can say is that it is akin to that.

Max leans against the wall, knocks the light on by mistake, sees too much of her, and quickly recovers it. She has knit all the blankets on her bed. He wonders if it's a disappointment to be under them, in this way. It would be, for him. He watches her breathe.

Jane? he says, but his mother doesn't flinch.

I came to see you.

On a small table is a string sculpture she's done of a man balancing on the roof of a tall building. The thread is so white it's nearly incandescent. Max walks over to it, strums it like a guitar. He has never valued her work—though some of it he has liked. He has never sold it, though he could have. Why didn't he? When people make the connection between the two of them, he always says the same thing: those who can't make art sell. It isn't how he feels precisely, but it works. They always say how lucky he is, to have her.

Max takes two of her pain pills, good stuff, sits on a stool until the light goes down. He doesn't say anything. The pain in his knee gets swallowed by the stream. He is not sure what he's thinking about or if he is actually thinking. Is it possible that conversations happen subconsciously in moments like this? Or that thoughts happen outside your head? Like tea being poured onto a table? It is not that he can't imagine his life without his mother. It is that he can't imagine the world without her. She has interns and mentees, donates to everything. There is a reliance on her but also a light from her. If a person dies every second, even if a new one is born at the same time, how does the world not go dark? It isn't a one-to-one. At least not with her.

Max gets close enough to hear her breath. He puts his hand to her head. He has to steer himself away from thoughts of her in the bath. He has to steer himself toward her in galleries, pointing and laughing loudly and being followed by a throng of minions. The golden dazzling light beam that she was. If only he could have known her from the outside in first.

You came, she says, but her mouth is a broken jar. She looks Fauvist. It occurs to Max that his father is overmedicating her. He should say something or maybe not. Max takes a bottle for himself. The whole thing. He is not sure whether or not she's asleep or aware when he backs out of the room, closes the door behind him, says, Night, Jane.

He knows that he should do something else. He cannot.

Max would like to drive home with someone. Instead, he turns up the music so loud that the convertible top trembles. At home, he realizes he has killed the money plant. How long has it been? The man at the store told him that demise was impossible. See?

The next morning, Max shows up at Jaclyn's apartment. There isn't really another way. She is an early riser, like him. And it's just dawn, light coming up behind the buildings like a wide eye. He opens the door. She is standing at a bird cage, eye level, her fingers inside, twiddling. There are two canaries, layers of white feathers like wedding dresses on their backs and downy heads. Jaclyn resembles them in her billowy nightgown, hair loose and wavy, feet socked. She looks at Max as if he's just come back from a trip down the block for bagels and juice. Which he hasn't. He's brought nothing but an art book that was dropped by his office in yellow ribbon.

Hi, she says.

Before he can ask her if she needs anything, she says, What is it that you need?

Max puts the book on the counter. He wants to ask her how she is but he knows better than to ask a question he will loathe the answer to. He wants to ask her if she's forgiven him too. That's really what he needs: a pass on all things. He wants to say something about his mother—not to prove anything but just to talk. Instead, they stand and watch the birds. She does not yell or look at him. The kettle whistles. She does not make him tea.

After a while of silence, standing apart, Jaclyn goes to the bathroom. One of the birds sings to Max in a high trill. How does he know that she is female even before the sound? He does. Without thinking, he opens the cage. The singer hops onto his shoulder, and Max picks her up, holds her in his fist, not suffocating her but tightly. She feels like a cloud or maybe a bomb. Something awful is about to happen. He puts the bird back and leaves.

Max has a dream about the color purple. He can't explain it exactly, but purple is the color of his heart. It pours out like ribbons onto dark, glistening pavement. What about red? he thinks. What about black? What color is the inside of his mother's mouth?

The next week, he sees Jaclyn at a show—*Clocks and Watches* at the Frick. She waves to him with two fingers. There is a crowd of people. Max goes up to her, kisses her on both cheeks. How are the birds? he asks. She nods, looking at someone else. There is an invisible moat around her, which she's made with her chest and mouth.

Jaclyn, he whispers in her ear, though he's not sure what he's going to say.

Yes? she asks, whipping around, as if surprised to see him.

He has been here all along, hasn't he? He tells her she looks great.

She looks at him like he's said something in another language.

What? he says, teasing out a laugh.

I think I thought, she says. That because of your parents . . .

She trails off. She shrugs. She moves her hands in front of him, up and down, up and down. There is a tick tick ticking that sounds like half clock, half heart. It does not stop for anything.

21

One summer, Max's mother worked with flowers as her medium. She'd pluck white ones, dip them into resin, and create layered bouquets that were also shapes, surprising and dense. A door, a shovel, a bookmarked book. She worked on them all day long in the sun at their North Fork rental. He remembers her back, shiny and pink, as she leaned over a large wooden door that she'd fashioned into a table outside. She'd shear and cut and paste and mold. He remembers that her hands were always rough with something: glue, paint, petals. He remembers there was a finch flower sculpture that she was partial to. She kept coming back to it. One night, his parents went to a cocktail party and Max brought the finch into his room, plucked just a few petals. Why? Because he was jealous. Because he was fifth on her list. And because he was like his mother in certain ways: silent, effective. He had her dexterous fingers too. Sometimes, a feeling like have-to would rise in his chest. To ignore it would be like walking around with one shoe off.

Did his mother ever hurt anything? That is something Max would like to know. One two three four five.

In her show, his mother included the one Max had vandalized. What a word. Of course, she never said anything. Never would. The finch sold first. His mother left the money under Max's pillow in a bulging envelope. It was a lot. She never said anything, never would. Some people would call that the beginning of Max's fiscal tendencies in art. Some would not call it that. Max is not sure what he would call it.

Max's new assistant doesn't pan out. He finds another female. Younger, girlier, does a kind of yoga that involves electrodes on the body to eradicate fat, of which she has none.

Max knows that Jaclyn will marry. He knows that he will think of her for many years. Not their relationship exactly but of the moment he imagined being a father. It was the first time. She will be the only one like this, etched in his brain, a visual branding. He knows that once she's found her right match, Max will ask around about him. He'll be wealthy, aloof. Jaclyn won't have to lift a finger again but she will. Sort of. Foundations and such. Max will spot them one evening. He will go up to the man. Max will be strong from triathlons again. Healed in certain ways. Which? Max will be just drunk enough to say what he really feels.

What else does Max know? That Max will win. Whatever there is to win besides her. He'll win all of that.

His father says his mother is on her last legs.

Max goes to Orient, stays at a hotel nearby. The idea of watching his father's shoulders, robed, kitteny, making tea is too much—though the right thing. But he has work to do. Calls. The hotel is nearly empty. Off-season vibes. There is a decent-looking bartender. And yet. After a while, Max gets just drunk enough that he goes outside, takes what is left of his vodka, puts his feet up, sits under the stars. He smokes three cigarettes. His mother hates that he smokes, but does she say anything? She does not.

Max remembers four of the constellations that his mother gold-leafed on a bathroom ceiling in their apartment decades ago. Cassiopeia, Vulpecula, Draco, Lynx. He is drunk enough that he doesn't notice the teenagers doing wheelies in the wet street, playing Drake on their iPhones. He doesn't smell salt or dead fish, feel the cold from the pavement up his denim into the small of his back.

Instead, he longs for what could have been in the way someone longs for a hit, or fresh air. A delirious urge, an itch, an actual heave. He could have driven Jaclyn here, taken her to the sea, bought her a book and a postcard and an ice-cream cone with nonpareils. He could have remembered that every woman wants to be a mother. Don't they? He thinks of his own mother then. Didn't she? For a moment, brief, confusing even, he longs to hold her too. Perhaps it is too late. Perhaps he wouldn't know how to do it. He's mastered such a particular kind of intimacy, inert in the daylight hours, impervious to grief.

Max grasps the cup of melting ice. It reminds him that he's alive. He closes his eyes and lets his head fall back. The longing weighs even more than he can imagine.

Back then, in the interviews, they never asked about motherhood, did they?

It is Todd who tells Max about the article. Jennifer has told Todd. Everyone told everyone, and knows. The whole thing has gone viral. Max had no idea. And anyway, it is not really about him. Jaclyn does not mention his name or profession. Never would. She talks about love and loss and sex and societal expectations of women. She talks about disappointing herself. Todd asks him how he's holding up with everything. Jennifer lost a baby years ago too, he says. It was rough.

The rage that Max feels is toward Todd in particular. Asking him like this. It feels solicitous and out of character. Max knows they won't speak again. He imagines someone, he doesn't know who, telling him: this is your pattern. At least he knows, right?

Max's assistant pretends she's reading something else. She slaps at the keys. She looks at him differently though not with less lure. In a week, they'll go out to dinner but skip dinner. This is also his pattern.

Be good, Max!

Years ago, Max's mother painted an impressionist piece: cormorants carrying green bouquets in their mouths, making a zigzag formation against the gray winter sky. It hangs in some admissions office at a fancy private school somewhere. Max doesn't remember where exactly. And he hasn't seen it in years, or thought about it. But then, here it is. On Max's last visit to see his mother, he stands outside for a moment. In front of him, eight of the rubbery birds appear. They are arranged as though they've been tacked just so with pins against the winter sky. There is green hanging from their mouths. Are those fish or plants? Max is a city kid. He doesn't know. There are lines like slats separating sky from water from sand. There is no sound but a blanket of wind. Life imitating art, he thinks. Momentousness like a warm gust. Max doesn't move. He has the syrupy urge to tell Jaclyn—his mother even—but it is too late. Also, for some reason, he just wants to see it. And have them know. To have a bond like that. Stronger than blood, than love, than everything else.

Upstairs, his mother doesn't open her eyes but she is breathing. Max matches his breath to hers at first as a sort of game and then, imagining how he must have done in her belly. Is that how it happens? This is the sort of thing that would matter to her, wouldn't it? This kindness. Either way, he feels it too. For a moment, he tries to imagine her as she was because it feels adulatory. One year ago, she went to the desert. One year ago, she yawned in the Park. One year ago, she floated on her back in the ocean in November. One year ago, he told her that it confused him: all her mediums. And she said, I confuse myself. Isn't that the joy of it?

No, he'd said. At least it wouldn't be to me.

Max looks outside for the birds. They're gone. Everything is dying all the time. Max is too late.

His assistant calls. They've sold three more Reynaud-Dewars.

Fine, he says. Super.

In the dark, Max has a bourbon with his father. His father plays jazz. He seems to float, with Jane unwell. He is a puddle that doesn't reflect. He used to always hold her socked feet, Max remembers. In fact, Max can barely remember a moment when they were not together. Foreground, background. Shadow, light. Maybe this explains something? Max is fine. What he means is, what choice do you have about the formations of things, really?

Do you remember, his father says, those beautiful little men you used to make with your mother's clay? You'd make them ties and suits and briefcases? Was that just to spite us?

What made you think of that? Max asks.

I don't know what else to think about, his father says. His palms are facing up. There are no one's feet inside. Max wants to apologize but he is so tired he can't muster the words.

Max is a child, walking down Broadway, screaming for a cookie and then throwing the cookie down the subway grate. At the same time, Max is eating a black-and-white cookie. It is late. Max and his father have had a lot of bourbon. Who brought these? Max asks, eating cookie after cookie, nearly asleep. His father puts the kettle on. Small back, robed. No idea, his father says.

Now Max's father is by the window, looking out, holding a blanket that Max's mother made in his arms like a child, but also like her life, work, art. She could make anything. Max knows this. The water boils. Thanks, Pop, Max says. Max picks up the tea, sips it. It's too hot. He spits it back into the cup. Some gets on his shirt. He is so tired. He is so wired. He makes his way to his father, puts his face into the blanket, his mother's smell, also her art. There is no money in blankets. He could have helped her. She never needed it. He still could. He has his whole life ahead of him, doesn't he? Her work behind her but not him. Drink your tea, his father says.

What would your father have said? Max asks.

To what? he says.

Your own mother dying.

No, his father says. There is a divine order. An ordained chronology even if it's shit.

Jaclyn gets married. Surely, there will be a baby soon, somehow. She deserves that. A divine order.

There are a lot of very long nights.

What bothers him the most? Everything. But really? That the thing
Max wanted most in the world—safety from unwellness—was also
the most impossible. It could not be bought or ascertained. What
he would have done for a silent deal on that. Anything. Everything.
To be one hundred percent that Jaclyn would never crack. That his
knee would not give out. That the markets wouldn't tank. That his
father would not get smaller and smaller and smaller and smaller
and smaller. So small, in the end, that Max would need to squint.
Pop? And that art would not be most significant here, most imper-
ative, at his parents' home, with nothing at all for Max to sell. Max
could not imagine a world indifferent to that longing and yet the
world was always indifferent, wasn't it? The world turned despite
anything his heart might murmur. Despite heartache and whenever
a heart might simply, impossibly stop.

Years later, Max will remember one night. His father is out somewhere. Bubbe too. Max is home with his mother, just them. It
wasn't usually the case.

After dinner, they find themselves painting in Max's mother's
studio, windows open, leaves crinkling. It is autumn. It smells
like that. Rust. Max is ten, maybe twelve. The light is low, as his
mother liked it. There is a candle and Joan Baez playing or something of that ilk. Max is using the color blue on a giant canvas on
the floor that his mother has set up for him, for them. His mother
is using yellow nearby. Max is using a brush and his hands. His
fingernails even. After a while, his mother comes close enough to
whisper.

Tell me, Max, she says. And Max knows. She means about intention, inspiration. She was always thinking about that.

For a moment, Max isn't frustrated; he isn't jealous. He doesn't have a plan. And his mother isn't sentimental. She is curious. She is well.

Max thinks. His mother is asking him something.

I can't, he says anyway. Jane nods in response. It is just how I feel, he says, not because he knows that she wants him to but because it is true. It is what he is sure of. He feels moved by the color as much as anything.

His mother's face is full of encouragement and grace. It is open like a window to light.

That time, Jane doesn't cry. She doesn't beg him or try to hug him. She doesn't walk away or find his father. Please.

For once, Max hasn't broken or shaken her. For once, where he is concerned, there is something strong inside her, a spine of light or steel that he doesn't recognize but that he loves. Truly. There is no quiver or collapse. His mother is stronger than him. He can recognize that in this moment, even if it wasn't shown to him in many others until much, much later.

It is no one's fault, he thinks. Life is impossible. Love kills us. The color blue. The color blue.

Good, his mother says, or maybe that is the fall wind or maybe her knees or his heart. Who knows.

In a moment, Max's mother stands up. She runs her hands down her front, squeezes Max's shoulder. Max doesn't swat her away or recoil. He feels it. Her touch, affection. It is safety, a stingray baked in the sun.

Jane?

Max's mother gets back to her work. Not as a distraction or punishment, but as a way to create more life, to make life longer, better.

Max gets back to his.

22

CENTRAL PARK

In the Park, if you look closely, you will find scrawled Rumi quotes, Etta James lyrics, the first sentence of *Lolita* etched vertically down a black tupelo. And although the tree has nearly healed over three times, Park-goers won't let the message fade. They re-carve it. And re-carve it again. It is as if the act itself is stimulating, or as if to remind themselves, as if sentimentality and superstition can keep romance, even the questionable kind, from decaying, from going slack.

Under the benches, where the streets meet the sidewalks, there are condom wrappers, undies, and phone numbers scribbled on ticket stubs. There are red, pink, nude lipstick tubes discarded or dropped near oak stumps by Gapstow Bridge. All have been used with love in mind in some way. There are francs (he can't know I was there), dinner-for-two receipts (it wasn't with Bob!), jewelry boxes, oyster shells, tennis permits (that only means one thing), and lube bottles.

There is a bottle of Viagra, half-used. There are ripped photographs with a smattering of black *x*'s across a woman's face; she didn't cheat but it seemed like she did and that was enough. There is the entire manuscript for a romance novel, scattered between Eighty-First and Eighty-Second, three blocks in. Vampire meets vampire. They fall in love. There is a copy of a matchmaker's NDA. What goes unnoticed? What is missed? The phone number scribbled on a takeout menu, one lipstick in shade Orgasm, and the oyster shells. I was saving them for our love box. How else will we remember our first time?

In the Park, there is a dedicated team of cops, gardeners, and arborists. There is pest and waste management, and custodial services. There are monument conservationists, directors and assistant directors and assistants to the directors of Parkwide Support. There are three provisional wild animal keepers at the Central Park Zoo, and they're looking for a fourth. Eduardo met his wife as he was doing stone repair at the Delacorte Theater. She's a singer. You should hear her Tina Turner. Sergeant Ramirez and Lieutenant Johnson-Ramirez got married at Cop Cot. Tyrone proposed on a gondola. The assistant manager of Natural Areas cannot believe the beauty of the mother of two at the Pinetum. He is reminded of her whenever he smells pine. The gardening interns pretend that touching knees over the daffodils is not part of the job. How they long to take off each other's overalls and roll around in the moist soil of the Olmsted Flower Bed.

If one is alarmed by the raccoons near the Reservoir—what is happening? are they rabid? mating?—do not hesitate to call the Park's Urban Rangers. If the Stroke It Like a Pro demonstration gets out of hand, try 311. Always report lost engagement rings, expensive-looking bridal shower gift bags, and a honeymoon photo album to the NYPD Central Park Precinct by the 86th Street Transverse Road. They will meet you if their schedules permit. If Quincy, the black Newfie, gets away again, please know that he loves hot dogs and will respond to his name but only when it's whispered softly. Then call the animal care center. If people are screwing in the Merchants' Gate comfort station, check the Restroom Guide for protocol. There is more information there. It is illegal to film porn in the Park. Even the soft stuff. Check the Film Guidelines and Contact Information for specifics. The NYC Parks Enforcement Patrol is here for all questions about mating and peepers and creepers and unauthorized anniversary celebration mariachi bands and G-strings. They want to help.

Important to note, despite all the love in the Park, there are certain lovers best to avoid. There are couples who meander, stop abruptly, stretch their arms out long, keeping their fingers entwined so one never knows which way to go to get around. There are partners who scream at each other, take up the whole walkway; one has to dash around them, ducking down, pretend not to see. There are lovers who French-kiss right in the middle of everything. Get a room! There are kids around! This is the bike lane! There are mating cats. If they sense a threat, they'll turn their passion into aggression—and typically not toward the other cat. There is an ex-UPS driver in a pink dress who stands on Umpire Rock and proclaims the love fortunes of anyone he sees fit, whether they like it or not. News flash: it is never good. There are guys with their dicks out in the North Woods, including Sammy, who also volunteers at the basketball youth group. There are creeps, letches, pervs, and stalkers everywhere, and it's hard to know who is who, but a good place to start is to notice eyes and pacing and breathing and location of hands.

For those who know, for those who feel it, the Park is more than just a park. It is evocative, a symbol. It reminds them of something else, someone else. After many months, two men from Tantric Stretching try meeting for coffee on Columbus. It doesn't work. Without the Park, they don't make sense. Their faces look different. They prefer to be upside down together. The mommies go home. There, it is not that they change their minds exactly. It is that motherhood is hard enough. There is so much to clean. They'll discover their own needs one day. But not today.

Near the entrance to Strawberry Fields, Alice's husband sits on a bench dedicated to Jane, though how could he possibly know? He is reading the Saturday Profile and drinking orange juice with a straw, no pulp. It is about a priest who officiated a marriage every day for fifty-five years, come rain, come shine. Alice's husband loves a good love story, leans back in appreciation. His marriage has always been good; they've always been happy, despite their lot. Still, on Jane's bench, Alice's husband feels a romance like he's never known. It is in the hushing leaves on the trees, in the light catching on the San Remo as if there's a god on each tower, radiating. Or perhaps the towers are the gods themselves at an altar, he thinks. I do. I do. Alice's husband puts down his paper, his juice. He listens for birdsong but there is none. No ballads either, though it feels like that. He is desperate for nothing. And yet, here, there is acknowledgment anyway. A promise as if from the gods themselves for what he could not know. You do, they say. You do.

23

JANE

On the night before Max is born, Jane sits by the window. There is a sketch pad perched on her belly and opera on low as Abe snores upstairs in a sleep so deep and blue he's underwater. Outside, the sky over Columbus Avenue is bruised, flicked with dark slithery lines that remind Jane of her own veins and ankles at forty weeks. Behind the clouds, there is a tiny moon, pulsing. Jane realizes she missed it entirely the first time she watercolored the scene. Pregnancy has hijacked her ability to observe. Also, her inspiration, tastebuds, circulation.

She starts over on a fresh page, drops the first one on the floor. This time around, the sky is more ominous. The moon is a tiny tooth lost on pavement. She paints what she sees. When she paints, there is an unlocking in her chest, a lightening in her forehead. It relieves her but it also revives her. She has been so blurry for the last nine months—frosted over, the Arctic.

After a while, she stands up, all knees and elbows. At this stage of pregnancy, there is no grace. There is effort and will. She goes into the kitchen, makes herself a cup of chamomile tea in the dark, stirs in milk and creamed honey. Her mother was a great believer in honey for all things: rashes, insomnia, shivers. Lately, Jane thinks of her mother as often as she does not. She counts the years since she's seen her. She was twelve when her mother died. Since then, Jane had always thought that she would not be able to have children of her own. Her mother died in a quick, brutal fight, rigged from the start. And though no one ever told Jane anything specifically—who would have? it was just her and her father, her father and her, and he was so detached, disinterested, disheartened by Jane, Jane alone—Jane assumed it. She had watched her mother writhe in pain, holding her belly, blood in the toilet. She'd uncross her mother's legs when she fell asleep. Don't hold on, she'd whisper. Somehow, Jane imagined the clenching making it worse. For Jane, it was a felt sense, like an imminent storm, or the last step on a staircase: Jane would not get pregnant. Jane's mother considered Jane a miracle in more ways than one—and it had made Jane sure of this one thing. Until she wasn't.

Two years ago, Jane lost the first baby. When this pregnancy held, week after week, month after month, she had to constantly remind herself that it was only her mind that had tricked her into believing something was wrong with her. That having a child was impossible. Sometimes, she would repeat over and over to herself: you are having a baby you are having a baby you are having a baby. She would look at herself in the mirror, check her profile, collarbones, as if knowing oneself as a mother had to do with one's face. And although, in all those years, Jane never imagined pregnancy exactly, this certainly would not have been what she imagined. Jane is not in pain. She feels lucky for that. But her body has changed. Her thighs and arms and neck are soft, nearly purple. She is overripe fruit, touchy around her armpits and knees. She retains nothing. Creativity is slippery. Her work has suffered. She shuffles around in her studio, exhausted. She longs to nap but cannot get comfortable. Even the freshest strawberries taste woolly and dull in her mouth. She does not emote: cry or rage or laugh hysterically. Her face, too, as if to reflect her insides, has gone wan, especially around her eyes, as if she's been powdered over, chalked.

Because of her belief, and because of her first pregnancy, Jane limits what she does. She treats her body as though she is something shatterable: old crockery, spectacles on the street. She's quit smoking, stopped stretching her own canvases. She can't stand high on ladders without feeling woozy. She doesn't jog in the morning anymore—the shaking is nauseating—and she drinks so much water that she may as well float, but there is nowhere to do that. It is winter. The tub won't stay warm. She was filling the tub? She's thirsty again. Her thoughts are like fireflies when you turn on the lights.

Still, at this hour, in the dark, there is nothing to keep track of. The apartment is silent, safe. Jane's paintings are all over. In ceramics she's made, there are greens she's cut from the Park: dogwood, reindeer moss, and wintergreen. Her studio is upstairs, neat and silent, the door closed, everything in its right place. There is the old photo of her mother on her nightstand—the almond Iraqi of her eyes—and also portraits in ink of Abe, inspired by moments that she committed to memory. He is eating watermelon and writing on a bench—final edits?—pointing at a cormorant in a stormy sky. Jane is in one: Abe has his arms around her from behind as if keeping her from a ledge or a fast black car.

By the front door, there is a large linen bag holding her favorite dyed pajamas from her shibori phase, rose water (the kind her mother used), a box of Californian dates from David, a book of Picasso's sketches, ivory slippers, the tiniest yellow sleeping set you've ever seen, and a stuffed frog. Will her son like frogs? She doesn't feel like she knows him yet. He is so active, intense. She is sure of that. Perhaps he'll do hurdles, boxing. He is particular too. Whenever Jane eats anything other than grapefruits, he flails in disgust. She has lost weight, unbelievably, but if she even tries asparagus, walnuts, or a bagel, he rages. What a juxtaposition he is to her. Jane: content with fresh air, toast, and paintbrushes. She could sit here, right here, and watch the sky until dawn. She could move only to get into the sunlight, and another fruit.

He kicks her again, as if to chime in. Jane feels, and has felt, ever so slightly sick.

And though Abe has been helpful, supportive—what can I get you? she doesn't know—he cannot understand. It is a feeling from the inside out, Jane thinks, and deep within her. A place she never knew was there. It howls. Abe continues to sleep and work and write and eat normally. He is a person in the world, unchanged biologically, physiologically. Jane wonders if she'll ever do anything normally again. In the beginning, she was so sure she would. She is less sure with every passing day.

Jane sips her tea slowly. She sways, standing. Soon, she moves through the house like a moth. In the library, on Abe's desk, leaning on a string sculpture Jane made forever ago, is Jane's old pack of cigarettes, half-smoked ten months ago. She picks them up, smells them, wonders if they will appeal to her after her son is born as they've appealed to her every day since he's been in her belly. She's heard of tastes changing dramatically after labor. She feels suddenly protective of cigarettes and milk. Cigarettes and milk and honey.

Jane opens the window. On the side of their brownstone, up high up here, there are lighter-colored rectangular stones, fanning out like sculptural flowers, heavy, grand. Jane takes a permanent marker, thick and moist, from Abe's desk. She strains to get half her body outside the window. Her belly accommodates; the baby stops kicking for once. The cold is enlivening. Maybe he likes that. There is light from the moon. She is Santa's sack, bulging and ungainly. She holds on with one hand. With the other, on the sandy stone, Jane draws a tiny nude, all breasts and belly. Underneath, she signs her name. Below that: JANE DREW THIS WHEN SHE WAS ABLE. She dates it. No one could ever see it from the street. Won't. Still, it will remain. Jane will know it.

Jane closes the window. The room sucks in on itself again. It insulates. The woman is outside still, Jane thinks, permanent and lined. The baby shifts.

Jane isn't alone exactly, but at this hour, in this room, it feels like that. Months ago, when Jane was the sickest of sick, heaving and shuddering over the toilet, begging for it to be over, Abe had come in. I want to be sick by myself, she said. Abe can be too kind.

That's too bad, Abe said. Our child is in your belly.

It isn't as simple as that, Jane thinks. Abe is asleep. Could not be roused. If Jane dies at this very moment, she thinks, the baby will die too. A mother is always and never alone. Responsibility strikes her like a silver spur to the back. She goes to the living room again, to her watercolor of the sky. She isn't finished yet. She must make something.

Jane watercolors until she doesn't know when. All she knows is that she wants to finish. The desire goads her like a strong wind. There are drafts on the floor, a steady hand behind her. Perhaps it is her mother.

When does Jane go into labor exactly? It is hard to know.

Jane is watercoloring, and then it is morning and there is something happening, low and animal-like, in her body. She must go for a walk. She walks the west side of the Park in the sunshine, alone, full of purpose. Abe sleeps on.

Jane carries a book; she doesn't wince. She is a penguin, a hard-boiled egg. She is able to watch her own breath. It is the tide, she tells herself, as it suggests in the book. Jane is the shore.

When the pain feels like a jab, Jane exhales loudly. She shakes her pocket for change. She considers finding a payphone, calling Abe's mother, who would know what to do. But it is out of routine more than need. Jane inhales. She knows.

By the Seventy-Second Street entrance, Jane passes two men in khakis, shiny shoes, and crossed legs. They must think, she thinks, this is a very pregnant lady. I hope she doesn't give birth here. They would never think: This is an artist. This is a woman who can make anything. And when she makes it past them, no labor right here, right now, they won't think of her ever again, will they? Jane wants to tell them something. It feels critical and pressing. I make things, she wants to say. I have always made things. I made a three-foot Great Dane out of paper clips and twine.

Exhale.

When is it—Jane will never know—that the pain intensifies so much that all she can do is stand outside their building, put her cheek to the cold of it, rock and sway and pray and rock? How did she get here? Abe is with her. Did she make some sound? Did she call his mother? How did he know?

When she cannot feel herself in herself, when she is afraid of losing her mind, she asks herself her birthday. The name of the president. The ingredients in her mother's orange-blossom cookies. Her favorite line from Abe's first novel: about the suburbs. She would be able to tell you her name if you asked her, but no one is asking. Jane, because my mother wanted me to be American on the page in case I wasn't American in the eyes. She was so afraid of a pogrom, a long list because of growing up in Baghdad, being a Jew. Don't be a Fakhria, a Smadar, a Samira, she'd thought. Safety over grandness in a name. Grand, she said, Jane would just be.

Now Abe is rubbing her back, asking if she'd like a grapefruit.

Soon, water floods out of her. Jane closes her legs to keep her baby in. Abe wants them to go to the hospital. It is time. No, Jane says. She is sweating. She is freezing. She thinks of her mother. She has occurred to Jane during every moment of this pregnancy. She never got the chance to ask her what it was like for her, this part, any part. Jane was so young when she died. She didn't know the right things to ask. Now those things are the only ones she feels she must know.

The sky is bright and colorless, bleached with cold. Jane does not want a grapefruit. She wants to ask her mother what is coming: if it is, in fact, time. If she will be all right.

Jane wakes up, or maybe she was never asleep. Later, Abe will tell her that there were eighteen hours of agony. Maybe it never really ends. Some of it, Jane spends on the front stoop. She will not leave. Abe, bless him, listens. He knows her well. People walk by, but Jane doesn't notice them. She sits and she stands. She holds Abe and asks him questions, or maybe she's asking her mother. She throws up and he wipes her face with a towel he's brought from inside. She eats two dates. She walks around the block once, and then the sun sets.

When they finally get to the hospital, the baby goes upside down. Downside up. He swivels. This feels like a mutiny, Jane says to a nurse at some point.

It always does, honey, she says. Always.

When Jane swims out of it, upstream, everything feels like slicing. The baby is shrieking. Jane asks for her mother and then closes her eyes.

Abe is holding the baby. Has she held him yet? She's afraid her arms cannot bear his weight. She is afraid of him. Or is it that she's afraid of herself? She cannot do this, she thinks. She wants to reverse time, turn off the volume, shut everything off.

He is healthy, Abe whispers.

Thank you, Jane says.

But she doesn't want to hold him. Not yet.

On the first night and every night after, Jane closes her eyes against Max's crying. She knows it is wrong but she cannot help it. His voice makes her itch. Worse. It makes her ache but not like longing. Like disgust. And Max will not latch. Jane cannot feed him. She cannot nourish her own son.

Jane has heard other mothers talking of the deliciousness of babies. Jane doesn't think Max smells delicious; he smells rotten. She gets close and then squinches her face as though she herself is rotten from the inside, vinegared, soured. There is something wrong with her to feel this way, and yet she cannot help it. She doesn't want to hold him, be alone with him, rock him. Everything is all wrong.

And though Jane longs to feel peaceful, strong, despite, she cannot. There is no break. It just starts up again. It hurts to walk, to eat, to cry. The only thing that doesn't hurt is dreaming. At the window, Jane dreams of her watercolor. It is unfinished. She dreams of her mother. Sometimes, she can hear her. Sometimes, she cannot. There is so much crying.

And yet, Abe is here. He is holding them both. His mother comes. Takes the baby. But still, there is no rest. Jane is not dreaming but it is a nightmare, this. No sleep. No waking up.

24

The first time Jane leaves the house, it is months later, though she's lost all sense of time. It takes her hours to get out the door. She has forgotten how buttons work; she keeps having to change her pants; they hurt where the elastic touches her skin. She gets lightheaded tying her shoes and needs to sit down again and again and again.

Upstairs, Abe is giving Max a bath. He is taking a break from working, from writing, which he has done so much of lately. Despite everything. Jane cannot believe it would be possible to make anything at a time like this, much less be creative. And yet: biology. This is the difference, she thinks, between you and me.

Every so often, Jane thinks she hears Max cry and a flare goes off in her neck. A slightly sick, metal feeling as if a shot has been administered there. But Max is not crying. Instead, it is a bird on the sill, the screech of brakes outside. Jane exhales, not knowing she has been holding her breath, or for how long.

She gets to the grocery store before it opens. She is unsure how cold it actually is or if it's just the sensation from all her time inside, sweatered, socked. She feels like she's been awake for weeks. Perhaps she has. This year, this winter, is endless. There has been no snow, only wind. Every morning, the sun rises late, and Jane waits for it, sure of its salve. When it comes, however, instead of relief, the cold bleaches everything white, and Jane longs for it to be dark again. Less shrill. But at night, Max wails. He will not feed and when she gives him a bottle, her chest aches. And so she doesn't pick him up, mostly. Abe does the mornings. Then Abe's mother comes for hours every day. Sometimes, when she leaves, Jane lets him cry himself to sleep.

It wasn't supposed to be like this. Jane is not sure how it is supposed to be. When she sees them—Abe and Abe's mother—she doesn't feel the appreciation or jealousy that she should. (What would she possibly do without them?) Just utter weariness, resignation, defeat.

The street outside the grocery store is quiet. Jane closes her eyes and puts her face toward the sun. It feels as if something drains out of her ears, warm and thin. But that, too, is just a feeling. She reminds herself of the list: bread, milk, oranges. Abe repeated it to her as if she were a child, though he didn't mean it that way. He was excited for her. Get out! Get some air! Their tolerance is different. It has everything to do with their childhoods. Abe's family is loving, sound. He has feelings in all the appropriate doses. When the baby cries, Abe continues to talk to him as if he's not. He doesn't cave in, lose his voice, go dark. He sleeps still. Jane cannot imagine that. Releasing.

Jane is different. A maroon balloon, opaque, quivery, alone, and high, high up.

There are moments when Jane would like to confide in someone, to tell them that she isn't sure about anything. To ask. But there is no one. Abe's mother is so expert at mothering. She should not have to take sides. Jane's father: what a joke. He is remarried, always on a cruise. Jane's friends from art school do not have children. Likely, they never will. It has put a wedge between them. Like, why did she do it? Shouldn't she have known? Even Bea has always said, Babies become humans when they can appreciate art. Jane can surmise her feelings to Jane's situation now. Abe's friends' wives are easeful, graceful, dozens of kids among them, dressed, fed, and brushed. They keep sending gifts. Little onesies and socks. Where to even begin?

Bread, milk, oranges. Jane wants to buy lemons too. Jane's mother believed in yellow and orange fruits for happiness. Dates and walnuts after birth. Jane wishes she could ask her mother everything. About her milk, for example. If there is something wrong with it perhaps.

Bread, milk, oranges, lemons. Lemons, oranges, milk, bread.

Soon, a man shows up in a newsboy hat, cuffed pants, and a plaid jacket. Jane marvels at the pattern. For months, she's only seen her own clothes, Abe's, and Max's. Everything has been a shade of dairy and dirt. She's been wearing a brown linen shift for weeks.

No one here yet? the man says, but he doesn't wait for Jane's answer. Instead, he moves on toward Columbus Avenue. This moment, the store closed, means nothing to him, Jane thinks. He will forget about it in no time, has places to go. Jane tries to imagine herself with something she must do besides feed and eat, bathe and wash over the sink. To get on the subway, she thinks, would be wild: the speed violent even as she longs for it. She longs to be broken by rage that doesn't come from her child or from her—to be overwhelmed by something that isn't them.

Finally, the door is opened. Inside, the lights are harsh, the music tinny. Jane is sore. Something is leaking. Blood is an entirely different liquid, and she knows it. What can she do?

Every now and again, she is sure she hears the baby shrieking somewhere. He is or he isn't. But he isn't here. Jane has to remind herself of that. In here, it is a freezer opening, the turn of an old shopping cart. Each time, Jane startles. She drops the groceries twice. The fruit scatters, bloody berries at her feet.

Bread, milk, oranges, lemons.

In the dairy aisle, there is a giant butterfly etched into the floor. Jane thinks of her own art. She wonders how any of it actually came from her. She would have had to be a different person, not because of how good it is necessarily—only because it is. She can make nothing now. The baby cries. She is leaking. How much of her brain must have cracked off like crumbs in the last months. When will it stop?

Every time Max falls asleep—he cries himself into it and out of it—Jane promises herself she will make something. A doodle. A knot. A wire boy. Motion is a virtue. But every day, instead, Jane falls asleep—standing, on the toilet, lying down. Sometimes, she dreams of walking alone in the streets, getting soaked in the rain. She dreams of a tub of blue paint. She hears the tiny slosh of a hog-hair brush in oil—and when she wakes, though she doesn't remember it, the sound sloshes inside her like a ghost or maybe an angel, making indigo shapes with its wings. Sometimes, when she wakes, she is covered in a blue blanket—and Abe is at the desk, writing like a madman, fully absorbed.

Before she left, she checked the second-story stone out the window where she painted the nude. It is still there. Why not? It feels like a million years ago. Something destructive has happened. But only inside.

Jane forgets the milk. She gets chocolate cookies instead. Abe will understand.

A woman in heels is smoking a cigarette on the street. Jane had forgotten about them too. The smell nearly makes her retch.

Even that, she thinks. She cannot get back.

At home, Max is sleeping in his crib. Jane feels gratitude well up behind her eyes for Abe. Whenever Jane calls to Abe, even now, he puts down whatever he's doing and comes.

Tell me, he says, as if his whole life is to be there for her.

The thing he loves most about her, he always says, is everything. Sometimes, it feels like the thing she loves most is that it feels like he's saving her life.

In the living room, with the baby not crying, Jane takes off her coat, her scarf, shoes. She leans back on the couch, this couch that has become part of her. A limb. A womb. She marvels at the ceiling. White. Plain. This place, once so serene and safe, has come undone. It was forestlike in how it made her feel. Now everything is on glass.

Jane whispers something; she doesn't know what. She won't remember. She falls asleep instantly, dreams instantly. In it, there are birds against a stormy sky. They are high up and in choreographed formation. They are carrying fish, each one, heavy with seaweed in their mouths. And her mother is watching from the beach.

I wasn't here is the first thing Jane says when she wakes.

Where were you? Abe asks. He is holding her feet. Tell me.

I was a bird.

What kind?

It doesn't matter.

How did it feel?

Jane can't get out the words. There is gauze in her throat.

Abe puts a hand on her leg, on her cheek, says something full of promise with his face.

It doesn't matter what he does or does not know. Jane tries with everything she has to believe him.

Later, Max is crying. Jane knows that there is nothing that she can do. Sometimes, she tries. But she feels the anger stir up in her and she knows she has to put him down. After a while, she sits in the bathroom, a tornado whizzing in her chest. She has never been a person who yells. Now it comes out of her like flames.

So she lets Max wail. She knows it isn't right.

Soon, someone knocks. Jane's first thought—illogical, insane—is that it might be about her art. Jane runs downstairs, opens the door.

It is the neighbor, fully dressed.

She was just walking by, she says. Is everything all right?

Jane doesn't like to lie. She wants to ask the neighbor if she has any tips. She looks like she may have grandchildren, many, and can rock them all to sleep.

Instead, Jane fusses with her sweater, the brown shift. She apologizes. She realizes she needs to eat. How long has it been? She feels faint.

It isn't his fault, Jane says, not knowing where the words came from or even what they mean. They're like a phone ringing somewhere in the distance.

The lady nods, but Jane can tell she doesn't understand. She doesn't have to.

Jane closes the door.

She goes into the kitchen. Abe has done most of the dishes. But not all. Jane is thrilled by what's left. A task while Max cries himself to sleep. The splash of the water dims the sound. As she washes, Jane sees a woman across the way, zipping up the back of her dress herself. Jane has seen her many times over the years. She seems to be a teacher. Something about her gait. Sometimes, Jane is doing dishes and the woman is doing dishes too. Jane is getting out of the bath. The woman is in her robe. But she leaves at eight in the morning, is home at four. Unlike Jane.

Jane imagines herself zipping up her own dress. She misses a particular wool green one she used to wear with a suede coat. What would it feel like to have fabric like that on her body? What would it feel like to zip herself up?

Jane is drying dishes; the woman is on the street, walking in purposeful, tight steps like snips with scissors. She is headed west. She has a large leather purse and a piece of paper in her hand. A list maybe? A love letter? Jane longs to know. She puts the dishes away.

Max is quiet for a moment. And then? He starts again.

Stop, Jane begs. Please, just stop.

Jane goes into Max's room. He is in his crib. Where else? Jane lifts him, tries to pat him, sing to him, soothe him. He flails. Jane has to breathe through an urge to drop him. Just like that. It's not that she wants to drop him. Or maybe it is.

She doesn't.

Jane thinks of Abe, who doesn't lose his mind over anything. But even he has taken to apologizing before he leaves for work, or to write, knowing . . . just knowing. There is a high stack of pages on the kitchen counter that he's completed in the last—how long?

Recently. Every once in a while, they pop into Jane's head. The weight of them, their density and durability. The impossibility of that, she thinks, like a reminder, a taunting, an impossible, unfathomable feat.

Jane puts Max back in his crib. She closes the door. She clenches her hands to be sure she is awake. Or alive. There is a sandstorm between her eyes, scratching and spinning. She goes to the window, peers down at the sidewalk, to see what anyone else is doing. No one is there.

She goes to the front door, opens it, traces I AM HERE in big letters in the frost. The chill makes her ribs twinge.

In the bathroom, she lets out a hollow moan that sounds like a cry of torture but is not. The toilet is the only place where she feels safe. With the door closed, she can barely hear Max. From here, she can talk to him. Tell him what she wants to say.

It is going to be all right.

She sings him a song. The same one Abe's mother likes to sing. You are my sunshine. She is not sure she believes herself.

When she opens the door, the screaming hits her in the face like a smack.

Eventually, Abe's mother comes. Jane has known her for more years than she knew her own mother.

Her mother-in-law has brought kugel, baked fish, orange juice, and milk. She hugs Jane, looks her in the eyes sympathetically, gives her a squeeze. She goes into Max's room, and as soon as she does— like a light—the crying stops.

There is that draining again in Jane's ears: a soft release.

Jane stands at the door, watching them, careful not to be seen by her own child. She looks for clues. She has bought the same shampoo as her mother-in-law. She wears the same colors. She holds Max in exactly the same way. Rocks him to the same beat. Jane stands and sits in the same places. It is not that Jane is trying to trick her child when she does this. She is just trying to conform. She knows that he is not the problem. Neither are the clothes.

With Abe's mother here, Jane can almost rest. She goes into their room, lies on the bed. She is too tired to get under the sheets. She longs to be held, but not by Abe exactly or at least not as things are now. She longs to be held by Abe before Max, when holding meant security and not protection.

The room has changed. Jane has taken down the cuckoo clock. The wall is now naked, raw. She has pulled all the curtains shut, taken down the fruit collage she'd done in school that Abe inexplicably loves. Too much color. Even Abe's watch is in the other room. Jane kept asking him what that racket was. It was in a drawer, barely audible. But it was that.

When Jane closes her eyes, she thinks of her mother. Jane is maybe five. They are on line at Sahadi's, buying pistachios and apricots and loose black tea. Jane's mother is in brown heels and a yellow dress, with a white cardigan. Her hair is pulled into a low bun, tied with a red scarf. Jane's father bought all her mother's clothes. They met at a country club when her mother had just come from Iraq. She cleaned the club kitchen at night. Her father wanted to keep her like a bird in a cage. Instead, because of her strength of spirit, he kept her like a cat. She was quiet, but intentional. A housewife who went to museums with her allowance. Who loved modern art. Her father was fastidious, uncreative, detached. It never felt as if he chose her mother though he did. Specifically. As a child, Jane felt as if at any moment he might choose someone else. A woman with a return or exchange option. An entire family.

At Sahadi's, Jane's mother leans down and asks Jane what she might like to eat. Dates, Jane says. The juicy ones. Jane's mother orders them in Arabic from the man behind the counter. Just then, Jane notices the button on her mother's cardigan is broken, halved.

Your button, she says.

Her mother looks down at it and, without a breath, picks a blanched almond from a bin, snaps it over the top of the button, and voilà. A new button. Her mother's hands. They could do anything. Jane imagines them. They are jotting an address in Arabic at the post office. They are peeling a grapefruit. They are putting a bandage on Jane's knee or counting money, putting a stack of bills under the bed.

There were things Jane knew about her mother: she loved color, nuts, music on the streets. It aches: the things she doesn't know.

On the way home, Jane's mother buys her a sketchbook and a pen with a felt tip. They sit on a bench, eat apricots, green olives, dates, and sip orange blossom lemonade with sturdy leaves of mint.

What should I draw? she asks her mother, whose weight is warm and quiet against her. Her mother always says the same thing but Jane asks anyway just to hear her mother's voice.

Draw love, her mother says.

Was it because of the constraints of language that she was never specific? Or perhaps a craving so piercing that it severed her throat? Either way.

In response, sometimes, Jane would draw an artichoke, the sunrise, the neighbors' gray cat. She would draw a star made of stars, gloves in a sandbank, a large door with a strong knob. The night before, Jane's mother had told her about Baghdad—a story about her own mother, praying under a lemon tree. They would stop there anytime they went anywhere. It felt sacred. Jane had fallen asleep to the language of curved balconies, the tulip top of the temple, the stone school with broken panes, and Jane's grandmother, plucking feathers from a chicken, a white apron over her lap.

Now she tries to draw it all, pulling from memory as much as imagination.

Like this? she says.

Like that, her mother says.

And like this?

Like that.

Jane draws until the page is full, flecked, shaded. There is a whole city, and maybe it is Baghdad or maybe it is her Baghdad. Theirs. Her mother runs her finger over a flower growing between the cracks. She makes a sound that is as much pain as pleasure.

When she finally speaks, her voice wobbly and frayed, she says that it is even better than she'd imagined.

Why? Jane asks.

Because you are there too.

After Jane's mother died, for months, Jane thought she saw her everywhere: running toward the sun at dusk, skirt flying behind her like fabric wings, humming hallelujah amen to a baby that wasn't Jane in the produce aisle, in front of the pears, swaying back and forth and back and forth, boarding a bus. Always, always, Jane would stay up late drawing the images. To keep her. To be there too.

When Max comes, it is the same but it is different.

Jane sees her old self everywhere. She is not at the Guggenheim, wearing boots with a heel, making art in the studio, grazing the tiny scar on Abe's face as though he were a Buddha or a small rabbit, or in the throes of orgasm. She is not cupping her own son's warm head and dabbing his face with a wet cloth. She is not zipping up a dress.

And she cannot draw. She isn't there either.

Instead, Jane is doing dishes. Jane is rubbing her eyes. Jane is sleeping on the toilet. Jane's mother-in-law is rocking the baby to sleep because Jane's body is misery and she might drop her son but not just because she is so depleted. Because.

What she wouldn't give, she thinks, to hear her mother's voice again, Arabic curling the outside of her letters like heat. What she wouldn't do to hold her mother's slender fingers, chilled from the faucet. What she wouldn't do to look her mother in the eyes one more time. To mouth, I love you. To draw for her. To rebuild her a world.

What she wouldn't do to be herself again too. To have someone waiting for her and to come late, apologize, and say, I'm so sorry. I got carried away. I was busy. I was eating pistachios. I was drawing love.

25

The time when Max is old enough to stand, but he won't, and he won't be held by Jane. It is not a skill they've developed over the past year. They have done it hardly ever. Abe's mother is so often here, making it easier. When Abe is here, Max goes to him. They have a special bond, perhaps born in spite of Jane. Also, Max is so self-sufficient. Crawling and then teetering to whatever he needs. He is strong and assertive, capable. Even now.

And so, they aren't used to it—Jane and Max. It is as though their bodies brake hard before contact. As though a small red thing darts into the road and they slam to a mutual stop. Negative space between them. Definitive. Resolute.

Please stand up, Jane says. Please. Her back is aching. Max is heavy now. A big boy.

But Max doesn't stand up. Instead, he writhes so Jane can't hold on to him but cannot let go either. What does he want her to do? She fumbles, isn't strong enough. Never was. She cannot sing to him or rock him. He would never let her though she can still—a protective mechanism—imagine doing it, and the delicious quiet that would ensue.

It is all too late.

Max's face is hot as a storm and he is kicking—he needs comfort from someone else. There isn't someone else—and Jane, it only takes a second, lets him fall. Maybe she has a choice. Truly, she would not know.

What happens is that Jane releases her arms from underneath him and down he goes like a sack in front of her feet. Jane feels the thud of his body in the floor, not once but twice. And then there's a startling quiet. Shushed as a painting.

For a moment, Jane fears that she's done something irrevocable. She can't look down. Then the crying starts up again, this time with vengeance. Or at least that's what Jane hears. Utter disapproval of the person that Jane is and isn't, and for what she cannot provide.

And can she blame him? She cannot.

Max grabs at his mother's legs as though he wants fistfuls of her flesh in his dumpling hands.

Jane looks at the ceiling. Please, she says out loud. She prays.

There is the time after Abe's first novel sells to Spain, the Netherlands, France, Italy, and the UK in a day that Abe suggests they go for a drink. Jane and Abe alone. Just them two.

Jane will take any excuse.

But they do not have a babysitter. Abe's mother is Max's only caretaker—and this week, she is in the Bahamas with Abe's father and some couple friends.

And yet, the yearning to go out for Jane, to be in the world again and in the world with Abe, is tangible, acute. A cool blue body of water on a hot summer day. Jump.

Truly, Jane is happy for Abe's success. She is, in part, the reason for it. She has goaded him, supported him, over all these years. He would have given up, surely and otherwise. And even if it feels so wildly remote to her now—art as fulfillment, fulfillment as fulfillment—Jane longs to tell him how proud she is of him. And also, to have a drink.

Abe is going to figure it out, she thinks, as he does. He always does.

For Jane, it has been a day. A month. Many months. Lately, Abe has been busier than usual, leaving Jane, the default, at home to care for Max alone. Jane does not envy Abe exactly unless she thinks of things directly. And she does not. If she were in her right mind, perhaps she would have found direct fault. But Jane is nothing if not a woman who can follow through. And she wanted this baby, didn't she? She wanted to be a mother, right?

There was the time that Jane and Max finger-painted together at the kitchen table. Orange and red. Jane watched Max's intent face—lips pursed in focus, cheeks heavy in contentment—and longed to touch it. Share her pride. But she knew how unwelcome a gesture like that would be. Instead, she stayed silent. Support in non-presence even as she sat right there. She knew.

Too, there was the time when Jane locked herself in her room for nearly an hour just to catch her breath. Max wouldn't have dinner. Wouldn't have a bath. Wouldn't be read to. Jane had nothing left. The thing about parenting, Jane thinks, is how often failure is on the line. All the time. Every time.

Jane kept imagining that after a while, they might fall into a rhythm: Jane and Max. Max and Jane. They might have to.

They did not.

We will put him to sleep, Abe says. And just lock the door. He'll be fine.

A gin martini. A bourbon. Jewelry. Shoes. Jane quivers with hope.

Max goes to sleep at nine p.m. Jane and Abe lock the door.

On the bar there are peanuts and small white napkins with the letter *P*. Jazz is playing quietly. Jane's first thought is that no one else here feels quite like they do. These people sip, wipe their mouths with little dab movements. They haven't fled a fire, wouldn't have any idea of what Jane and Abe are doing, Jane thinks. Or of what they are not.

In his room, locked in, Jane doesn't worry that Max will get hurt. Instead, she is afraid of what will happen if she doesn't come here, get out. It is like that so often. The doctor had said it would get better. The medicine would help. It has and it has not. On the inside, the storm rages less. But the relationship—Jane and Max— remains stormy, at best. That, the medicine, it seems, cannot repair.

Jane and Abe don't stay longer than twenty minutes. Their eyes are attuned to sharp movements, ears to sirens, alarms. But nothing triggers. Max seems smaller and farther away by the moment. They hold hands. Jane can imagine getting in a cab, on a train, on a plane. She can imagine cocktails far, far away from here.

Congratulations, Jane says to Abe. She means it. Somehow, saying it feels as much an acknowledgment as a prayer. She says it again. She touches his face. She doesn't think of forgiveness. Just relief.

When they come home, Max's door is still shut, locked, but there is light around the perimeter, leeching out. For a moment, Jane fears he's set himself on fire. He has not.

Inside, she sees that Max has turned on the light and fallen back to sleep like that, in the middle of his floor, clutching a soft monkey and a toy fire truck. Jane crouches down next to him, runs her fingers through his hair. He smells like milk and grass. She puts her face to his cheek.

What she wouldn't give.

Max rolls away from her. Jane moves closer. He rolls away. She moves closer. She puts his arm across her back.

For a moment perhaps too short to measure, there they are, almost holding each other. Love born from presence if not affection. Born nonetheless, she thinks.

Max doesn't wake up. He sleeps right through. Jane is too tired to stay and also too tired to sleep.

It will be tomorrow soon. After a while, Jane turns off the light. She sits for a long time alone in the kitchen and thinks or doesn't think. She does what she can.

26

The first time Jane goes into her studio after having Max—fourteen months later—she is surprised by the smell. It is earthier, woodsier than she remembers. And quieter. And brighter. It is morning and sunlight splatters on her giant table like flattened white petals. It lands between the sketchbooks, wooden paint boxes, and a desiccated plant, the soil like magic powder in the light. There is a glass of water, half-full, covered in a layer of dust, on an easel. There is an art book, open to Miró, and a magnifying glass, tentatively balancing on a smattering of red beads. There is a half-finished abstract charcoal sketch that Jane cannot, for the life of her, remember the inspiration for. She doesn't even remember doing it. Did she?

Her brushes, in a dirty mason jar, are pale and dried out, like the flesh of an apple left in the heat. There is a cup of light blue paint, sweet, innocent even, that feels unlike anything she'd ever use. There are splattered buckets, uncleaned tools for clay, and, lining the entire floor, pages and pages of newspaper. Jane checks the date. One full year ago, plus a couple of months.

Jane finds her radio on the windowsill, the spiral antennae

making the whole thing ungainly, insect-like. She turns on opera.
It blares. She turns it down. She turns it off entirely.

There is a yellow Navajo blanket that Abe got for her at a street
fair, folded on a chair, and Jane wraps herself in it, sits on the floor.
She's not sure what else to do. She isn't in the mood. It isn't the art
that she can't do. It is the failure in its face. The day looms.

For some time, Jane makes shadow puppets with her hands.
Soon, she tries to draw a shadow puppet. She can't. She trickles
purple paint into the water glass and splatters it on paper. The
washed-out effect is depressing, reflective. She takes two fistfuls of
clay and squeezes. Time goes by. Disappointment is doubled by the
fact that everyone is rooting for her.

Downstairs, her mother-in-law is making matzo ball soup.
Max is asleep, or feeding himself cheese, or propped up with pillows on the sofa as she folds laundry. Later, Abe will come home
early from work, take Max for a stroll outside. He'll pick up cookies
and flowers. Maybe he'll have some time to look over his manuscript while Max plays with blocks. Lucky.

When Jane leaves, all she will have to do is have dinner with
them at the table, comment on the flowers, the smell of the place.
Delicious! Likely, there will be a glass of wine poured for her.
There will be a napkin. It won't take much for Jane to sit down, be
polite and appreciative, to look like a nice mother having a nice
dinner with her nice family. Still, it is too much. It bears down.

She's been given the day.

Jane makes nothing. Instead, she sleeps.

The second time Jane goes to her studio, she eats a bag of pretzels,
reads the old newspaper, tries her hand at collage. She cannot get

the scale right. The glue is dry-tacky. Her fingers aren't used to texture and she just wants to pick. She throws out four rounds.

She picks up the phone to call Bea, but when it just rings and rings she imagines Bea in the world, searching for bottlecaps, paging through photography books, seeing a thought fully through—start to finish. Rain to gold.

What would she even say?

There is no noise outside, but Jane keeps looking down at the street as if someone is coming for her, someone who can help. Ever since Max was born, Jane has seen no one she knows—not a family member other than Abe's parents, not a friend. Not even Bea, who has twice nearly banged down the door and then finally given up, calling Abe at work. Is everything all right?

She's stayed at hotels and hurried to and fro, hoping not to be caught. And though the excuses are not untrue—we're not feeling so good today, there is so much to do, the place is a mess—it isn't just that. Jane doesn't know what to say, even how to say. The sensation is being too exhausted to speak but it is also that if she were to be honest—and she can't not—it doesn't sound good.

I don't want.

Today, Abe and his mother have taken Max to the carousel in the Park. There is laundry to do. And dishes. Jane tries making something with clay, but the smell itches her nostrils. She washes her hands three times. There is nothing to accomplish in here and accomplishing feels like the only thing attainable.

Jane heads out. She closes the door to her studio behind her and makes her way to the sink instead. She does the dishes.

When Abe comes back home with Max, he puts the stroller in the corner, tucks in the blanket below Max's sleeping face.

Tell me about your day, he says. His eyes are rich, rooted brown. Love like soaring. Like gaining footholds too.

Jane doesn't have to say anything.

You'll get there, he says. Jane is wearing his socks.

On the third day, Jane dips her brush into white paint. But she ends up doing her fingernails instead. She relishes the smell of acetone. Later, she does some yoga, push-ups, and dances to three songs. She reminds herself to bring real polish the next time and etches a haiku about honey into a mound of old clay.

On the fourth day, she dips her fingers into paint and closes her eyes and moves her hands and torso against the paper. She is the brush. She nearly rocks herself to sleep.

On the fifth day, the sun is out. The house is empty; birds are chirping outside. Jane locks the door to her studio just because. She feels different than she has—like she's wearing silk instead of wool. It might be because she's had some space: she's stayed at a hotel three of the last five nights—as she has so many of the nights over the past year. But it is more than that. It feels as though her heart has settled into a reasonable pace, and Jane is aware of space between the features on her face, as though they'd been pulled taut with string, and the string has snapped.

Jane opens the window—it is the first time in such a long time—and the air comes in, softly, teasingly, like a stray cat. She sits down at her easel, feeling if not ready, then curious. She notices the raw floorboards, splattered with remnants of work she's made, the strong legs of her table, a cracked plate from which she once made her way through an entire mound of cookies as she drew and bound a book of fish. Today, the noticing feels different. It isn't just noticing. Her brain is a sieve, not steel and deadbolt. She can hear the leaves in the trees. Her hands are yearning.

She picks up a gray pencil. She remembers its weight, her favorite for so long. How many times has it been sharpened and dulled, sharpened and dulled over the years? Jane begins to draw. It is nothing at first, a slender figure, not a body so much as a shape. She keeps on. Soon, she feels herself not just here, in this seat, but in a lighthouse, in the sand, planting flowers. She draws flowers. The birds are chirping outside; she is drawing a bird. She runs her fingers over it. She thinks of her mother's fingers. Soon, the fingers become part of the wings. She pulls out the red pencil and then the black. She shades and smudges, flicks and hatches. She draws a deer and a body, a tree and a baby's mouth. She draws a room with a crib. Not Max's room but a child's room all the same. There are lambs and books and a small light with a shade that looks like an apple. There are no frogs. There is a shadow cast by a large tree outside with magnolia flowers, blushing pink, in full bloom. She doesn't stand up. She draws pajamas, cast aside in a lump, and blue and green crayons and a small wooden stool with some letters that can't be made out. She draws signs of a mother. A stained coffee cup, one slipper, bra like a broken shoulder, unfolded laundry, a tissue, crumpled.

She draws for hours. In the meantime, there is no resistance. The work comes through like silk thread on a needle. Jane is folding something together or unfurling it. She is content, peaceful. It is quiet, but that is a feeling too. The work itself, and also doing it, feels inevitable, but not predictable. She thought there'd be something, some fastening that needed attending to. There isn't.

Jane makes things.

Soon, it is not just the figures, but the words come too. One at a time and then in phrases. As if from a vein. She goes through page after page after page.

Make different milk.

Be stronger.

Have a different body.

Comfort me.

I'm the child.

Take your art off the walls.

Stop crying.

What is wrong with you?

You should have done everything differently.

You should be a different mother.

It is dusk when Jane lifts her head, realizes she needs to pee.

Max's cry comes through, but Jane yawns against it. She realizes: nothing hurts. She isn't afraid of swirling into mud. There is an echo in the trees. There is a breeze. It is the world itself, she thinks, abiding. It does that when we make things. It says, Okay.

Maybe she can do things differently now. She goes.

27

It is just after Max's fifth birthday—fireman-themed, in the Park—that Jane begins to feel faint. At first, it happens infrequently, every couple of weeks. Jane doesn't wonder if it's her period, which has been heavy, hard; or her back, which has been aching something fierce; or her art, which has been demanding and torturous some days. She knows it has nothing to do with forgetting to eat. These days, Jane is rarely hungry. She is distracted, focused. She has been on an airplane to and from California to see David, Abe's brother. It is no strange virus, she knows, caught midair.

Jane knows.

Also, she is in the thick of it, finally. It has taken so many years. She eats more honey, drinks more tea.

But it will not quit.

In fact, it gets worse. Soon, Jane is passing out. It comes out of nowhere. First, she is fine, checking her face in the mirror or putting on shoes or stirring marmalade into oats. She is on the A train platform, assessing the ripeness of bananas at the supermarket, or listening to the news. Then, suddenly, a sensation comes over: it is like lead hands, little birds along her back. There is no feeling from her waist down. Everything drains out of her and Jane is stockings, no legs inside. She is standing and then, suddenly, not. Jane is on the floor, drenched in sweat, freezing cold.

Sometimes, she is able to stay alert—her body very loose, then very stiff. Sometimes, she wakes up, remembering a vivid dream of frogs, or a graphic-books bookstore on Avenue B, or the Jackson Five, of all things. Once, she hits her face on a chair on her way down. For weeks, there is a red smear on her cheek like someone has pulled a jammy spoon across.

Of course, Abe is concerned.

At first, Jane tells him that she slipped in her studio. Once, she faints in the bedroom when he is in the kitchen. He runs in.

I forgot to eat lunch, she says. It is not a lie.

That evening, Abe packs almonds in Jane's purse and leaves a bag of oranges at the door to her studio.

You should get checked out, Abe says. He is not wrong.

Jane does not get checked out.

Instead, she goes for long walks, has tea with Bea, focuses on kaolin, a new favorite style of hers; she buys underwear that won't show stains and large packs of sanitary napkins, which she goes through with an alacrity she never thought possible. She is courted by the dealer Collette Cooper, who has been Jane's dream dealer for many, many years. Jane is beside herself with hope. Collette is a unicorn in her field.

When they finally meet, on a snowy day at Collette's Upper East Side co-op, Jane makes sure to eat first. In Collette's blush living room with a round satin sofa and calfskin rugs, Collette promises she'll sell the hell out of Jane's work. Minutes later, Jane faints in Collette's bathroom. She has been bleeding for two weeks straight. When she comes to, Collette's assistant is there, fanning Jane, who begs her not to tell. For all she knows, she does not.

Collette Cooper, always in leopard and lipstick. Always talking so fast. A golden ticket. A breast cancer survivor too.

The feeling, in the beginning, is that Jane does not have the luxury to stop. She has just signed with Collette. She has a show of her porcelain boats in two months. They will not finish themselves. There is an article coming out in which they call her the "Next Best." There is such momentum and what a waste not to ride on it. Jane has worked so hard for so long and for this exact moment. It feels like fleeing something. It feels like coming back.

Lately, she and Abe have been on such different pages, crossing paths less and less, or crossing paths and forgetting to engage. On evenings when they might have real time together, with or without Max, the thought of being with Abe makes Jane uncomfortable. She feels pressure, as though they haven't been a pair, happy, together, for so very long. As though they may not have enough to chat about, it may be awkward, or Jane may be bored. It is as though small talk with Abe would take away from Jane: art, time, inspiration.

As though he may ruin something holy.

The only true intimacy Jane can imagine with Abe is sexual, but it isn't even about him. It is about urges, fury, sweating out a fever. It would have to be forceful and quick, Jane thinks, which is unlike Abe and which, frankly, she doesn't have the spunk for. Where would she even begin? Never mind.

In the meantime, she is sure Abe feels the same way. He is working working working, writing writing writing. His books have done well, incredibly so. They are smart but accessible. His female characters, Jane thinks and so does everyone, are particularly strong. It feels like a moment of momentum that is both tenuous and unsustainable for them both.

And so, Jane thinks. And so.

Most days, lately, Jane suggests that Abe stay late at the office. She makes pasta with peas and Parmesan as Max practices chess on the floor. Their time together is neutral if not connected. Jane doesn't feel herself around him. She is off-kilter, nervous, one shoe on, one shoe off. She is never sure when he will challenge her—and what she will lose. But he gives her less grief when Abe is gone. It is certainly easier.

When they are alone, Jane does not ask questions about his day at school, his friends, the weather. Max doesn't offer his thoughts. Sometimes, she imagines other families, this time of night, sweet interchanges, affections, reading, feet intertwined on the couch. That thing about witnessing your children's brilliance through their observations. But no. Max doesn't make them—at least not to her. And so, she watches him. She finds solace in his diligence and focus, precision and obvious intelligence. When he goes to bed early, reads for an hour alone, as he likes it, and Jane goes back into her studio, leaving leftovers, a cookie, and a note for Abe—Enjoy! On deadline!—Jane's balance is restored. She doesn't feel full but she doesn't feel broken either.

Hours later, Jane goes to bed only when she is sure that Abe is asleep. There are student manuscripts rising and lowering on his belly as he snores. Jane moves them to the nightstand, turns off the light, gets in bed with pants on, and faces in the other direction. She sleeps. In the morning, Jane and Abe exchange niceties. One of them is always rushing out the door with Max or some paper work or a piece of toast, coffee mug, apple.

See you later!

Any real details, any real content of this time between them, goes in one ear and out the other. When was the last time they had a real, connected conversation? Sex? Jane cannot remember. And trying feels like a distraction.

It gets worse, and not just with Abe. Soon, it is not just the bleeding and the fainting, but a deep pain behind Jane's belly button, above her pelvis, purple and vast, that she cannot ignore. The pain is akin to bricks being dumped on there, rough and sharp, heavy and harsh.

Of course, Jane thinks of her mother. She does the math. Jane is two years older than her mother when it started for her. For a moment, Jane feels like she's gotten away with something. What exactly? Two years.

Jane holds the side of the sink. She girds herself against a building or squats down on the subway in a crowd. The cramps. The nausea. So much fog, but it is heavier than that. It is those bricks.

In the spring, finally, Jane makes an appointment. It is not because she wants to but because she has to. The pain is interfering with her work. She cannot focus. She'll be painting and suddenly, folded over on the floor, on her side. The pain runs straight from her belly to her brain, which has gone foggy and slack and sometimes sharp and hot.

It is impossible to get anything done.

Abe's semester is finishing. His big book is nearly done, the important one, he feels—though he hasn't yet asked Jane to read it. Thankfully. He is able to help with Max more, but that doesn't fix things. Jane is still the one to coordinate Abe's mother and pickups, doctor's appointments, fruit, toothpaste, and playdates. She is responsible for Max even when she is not responsible for him. Jane has turned in her collection to Collette and it's not that there is time now—there is not.

On a rainy day in May, Jane goes to the doctor's office alone. She doesn't want to alarm anyone yet. And it feels somehow easier to gird herself, with just herself. Once there, she looks around the waiting room—child with the sniffles, grandmother, single man in sneakers and blue pants, old man in a wheelchair. Who helped him in? For a moment, Jane hopes someone will make eye contact with her. Tell her it's all right. No one does. Maybe she should have invited Bea.

In the examination room, Jane takes off her clothes, puts on a gown, lies down preemptively, is grateful to rest.

The doctor comes in. Short, glasses, heart-shaped face, unfazed but not unkind. He asks about Jane's symptoms. She tells him. She lies back down again. He palpates her lower belly.

Does this hurt? he asks.

Yes.

Does this?

Yes.

How much?

It does, Jane says.

The doctor nods, doesn't make eye contact, keeps on. Jane jumps.

Ouch.

Sorry, the doctor whispers. Jane can tell that he is.

Hmm, he says and then that they'll have to do some more tests.

When he leaves, it is hard for Jane to breathe. All the pushing, all the pressure. For a few minutes, Jane cannot get up. She wants to ask her mother if it started like this for her too. She tries to imagine her mother alone, undressed, so young still, in a place like this. She tries to imagine her in a gown and socks. She wonders if her mother was treated differently for her accent, her eyebrows, her long braid. She hopes not. How futile, useless to hope, Jane thinks. Jane will never ever know. Any clues, any remnants or treasures, have been scrubbed away by time.

A wave of exhaustion comes over Jane, and she nearly falls asleep on the table. She daydreams. A bonfire on the beach, good days of Max painting in her studio, his belly covered in purple, Abe driving, Jane in the passenger seat, a stack of books on the floor. Jane has to move her feet to accommodate them. Abe's hand is in Jane's lap and they are two hearts in wind, speeding, winding, with the top down. Jane's mother is kneading bread dough in their kitchen, sprinkling it with black sesame, turmeric, and salt. Jane's mother is singing in Arabic, wavy, cursive, as she only did for Jane.

Remember?

Jane wakes up humming, the memories like fish, flickering in a lake. Jane wants to hold on to them. When the humming stops, the fish sink.

Jane remembers that the only time her mother ever arrived late for school pickup, she came sweaty, frazzled, apologizing. There was a pink medical gown under her gray dress that Jane noticed immediately.

I rushed to you, her mother said. I didn't want you to worry.

Jane sits up. She realizes that she feels an odd freedom, a click-ing into place. As if perhaps she has done nothing but worry since then. And until now, when the doctor said, Hmm.

And Jane knew.

The nurse comes back in. She asks if Jane needs something.

Jane's instinct is to say yes. But what?

Jane lets the nurse help her to get dressed, though she doesn't need it exactly. She lets the nurse squeeze her shoulder. Say, Oh, honey.

Jane collects her things: scarf, hat, purse, shoes.

She leaves the medical gown, folded, neat, on the chair. As though she never used it. As though it might be for someone else's daughter, mother, friend.

Jane walks uptown on Columbus. Does she feel like she's dy-ing? She does not. The wildness of reality sometimes. Everyone always dying, all the time, and yet. Death as the most inevitable. The most unnatural. Power and powerlessness with these bodies of ours, she thinks. The way you can't keep your eyes open for a sneeze.

For now, only Jane knows of what's imminent. And what does she know really? That she and Abe are moving at different speeds, for example.

Hey, Abe. Wait.

For a moment, as Jane walks, she tries to imagine Abe alone. She tries to imagine herself gone.

On Seventy-Seventh, she turns into the Museum of Natural History, where they do not check her ID. They know her, smile and nod, and wave her along. She takes off her scarf and tucks it into her purse. Inside, her loupe tool, a comb, her sketchbook, yet another sanitary napkin, the nuts from Abe.

Jane makes her way; she could do it with her eyes closed. She comes here weekly, sometimes more than that. It isn't the animals she's interested in, the history, or the whale, but the Halls of Gems and Minerals on the first floor. They are tucked back past the Small Mammals and Insectarium, and precious, like a vault, dark and protected. Jane goes in. It is empty. A student with a sketch pad. A security officer. A woman with her back to Jane. That's it.

Otherwise, just hundreds of gems, pronged upward. They are lit up like baby suns, or hearts in an operating room. Important, kept.

Every time Jane comes, she falls in love with a different stone. Sometimes, she is drawn to texture, to rawness. Tsavorite garnet. Sometimes, the round, polished, shiny ones speak to her. Sparkly pink quartz. Each time, there is no rhyme or reason. But always, always, Jane feels comforted and a part of a conversation about art and beauty in here. It feels otherworldly, the bottom of the ocean and also womblike. Places Jane has been and also not.

Today, Jane longs to get lost. She feels so unlike herself, so unsure, that getting lost might be the start of finding. She walks around and around.

But she cannot get lost.

Instead, a young woman, no one to speak of, seems to seek eye contact, a connection. Perhaps she knows—like a cat—that Jane is dying. Is she the nurse? Jane cannot gather her thoughts. No, she is not.

For a moment, Jane feels her staring at her. But the woman averts her eyes as soon as Jane looks. She is pretending not to notice

Jane's bag and hands. Her ring? Maybe she's some kind of gemologist, Jane thinks. Or a surprising thief?

Jane goes into the gallery, thinking that surely the young woman won't come too.

But of course, she does. It is that kind of day.

The woman is in a long camel coat, cinched around her waist. She is teetering in heels that she doesn't seem fully comfortable in. She is young. Younger than Jane originally thought. Something about the clench of her face made her appear older. She is probably twenty-three or -four. Just getting started on who knows what. Whatever she wants. Anything.

They are the only two in here, and for a moment Jane senses danger. But it doesn't alarm her. Mortality, Jane thinks, can only be on the line in one way at any particular time. She is not going to die in here. At least, not yet. And not with her.

Hello, Jane says finally, maybe longing for evidence of her own voice.

Oh, the woman starts, but she stops herself, waves her hands in front of her face, then covers it. She apologizes, turns around, and goes.

Jane laughs out loud.

It is only on the walk home that Jane remembers she promised Abe they could have dinner together tonight, just the two of them.

Of all the nights: okay.

Jane hurries home. She still can and isn't that a sign of something? She showers, barely registering the water or the light or the walls. She scrubs her body of the doctor's office smell, rubs it hard with rose water and oil. She puts on fresh clothes, as though she might be going out somewhere.

It has been so long since it's been just Abe and Jane for dinner. Jane wishes they could do it another night. She isn't hungry. And that is the least of it.

Downstairs, Abe has already come in, washed up, set the table. The sky outside is gray and leaden; the apartment smells like duck sauce. Jane sits down, slightly nauseated. She forgets to say hi.

Hi, Abe says, focus narrowing his voice.

Sorry, Jane says. Hi.

Jane leans back. She feels she's lived twelve lifetimes already today. She misses her studio, longs to make something. What is Abe doing? Fussing at the counter, patting his own chest?

Soon, Jane is engrossed in classifying the shape of a magnolia blossom outside the window. It is because of that that she barely registers Abe saying that he needs to talk about something. What does it remind her of, the blossom? A starfish? A muscle, ripped? She cannot sort it.

For the next hour, Max will be at chess practice on Eighty-Fifth, which he seems to enjoy because of how good he is—wildly so, despite his age. Abe's mother took him. Abe will pick him up when it's done. They'll stop for chocolate ice cream. As they do. Jane has long given up on finding a precious ritual with her son. There will be other things, she tells herself.

On the table, in front of her, there is cold white wine, indigo napkins that Jane hand dyed as practice for something large-scale, and Chinese takeout, steaming. Vegetable lo mein, beef dumplings, egg drop soup, broccoli in oyster sauce. She would prefer toast and butter or nothing. Ginger ale or ginger tea or just water.

Does the magnolia blossom remind Jane of hospital gauze? No.

Are you listening, Jane? Abe asks.

I am, Jane says, but the words emerge without effort or consideration.

She is not.

Jane stands up. Do you mind if we go for a walk? she says. She feels like she needs some air. She remembers that she has tucked a pad into her underwear. She is safe. She is not safe. Is it because she knows what he's about to say or because of what she knows? Either way, she cannot stay here.

And this is the thing about Abe, Jane thinks. He is okay to ditch dinner. Everything he's done.

Sure, he says. Not a problem at all.

They put on their coats.

They've just entered the Park. It is dark but they stay under the lights. There is a loop they're familiar with, that doesn't feel threatening. A cop car is stationed at the halfway point and they know the policeman inside.

Tonight, there are birds or maybe bats and it is windier than Jane imagined. Still, the air is restorative, enlivening. Jane has forgotten that Abe had wanted to tell her something.

Okay, he says then, and stops her walking, reining her in by the hand.

What I'm trying to say, he says, and his voice cracks. For a moment, for Jane, there is grace. Jane imagines Abe saying that he knows about the appointment, the pads in the garbage, all the bleeding, the pain. She imagines Abe telling her that everything will be okay, they'll get through this together. As they have so many things, over so, so many years. That would be very much like Abe, wouldn't it? And Jane would be open to that, she thinks. She knows.

Why hasn't she just been honest all this time? she wonders. Why has she suffered so long, so much, without him? How silly. How misguided. It smells like cold and wood and fire. The Park supports and loves them. It has seen them through so much over the years.

Jane rubs her eyes though she isn't crying. The thought is nearly too much to bear. The surreality of it. The sweetness.

Right, Abe says, then claps his hands once.

It is only then that Jane realizes that Abe has been talking for quite some time now and not about Jane being sick. How long has this sort of thing been going on? Jane wonders. His talking, her on another planet. Weeks? Months? More?

This is fully Jane's fault. She should have been better. Could have. It occurs to her that it has been so long, Abe's words filling her brain like day-old oatmeal: nondescript, globby.

She will do better.

There is a bat.

What I've been trying to tell you, Abe says again, and clears his throat. And now Jane is ready to be in it with him, to fight for the rest of their lives. They'll be okay, she thinks. They just need to come back to each other. To get through this together. They can.

. . . is that for a really short while, it wasn't even a while really, it was a moment . . .

Yes, Jane says, and she is about to interject. But Abe's eyes are closed to her now. He doesn't hear her. He is focused inside.

There was someone else, he says.

Abe opens his eyes. Jane closes hers. The world stops. The Park.

For a moment, or maybe a hundred moments, it comes to a whirring, whizzing halt. Everything wobbles in response. The trees, Jane's torso, her brain, the road. She can feel it in her neck but in her spine and throat too, which is instantly sickened. Whiplashed. It is so cold.

Jane's eyes are magnetized to Abe's face, which looks as if it's been struck. His? There is no answer there though it feels like there should be. And what is even the question?

How could you?

Jane's hands tingle with something she can't yet name. Violence? Terror? Weakness?

Until this very moment, Jane was sure she'd have to explain her own self. And although she didn't have any definitive answer yet, she was ready to be in it with Abe. For a second, Jane forgets about her day, the doctor, the nurse, the physical pain—which feels, suddenly, like hers and hers alone.

It occurs to her that at any particular moment, you can only be most alarmed about one thing.

Abe drops his head and shakes it, as if ridding it of a bee or a bad thought. This.

There was what? is all Jane can manage. She wants him to repeat the words for content as much as emotion. She is not sure of what she feels exactly, the exact symptom or cause: a hollowness in her belly, tenderness not like love but like being socked in the throat.

She needs to hear him say the words again.

There was what? Jane says.

She was no one, Abe says.

No one, Jane repeats, parrotlike.

Does Jane imagine the sirens or do they really blare? Where is their policeman? Either way, the world is moments out of sync. There is dust, something, in Jane's throat. She coughs once.

They should go. Maybe they are in danger.

Abe reaches for her. The ever present instinct to help. Jane backs up. She looks around as if for help, but also, trying to remember what it looked like a minute ago. It is as if someone has come here and rearranged everything. There are new traits, angles, casts of light. Mice? Roaches? There is something perilous, is all Jane knows. Something unsound. How quickly everything feels unsafe.

Jane watches Abe touch his nose. She watches his hands across his hips as if he's praying but just a little. Jane considers how another woman might see him. He is a writer with merit now. A man who wears khaki and suspenders, gives talks, signs books, crosses his hands across his front in contemplation and, apparently, regret. Who knew? Jane did not.

Did she do this? she wonders. Did she push him too far?

For a moment, it doesn't matter. Jane longs to tell him about the doctor. Is it habit or desperation that compels a need like that? In a moment like this? Jane has no idea.

I'm sorry, Abe says.

You're sorry, she repeats.

How much does one miss when one feels secure? Jane thinks. It isn't self-blame or even a positive lesson. Not now at least. Not yet. Rather, it is a legitimate question that Jane would die for the answer to.

Then Jane's got it. The magnolia bud at home, she thinks, reminds her of paper, ripped open. The finality of it. The treachery.

Inside, she thinks, there are scribbles like pistils. What do they say? Nothing. Everything.

I was never perfect. You just weren't paying attention.

That night, when Abe is asleep, Jane goes into the living room. Usually, Abe leaves his briefcase leaning against the leg of the sofa. This, she always knew, she thinks.

Sure enough, it is there. Battered and brown, fastened with a burnished gold lock that is never locked.

Jane leans down, picks it up, is surprised by its weight. Perhaps, she thinks, this is something she should have known too. The weight of the things he bears. Or maybe it's just her body, giving out. Everything too heavy, too much now.

Jane opens it. Immediately, she is startled by the sound and sensation of something scattering on her feet. She spooks. But when she looks down, it is just four blue pens and one red—not a sea of roaches. Jane nearly laughs out loud. She nearly cries.

Shh, she says to no one, though Abe and Max are solid sleepers. They cannot be disturbed. Abe sleeps more solidly, too, in response to crisis. Ever since Max was born, he sleeps like the dead.

Jane goes over the conversation in her head. There was someone. She was no one. She repeats and repeats the words like an awful song that is stuck. As soon as Abe said the words, Jane knew it had to be one of his students. How? Abe, she is sure, would never seek someone out. He doesn't have that particular edge in him. Nothing wolfish. Never ever. For years, she has watched his eyes. Also, there are the things you know in your head, and the things you know in your heart.

Inside the briefcase, a yellow envelope, no name.

How does Jane know? She just does.

She carries the envelope upstairs in her arms. She keeps it inches away from her heart as though it were full of lice, or ice. She takes it into her studio, which smells like paint and cold concrete. How she likes it.

Jane closes the door gently behind her. Asylum. She is safe in here. She turns the lock. She sits down on her chair. It is covered with a sheepskin Abe bought for her in Finland on his first book tour. When was the last time he brought her a gift from his travels?

Or her him? Things have changed. That is true, though it is not an excuse. For goodness' sake.

Jane turns on the lamp. She looks out the window as if someone might be watching her. But there are only two lights on in empty rooms, furnished, still and quiet, across the street. No one inside, conspiring.

Who else is feeling this way? Jane wonders. And what are they doing about it?

Jane feels faint. She steadies herself by leaning back against the chair. Is it the sickness or the sentiment? Impossible to know now. Maybe forever now.

Jane is tucked in, legs crossed beneath her, duck-like. Her calves are throbbing a bit—adrenaline, or something else? But she will not stop or be distracted. She is guided by an energy unto itself. It is like searching the house for an intruder. The mystery, the compulsion, the fear of discovering something she never wanted to know.

She opens the envelope. She reads without pause. The writing is not not-beautiful. That is, the writing is lovely. Jane feels like she might throw up.

In the end, the story can only be described as one thing: an ode to Abe. Of course, Jane recognizes him immediately: suspenders, chewing gum, a history professor, as if. His name is Professor Park.

And the woman, apparently, is Ashley. A twentysomething from a broken home in an affluent New Jersey suburb. She has been writing her whole life, unsupported. Until Park.

Jane touches her throat.

In the beginning, Jane reads for clues. Ashley is petite, blond, freckled. She is great at tennis. In one scene, she is wearing a camel coat with a tie that Jane is sure she's seen on someone recently. Hasn't she? But today, every day—when did the morning even start?—is an absolute blur. She cannot remember seeing anyone except the doctor, and the nurse. And even then.

And yet, reading this, there is a weird feeling of déjà vu.

It isn't that Jane recognizes her, Ashley—how could she?—but something about Ashley feels inevitable. Neither lofty nor grand, scripted nor precious. Just small. And fated. The intruder in the tub, behind the curtain.

Boo.

When Jane gets to the end of the story, she drops the pages onto the floor. She cannot help it. They sting. She looks out the window for she doesn't know how much time. Ashley and Park do not end up together, in the story. But they've made such a mark that Jane feels the need to cover her own head and back up against the wall.

When finally, after who knows how long, Jane gets her strength back, she picks up the pages, finds the tiny part about the wife on page seven. There is only one mention of her.

Ashley is in Park's office on a snowy day when no one else is around. On the desk, a photo of the wife, blurry, black-and-white, with a plant in the background. Nonfiction. It is then that Ashley experiences some level of guilt. Doesn't she? Or perhaps Jane reads into that. Perhaps this is self-protective, or simply protective.

Jane puts this page on top, exposed, on her chair as she goes to find a needle tool in a desk drawer. She finds it. It is precise, sterile. Useful. She goes back to the page. Jane puts her fingers around the language of herself. Of Jane. And then, slowly, surgically, Jane steadies the tool on the words and slits down the part that hurts her the most. The part about her. The part about doing it despite or maybe because of her. The part about the three of them, then. A hideous triangle.

Jane leaves a mark.

The incision is tiny. It is vital.

Jane takes a step back, admiring her work. A black spider can get through now, she thinks. Or maybe breath. Or maybe the boil can bleed out in this way. Rocks over paper. Shoot.

Jane feels dizzy again. She sits down. She'll tidy up later. For now, she just needs a moment to settle into things. The plot thickens, she thinks. Or maybe she's lost the plot. She touches her belly. She tries to feel for unwellness in there. She tries to massage it back to health. As if. She tries to imagine what it looks like, corroded, crooked. The bottom of an old boat. The opposite of youthful. The opposite of new.

Jane's body is hot—inside and out. It is syrupy. It is weak. And isn't it something, she thinks, how we can long for something we weren't even aware of having. Time. Power. Health. Security. For a while. Before.

Jane wonders when she'll be too weak to feel hate like this, and what it will mean when hate shuts off. She thinks about her mother. Did she ever stop hating? She had to leave her country for her Jewishness. She never saw her own mother again, or her sisters. Jane's father was a steel blade in a drawer. Cold, if not deadly. He never saw Jane's mother, really saw her. Never asked questions. What hurts? He never held her in the night; Jane is sure. The agony of that. The preposterousness. Her mother's body gave up just when things might have gotten better, didn't it? Jane was just old enough. Her mother could have gotten a job, left. They could have. And what about hoping, Jane wonders. Did her mother ever stop that? And love?

Either way, for now, Jane's blood boils. She hasn't been perfect but she has, at least, been honest. And so, she can hold on to this— she is allowed—this feeling for as long as she wants. To not forgive, surrender—but instead, to cut cut cut, make holes, make something while she still can.

Jane Drew This When She Was Able.

28

CENTRAL PARK

Some people, though they haven't been to the Park in decades, dream of the dogwoods, the carousel, the sun setting behind the towers of the San Remo. During sex, the winner of Texas's most acclaimed peach pie contest must replay the moment her hat flew off and her husband ran into Terrace Drive to retrieve it. Aside from with the cattle, he is so rarely brave. Bethy in 7J dreams of fishing the Harlem Meer with Jason from 9E with a soda can, Christmas ribbon, and half a bag of sour cream and onion chips. He has the cutest mustache! Hundreds of thousands of people dream of childhoods spent in the Park, eating cherry Italian ices, feeding the chipmunks nuts, being barefoot for the only time in this city, the cold grass like wings between their toes. Some dream of first kisses at the Pool, white snow—for once it wasn't brown—learning to ride a bike because it was the only place their mother let them. It is the only place a kid can be free. Some people dream of the man with no legs who plays love songs on the Promenade not because of his no legs but because of the yearning heartache of his horn. It was the first time that music matched their feelings. Perhaps the first time they understood what those feelings really were. Some people picture themselves in the Park as they're on the subway, making a spreadsheet, flossing, standing at the foot of a ski slope in Denver, flying to Japan. It is as much a part of them as bone: critical and unchanging and knowable only by heart. The soap opera star who gets a lemonade in all her makeup and walks east thinks of the Park as she films. It is the reason she is so good: the longing, the melancholy, the blush.

Sometimes, leaving the Park feels like being stopped or stunned mid-pleasure, mid-sip, mid-step, mid-dream. It felt like a vacation inside. Why do all good things have to come to an end? Sometimes, for the first few blocks, one might shudder. The ESL teacher can't hear his ballads over the jackhammers. The detectives wonder, Was the sky like that when we went in? What is all that hissing steam on Amsterdam? Some hold their breath before they cross the wide avenues. The bright lights, precipitous hail of traffic, reminds the sous chef of violence, of being violated—and she buttons up her coat farther, wraps the scarf more tightly around her neck. She has been through so much and it is a privilege, she knows, to be romanced by the Park. But is it better to have loved and lost or never to have visited the Park at all? Abe hails a cab immediately. Everything but Jane feels like too much. He longs for home, if not his bench, if not his bench with her. The longing makes him feel frayed, like letters in the wind.

The Park isn't without its shortcomings. Some people consider the overt, ubiquitous PDA uncouth. The hot dogs are inedible; the mating calls of the yellowthroats are as cloying as the construction on Eighty-Third. He left bitemarks! She threw a shoe at my head! He read his breakup note out loud to me on my own parents' anniversary bench! The squirrels are rabid near the Reservoir. Who left behind that trail of chocolate kisses? And people come here to relax?

And when, after a few weeks, there's been not one single sighting of the Australian—let's call him Luke—the assistant producer gets desperate. She takes the day off, sits at the start of the six-mile loop for hours. At home, things have flatlined. Again. Her friends say she's in love with love. This is the fourth time this year. She doesn't know where love goes. Soon, it starts to rain. The assistant producer is about to leave when the Australian runs in. Mind if I join? she asks. He smiles, nods. Come, he says. He isn't Australian. Still, they run. They sprint in silence. They jog. They sprint again. Who is keeping up with whom? It doesn't matter. They know what they're doing. Eventually, they slow down. They talk about everything: running, family, the city. Turns out, they're both keto, love Southern California, fruity red wines. The rain stops. There is a rainbow over Engineers' Gate. They point to it at the same time. It feels like fate, doesn't it? Divined, supported, ordained. How lucky are we?

When the doctor loses a special patient, he comes to the Park too. He takes off his shoes, walks barefoot, eyes shut, believing, praying, promising, through the cold grass at Cherry Hill. When the sanitation worker files for divorce, he comes, spies an elusive scarlet tanager in the crown of the trees so bright it's a comet, igniting the leaves. When the unhoused throuple wakes up to three coats, folded, one hundred dollars in each, they jump around in a circle and embrace. When the sous chef meets someone at her meeting—she's been hurt in the same way—she vows never to stray too far from this place that heartens. That heals.

Of course, there are heartaches that the Park cannot fix. That is obvious, elemental. For the vegan, the Holotropic Breathwork will only do so much. Time is the real workhorse. And Jane, despite all Abe's diligence, cannot be made well again. The funnel of life for her, for everyone, but it's different, faces in. The Park is rife with trauma: grief, war, hate crimes even. She called the cops on me! I was just watching the birds! And yet, just when it feels like the whole world has gone insane, loveless, lovelorn—and it is just getting worse—the cherry blossoms bloom in the Park. Does it feel better in here? It does. Does it cure anything? It does not. Still, see how the sun flickers on the water. It's angelic, isn't it? As in, angels do exist.

At Cedar Hill, at dusk, the housepainter—Edwin—lies on his back in Strawberry Fields, his shirt rolled up, crisp corners, under his head. He is anticipating the fireflies. They remind him of his wife and daughters back home. They would sit on the porch, wait for the show. At home here, in New York, his bed is stiff, music blares from below. It is about loneliness and love, but Edwin is the only one really listening. Here, in the Park, he can rest. He brings a pint of blueberries. He stays until it is dark, and when he begins the trek toward Central Park West, his body aches. The work is unyielding. He isn't young anymore. But he is not scared or disappointed, fatigued or forlorn. The fireflies guide the way to the Park's edge. They beam, and just before the darkness fills his bones, they beam for him again. He feels love then like it is a place. Is it not? It is. It is within him and also without. Thank God.

29

ABE

The next morning, you want to keep remembering.

I ask you if you want to skip this part.

Some of it, you say. Some of it cannot be left out.

You remember, in the beginning, the pain like being hunted. It sought you out, held you down. It came in the night or in the morning. Some days, it stayed all day long. Sometimes, it felt like there was a grenade, heavy and metal, in you. Like it might blow and blow you up from your middle, from the inside out. There were two nodes, swollen and sore, in your groin. Was that them?

You remember, some days, wondering if you had any blood left in you. How you weren't already emptied out, and merely snakeskin now, or a dry old pipe.

You remember, too, how the weirdest part about getting sick was how it made you feel closer to your mother. You were suddenly in her shoes, her dress, were her even, decades and decades later. You could look in the mirror and see her see you. How are you feeling today? you'd ask. Same as me? Same as you. I miss you.

Stage IIIC2, they said. They didn't have language like that for your mother, you're sure. Or odds.

And you remember how hard it was, in the beginning, to be sick but also to be sick without me. You didn't tell me for an entire month. By then, I'd already told you about Alice in the Park. I'd ruined things. Ruined everything. I'm not trying to be dramatic. You were never dramatic. You never even screamed.

You shake your head. You purse your lips.

I didn't deserve to know, is the truth of it. You remember you couldn't bear my kindness. Tenderness is a question of giving up, you say. You just wanted to hold on.

And about Alice: you remember that it wasn't so much that you wanted to get back at me as you wanted me to take it back. Could I just not have. Could you just not have known.

Still, you remember that if not for illness, and illness then, maybe we wouldn't have been all right.

We take a break. I feed you buttered toast with your favorite jam. We made it together: strawberry peach. You have two bites. I finish the rest and wipe your mouth. I ask you if you want to listen to music. You say yes. But as soon as it's on—Paul Simon—I see your eyes squinch. I turn it off, shake out your blankets, hold your feet and hum to you instead. I want to beg you to forget what I did, and how I did it. It was so long ago now, but sadness carves deeper than happiness, doesn't it? That's what they say. Maybe it's true. But also, I remember you dancing to Buena Vista Social Club in our kitchen in an apron and socks, tomato soup on the stove. I remember that better than I remember almost anything else.

And doesn't that mean something?

You remember moving to the hotel, after I told you, for two weeks: white sheets, views of Central Park, French fries in bed. You wanted to do everything without me. Without Max. Without the guilt. More of it. Though that was impossible, wasn't it? You just wanted it more possible, you say.

You remember going to your first doctor's appointment alone. Is there someone who can come get you? they asked. You remember racing home, knowing I'd be picking up Max from school, and scouring my office for evidence of her. Her underwear. Her notes in my books. You remember wanting to know, and also the opposite of that.

You never found anything. I tell you, there was nothing to find.

You remember how, in the beginning, the angst was equally distributed between two things—Alice and sickness—and how odd that was. You'd remember one and forget the other. You'd forget the other and the first one would float to the surface like a body. Hers. Yours. One was fatal. The other just felt like that.

You remember on the day you told me about the cancer it was not because you wanted to but because you had to. You couldn't carry the groceries up the stairs, zipper your coat, brush the back of your hair. You asked me to help you. We were standing in the bathroom; I was working through a snarl, and you said, I have it. As my mother had it. That is why I'm like this.

I remember, after that, it wasn't you but me who reached for the wall—and how that made perfect sense, ridiculously. Truly.

You remember, in the beginning, niceties or maybe delusion. How we both said we were sure you'd be okay. Were we bound together by fear or hope or both, in the beginning? We were looking at each other in the bathroom mirror. Maybe you were looking past me at something else. Maybe you were looking at your mother, or your healthy self, or at Alice. I can only hope not.

You remember blue chairs in the doctor's office, wearing a cap, ice, burning, a nurse who kept saying she couldn't believe how young you were, and how good it was that you'd already had a child. You remember ginger ale and applesauce, needles, pink and white pills in tiny green cups. You remember not eating because you couldn't go to the bathroom, not going to the bathroom because you weren't eating. You remember trying to walk across the Park to your appointment and getting so tired that you had to flag down a horse-drawn carriage. He took you all the way east and between the buildings too, outside of the Park. And you told him. Killed my wife, he said. Hers was in the colon. He didn't know.

You remember getting very thin very quickly and that despite all the sirens and horns, waiting for a cab on Central Park West, you heard the ding when your ring fell off. You remember you wore it around your neck, after that, and despite everything.

When was it—months later?—that you let me carry you and tuck you in on the sofa so you could nap? I'll never forget it. It was the first time you let me touch you, really touch you, again. You were silk across my arms. I remember Max, in the corner, watching. He was holding a cup of juice and also a blue truck. For once, he didn't spill it or slam anything. For once, he didn't say something. Or ask. He just stood there. I remember how small he was, shoulders, feet, nose.

You remember we didn't tell him. Neither did my mother. She, too, felt like it was a bad idea—and said as much, though she so rarely forced an opinion. He'll be better off, she said. He was just five or six, and there was already so much distance between you two. But he knew. Of course he knew. It defined everything.

You remember when you were sick, he gave you a wider berth, but also, he made less noise. At night, he would ask to keep the lights on, to sleep with all his cars and books in the sheets. He would ask what was wrong with you and I would tell him nothing. You were just tired. I stayed with him until he was asleep and then peeled a truck wheel off his cheek. It had left a mark.

You remember that for the next two years, Max was taken care of by me, by my mother, by me, by my mother. You were asleep, you were staring out the window, you were on the toilet, dreaming of your own mother, rubbing your back. Sometimes, Bea would come over and it was the only time I'd hear you laugh. You and her in there, alone. She brought you a TV table so you could watercolor in bed. And you did, every now and again. You'd ask me to give the watercolors to Max and I always did. He kept them in a pile.

I wish you'd seen how Max rose to the occasion for us. But also, it feels cruel to tell you. And useless. Was it in reverence of you or me or because he was afraid? Not of his mortality but of how much we could all take. I remember he'd play chess with my father at their apartment. My mother taught him to make stews, do laundry, be a shark at blackjack, and also canasta. Not all kids can muster; that is what I want to say.

What I am saying is that everyone gave.

It was then, no surprise, that my father sold the business. He gave us money. Just like that. And it helped. We can both acknowledge that. All of us can. He didn't ask me, didn't have to. He just knew.

You remember sometimes wondering what that time would have been like without the cancer, without Alice. You and Max. You and me. What would we have done in the afternoons? On the weekends? There was nothing simple. Nothing obvious, you say. Everything was compromised because everything was broken.

You remember sometimes wondering if it was the art or the depression or the sickness that drove me to Alice. There is no way to know, you say. But I'd like to. What would have helped? What should I have done differently? In this moment, your voice is changed. You sound like a young girl. It cracks me open. I am yolk, on the floor.

Oh, Jane, I say. I cover my face. I don't know how to tell you that there has never been fault between us. Or at least never anything specific. You were. I was. We have always just been water, slipping through holes.

30

You remember when things started to loosen. Not for you, but for us. I hope you believe me when I say that I never saw Alice again. Not ever. That doesn't surprise me, you say. You were absolutely no fun during that era. What kind of affair?

You give a little laugh. You are amazing like that.

You remember, sometimes, in the beginning, and on good days, forgetting you weren't healthy—because some days, it seemed like you were. You could take the stairs two by two, eat a box of cookies. You could take a cab to Bea's studio just to be with her making things and with her. You remember, sometimes, in the beginning, on good days, forgetting what I'd done.

Was that the sickness or some kind of protective mechanism? you wonder. Perhaps that's the only thing that the sickness protects.

You remember how, in the beginning, sickness felt like more of a nuisance than an issue of life and death. Death too. Or maybe: you remember realizing how the opposite of pain isn't simply painlessness and realizing that you are never not depleting your quota of breaths. The realization that you've been breathing and dying your whole life.

You remember how the prognosis was horrible but you can't remember the numbers. The pain was the least of it, in a way. What was the most? Not being creative. Being a mother. Both.

You remember, on bad days, remembering what you missed already: coffee, the final chapters of good books, painting blue, hyacinths, chipmunks and how they looked toward the sky sometimes. Me (it took a while), my mother, Max. Sometimes, you'd wake up and he was asleep on the floor next to you. Never ever did you wake him up. You just watched him, trying to figure out who he was, who he'd be—as if you could tell in this way. And whether you'd live long enough to know.

You remember wondering about the last time for everything, checking the date on a tin of peaches and wondering if they'd outlast you. If you'd ever see Max in a grown-up suit. If you'd ever paint in a studio in France.

You remember how much my parents helped even though my father aged quickly and didn't know what to do with himself without work. Some days, you remember, he took Max to the Park. He tried to steer him away from the arts. But that is a different story. For a different story. This part is about you.

You remember, we came back together, slowly slowly slowly.

Like beads of rain? I ask. You're not sure you can imagine that.

I'm just trying to change the subject.

You fan your hands in front of your face. What a time, you say. We were holding on to so much.

You remember I didn't write for months, and didn't ever mention it. Instead, I followed my mother's recipe for chicken soup, talked to Max about you, memories he'd never heard and how he liked that. And how it helped us. You remember when Max asked you what hurt and how you tried not to weep in front of him and instead answer plainly. And you did. You were like that. Are.

I remember the bones in your hips and chest and wrists and how sometimes the longing felt physical. I felt that if I could just push something away, shove it, keep it from touching you. And then not. There were days when I didn't feel I could stand up. It is not the point. It just goes to the idea of power. And having none.

You remember months later, showing up to Collette Cooper's and how already she knew. You sat on her sofa, knees to knees. She was a breast cancer survivor. And you remember she did: she sold the hell out of your work. Because or despite or whatever. It doesn't matter, you say. She just did.

You remember the day she gave you your biggest check, you were in bed. She put the champagne to your lips. I remember listening at the door.

You remember at an important show in Chelsea, you were seated the whole time. You remember you had to buy new lipstick. Everything made you look like old melon, you say, or maybe dead. This makes you laugh.

You remember the first time you asked me to tell you about Alice, who she was, who she was to me. And I asked you if you were sure you wanted to hear it. And you said you weren't. And so I didn't tell you. I never did.

She was no one, Jane.

You remember one time asking Max if he'd miss you. He was seven. It was a dark moment; you wouldn't have otherwise. You remember how he said, Stop.

You remember sometimes, with him, keeping the words in your mouth like toothpaste water, wanting to spit. You remember wishing you could start over with him. Be a different mother from the get-go. You were more whole now, despite everything.

You remember that the cancer did do something to shift the configuration of things: you and me and Max. And the expectations.

You just couldn't. And in a way, you were grateful for that. I shouldn't have needed an excuse, you say. I am his mother.

You remember that time wasn't the worst time—though, in a way, it was. The newness. The shock of it even if you'd never not wondered. You remember that you were young, had a lot of fight in you. And you fought. It was not in your lymph nodes or pelvis that time. The tumor was the length of two nickels, a triple-A battery. You remember the exhaustion like an elevator closing on your head only to open and close again, and again. You remember the fear of not knowing.

That time, you did three rounds of chemo, six cycles each. You lost all your hair, and it came back within a year, no wave, lighter.

You remember—and me too—that time we hired a driver to take us to Orient so you could see the light on the oyster ponds in March. You remember imagining moving here, wind and the smell of rust and metal and fire, salt on the windshield. I remember how you looked at me, like an arrow shot. Let's end up here, you said.

Gosh, that was lifetimes ago.

You remember it was not long after that when they told you that you were in remission. You remember the relief, but also the beginning of eggshells forever, living on borrowed time. You remember that we went every weekend to Orient, sat by the shore, ate figs or crackers or passed a can of cream soda between us. It felt as if we were wishing, or praying. The water will do that. And also remission.

You remember feeling that you'd learned how to hold your breath for months at a time. You remember feeling like you'd learned to fully exhale too.

You remember Max being brilliant at school, telling you a long-winded story about soccer, and that if you ever tried to offer your two cents . . .

You remember one teacher: He is one of the smartest we've ever seen. And one of the most charismatic. But he's also got a temper. Perhaps it will serve him, you said to her. She was surprised by you. You remember never not being astonished by who he was.

You remember I was working on my fourth novel, the one about the two architects restoring an estate in Maine. You loved that one. I wrote in your studio sometimes. Sometimes, you doodled as I wrote on the couch.

And sometimes, you'd remember you hadn't thought about Alice in days.

You remember, once, finding Max staring at a painting you'd done of him in orange and yellow. What do you see? He just nodded. He was eating capers by the handful. That was the phase in which every day, he'd eat us out of house and home. Do you remember that? Of course you do.

You remember that when you weren't sick, he liked you more. Was more gracious. You couldn't blame him. He'd lean on you, sometimes, in the kitchen and ask if you could pour him some milk. It wasn't lost on you that on your bad days, your hands shook. You couldn't have helped him even if you tried.

You poured him the milk.

You remember thinking, At least I can do this. Your mother could not.

You remember my brother visiting. How he'd still not told my parents he was gay but he'd told me. You went for cappuccinos in Little Italy and you held hands across a rickety table and neither one of you talked about what was fair and what wasn't. That was something you two always had between you. You swam in the same sea.

You remember crunching leaves on Central Park West, the first time you did the Lower Loop alone, without losing your breath. You kept an eye on a horse and its carriage, just in case. You remember how everything was brighter after the chemo—the sun, orange trees. You remember how everything tasted sickeningly sweet: strawberries, herbal tea. You remember needing glasses for the first time. And wondering: Was that the cancer or was that the not dying?

You remember the first year we rented a house in Orient with Bea and her boyfriend, Lupo. He was an astrologer and said, about you and Max, Of course. It's in the stars. And wanting to throw him out.

You remember packing tuna sandwiches and berries, wading into the water deep deep deep and looking back, seeing me flattening sand with my palms. You remember Max reading alone on the beach and, sometimes, praying for him. It wasn't religious or even superstitious. It felt biological. Please, you'd pray. Be all right.

It seemed like he was.

You remember learning to knit, a neon sculpture installation on Canal, Saint-Saëns, peppermint oil when you got a headache, roasting salmon and fennel, and when I sold my fifth book—*The Material*.

You remember when my father died. You were in the room with him. My mother and I were in the kitchen. You remember how you'd never been close really, but saying goodbye felt important. It felt, to you, like you understood that in a different way. You were telling him a story that your mother had told you about a woman who sold chickens. When he went, you say, nothing changed in the room. It was silent before. It was silent after. And how that struck you. May his memory be a blessing.

You remember, after that, paying everything off. And that that was when David told my mother. You were with them both too. Hands in each other's hands.

You remember Max getting older and, some days, you two reading next to each other on the couch. It wasn't that you'd grown closer, but rather that you'd grown around a hole. You remember he still liked to make little sketches in your notebooks in black ink. He loved the coffee you brewed. He would sometimes ask to wear your

glasses because he liked the way they made the art look. Not specifically yours.

You remember that when your mother landed in America, she had
lice and fleas and the twig of an orange blossom plant that her
mother had tended in her pocket still. It was like a bone. You ask
me if I think trauma passes down like cells, but unlike bones.

I do, I say. I do.

You remember, some days, getting called into the principal. Max
had been writing quotes from Basquiat on the walls in your lipstick. You barely even wore lipstick. Maybe that was his point?

Here's a thing that we love: when he was tiny, he called it lip dick.

You remember when it was clear to us that he'd lost his virginity—
though he never said so. How he wore it like a cape.

You remember volunteering with the kids at PS 84—Max was at
334 for gifted kids—and how it made things worse with Max. He
could shut you out for days. But at 84: you remember feeling that
you were doing something useful, reciprocal. One gave you a black
eye. You remember, it was worth it. You could have been a kid like
that, you said. Angry. You remember telling him, Michael Dedo.
Your pain will be useful. Decades later, we saw his jazz performed
at Lincoln Center. His pain was.

It is interesting, but I do not mention it: how you could not say that
to Max.

You remember reading *Anna Karenina* on the M7, the record store on Amsterdam, the guy who sold purses made of rubber bands. You remember bringing the kids clothes you'd bought for Max and he never wore, and would never wear. You remember a girl named Lita whose father had tattooed her arm. An *S*. For what, you asked her. She didn't know. She was twelve. You taught her to make an apple tree around it with washable pen. Sometimes, you'd do it for her: a butterfly, a barn, a snake breathing lollipops and candy apples instead.

You remember when Bea moved to Dublin for three years to teach and how lonely it left you. Ours, you say, was a love story too. Some days, when you were really sick, you'd fall asleep and Bea would stay with you for hours, a hand on your hand.

You remember buying bras on Seventy-Eighth, keeping our citrus trees in the shower for moisture, washing windows with newspaper, losing your father. It was slow; he'd been in a home. It was my mother who hosted shiva for the second time that year. Both of Max's grandfathers. Good cop, bad cop but nothing's simple. My father did his best. And perhaps without you, I never would have even thought: he wasn't enough.

You remember it was not long after that that I finished the novel about a couple not unlike us but not quite like us. You remember not taking any of it personally exactly but it feeling exactly personal. You remember believing in it. And you remember that it was not just because you loved it and not just because you loved me.

That is the thing about fiction, I think. I'm not trying to make a point here, and yet. We were on the mend. You were all right, for the time being. Max was selling old copies of *Playboy*, was nationally ranked in chess, would run for fun, miles and miles around the Park. He was tall, charming, provocative. And we were hopeful. As in: there were so many reasons to hope.

Too, you remember how often I used the word *mistake*. Even many years later. I want you to know that's what it felt like. Just that. I want you to understand. I do, you say. I do.

Some days, it is late when we stop remembering. You've fallen asleep or your eyes get glassy or you keep moving your legs. Some days, you aren't asleep, but you aren't awake either. I'm not sure when you've stopped talking and what I've filled in.

Some days, I watch the rise and fall of the white blanket on your chest and I put my hand above it just to be with you.

Some days, I tell you about how the light is changing. It's indigo and orange at four thirty now. I tell you about how you've taken to setting one foot outside the sheets, socked. A kickstand. A refusal, betrayal of the rest of your body, so idle against the mattress. I tuck it in again. Out it goes. Wanting to keep you warm but also. How proud it makes me. Fight, fight, my Jane. Foot out forever. Some days, I whisper that.

Some days, I fall asleep myself, and when I wake up, I can't tell if it's because of your voice or because of mine or when my fingers stopped typing.

Some days, I'm not sure of where the memory ends and the story begins. Where the story ends and the writing begins. It's a Möbius strip. And yet, the more life, the more memories. The more memories, though, the less life. There's a mathematical equation in there somewhere. Or maybe just a mortal truth.

Some days, when you're asleep, I tell you what I don't remember. Which is also what I do remember, inside out. It's where story comes in.

I do not tell you that I've begun praying again. I can remember just two hymns in Hebrew. The mourning one we sang at funerals and the one for Hanukkah, which seems less condemning. I sing that.

For so many years, I'd forgone our faith, and though it isn't Hanukkah and there are no candles, it feels ceremonial, here in the dark, half dreaming, wishing, praying, singing or hearing the hymn from somewhere inside.

31

The next day, or whenever, it is midday on a weekday. I don't know which. One of the nurses has told me to say affirmations into the mirror and so I do, when I remember, in the bathroom.

I am strong.

I am full of ease.

I am hopeful.

I am hungry.

I do not look at my face exactly—that stopped years ago—but past it, past us, to a different time. It is not that I'm imagining youth. It is just that I am not imagining this.

In our room, you are in bright yellow pajamas in bed. They light up your face as though there is a spotlight under your chin. I'd like to ask you about color theory, about warmth and coolness. Instead, I reach for your hand and when I've got your stem fingers in mine, you nod, imperceptibly. Is this our secret language? I wonder. Or am I talking to myself?

Jane, I say. Do you remember that picnic in the Park—we were eating bagels and gravlax—when Max strolled through? He'd been somewhere on the Upper East Side, hadn't he?

Where? I ask.

Maxine Bentley's apartment, you say.

How do you remember? What were we celebrating? What about the sky?

That you don't remember, you say. Me either. I wonder about that.

I ask you if you remember the blue-and-white blanket we used for years for our picnics. The one with the mustard stain in the corner. Whatever happened to it? Why do I long for it now?

Then you say that sometimes in the Park, but only in the Park for some reason, you were sure you saw Alice. But you never did.

Did you?

You go on.

You remember when you got into the Whitney, we celebrated at the Carlyle. You remember your show in Madrid when you sold all but one. You remember painting on linen, the smell of glue, your staple gun and how it was splattered dark green. You remember when a famous gallerist asked you to lunch and called you Joan and you corrected him and that was the last you heard from him.

Do you think we should have included Max? you say. In everything?

He wouldn't have wanted to be included. He was a teenager. He was always with his friends.

But we're both thinking about the trade-offs between ease and commitment, hardship and giving up. No one knows, I tell you, how to do it exactly.

Still, you remember things feeling easier for a while.

You remember painting a round of carousel horses for a private residence in the South of France, clay again, and then watercolor. I remember that you could do anything, make anything, make anything into art. You were covered in gold leaf for a year or so. It looked so ethereal on your skin. That, you were. Are.

You remember lentil soup with purple carrots, down coats as light as feathers, working with magnets and tiles, a little cactus in your studio that bloomed every season, differently though consistently, for years. You remember how we would walk to dinner on Columbus when the street was slick black and it smelled like pine and also soy sauce, and how the lights reflected in the puddles and on the glass doors, and you thought, holding my hand, No one can take this from us.

You remember how Max always carried a notebook, as we did, and also a pen. You remember how he went out a lot and some nights he slept out. And even though he never told you anything about anything, you didn't worry that he wouldn't be okay. You trusted him and that felt like a feat.

You remember painting plates and how they basically made us rich. And how that surprised you. That you could never guess. You remember meeting other artists and always thinking they were either farther along or farther behind. Especially the men.

You remember how we used to sit on the sofa and read the same books so we could talk about them as soon as we both were done. You remember when we started cooking for my mother—carrot ginger soup, bean burgers, salmon cakes—and how you used to beg her to move in. I'm too young for that, she'd say. She was not.

You remember my teal computer, our corn muffin phase, standing outside Shakespeare & Co., the two of us, as they stacked *Pastiche* in the window at dusk. My book about deception. You remember not cheering, but clapping slowly. I'm not sure how you remember that, but you do.

You remember a moment when you realized we'd become what we'd always hoped. And at the same time, saying, I couldn't have done it without you.

I remember walking so many, many, many streets with you. Eating so many meals, sharing a tres leches, two spoons. And drinking tea.

And then I want to say something about how marriage is a relay race. Or long loops around the track. One gets ahead. Then the other. Then the other. Or maybe like the ocean. A wave crashes in two places at different times.

And, in between, you walk, even from the front door to the car, together. In every weather. So many, many, many streets.

You remember something you made during that time. Crochet and clay. It was you and Max. Slack and also restriction. You were in MoMA by then. And Max loved art, was sure to make a career out of it, but he never commented on yours. Why would he have? you say. But I know you don't mean that exactly.

What you mean is that you wished that you could have had an ongoing conversation about anything with him. One day, he'd mention a girl. But if you ever asked . . . One day, he'd ask about a certain artist, but as soon you said anything . . . It was a game of tennis but always, suddenly, catastrophically, he'd walked off the court. Sometimes, at dinner, all three of us, it was just you and me talking. Or just him talking. Sometimes, it felt like three was the most impossible number in the world.

You remember the New York Public Library at Christmas, gum stains on Seventy-Fourth, water fountains never working in the Park. You remember the tulips on Fifth at dusk, Pearl Paint, and an opal my mother gave you that had been her mother's. You remember learning to solder just to work it into a ring.

You remember stitching on canvas, spinning red wool, a lime orchid you kept for years, you and Collette and me at Tavern on the Green again. Of all the places. You remember three bottles of champagne, a silk dress, jazz, a fish tank, deviled eggs, and feeding leftovers to a carriage horse before we got chased away. Again.

You remember wishing you'd known Collette when you'd first had Max. Bea never had any children. People talk about villages. I would have died without your mother, you say.

You remember visiting your pieces at museums, watching people walk by, people stop. You remember your favorite studio tech, Leo Sinsky, and how he arranged all your work by color and year, knew better than you about what you'd made, what you'd done. What have I done? you ask. He was a vegan and lived on the same block where I first visited you in the city.

You remember 9/11—the smell, the footage; we were lucky to know only one—and how I wouldn't let you volunteer below Fourteenth Street because we couldn't take any chances. It is not my lungs, you said.

And yet.

You remember the perfect cherry red, an easel that always tilted right, when Leo Sinsky got stabbed (he was all right, though he died of an accidental overdose not long after), listening to opera, locking the door, and me showing up with grilled cheese.

You remember seeing your work in Paris (we both went, Max stayed home, took Bubbe to dinner), escargot and the Eiffel Tower and a store that sold only lavender oil. You remember when I did a reading in the Louvre. You remember your brief fascination with using butterflies, a needle tool that you had for fifteen, maybe twenty years, and when you dropped a roll of canvas on your toe and how, in the emergency room, the doctor had to drill a hole in your nail to release the pressure. Let me do it, you'd said to him. Let me, he'd said back.

You remember, when you weren't sick, we worried about you getting sick again but we never talked about it directly. I know because if we saw an ad in the paper for the hospital, or a person in a wheelchair, or we had to write down our medical history for the dermatologist (age spots!), our faces and voices would lift. Like hiking up pants. And suddenly, we'd talk more quickly, more superficially. Play it cool.

You remember your collection of pearls on tiny canvases. *Lulu*. It took you years and years and years.

You remember an article in which they called your success hard-won.

Why do you remember that? I ask.

It made me think of my mother, you say. How she struggled. What she had to show for it, at the end.

You? I say.

You.

I do remember Alice, you say then. Do you? I say. I don't know, you say. I can't know.

You look out the window. There is a copper beech we named Ginger Rogers, and a whole collection of birches, and birdhouses, wind chimes. You rub your ears. You rub your eyes. I want to ask you what you're thinking but I apologize instead.

Let's keep going, you say. Instead.

You remember your mother's hands. She smelled like jasmine and cigarettes and called you Habibibaby. You remember her slow walk, hands around a wineglass, hands in your hands—like birch branches? Tulip petals? Those twiggy dried things on the beach. You remember she told you that she used to sneak kebabs from the Muslim butcher. You loved to imagine her young. She used to rest her chin on her shoulder to think. You do the same. It always comes back to the mother, I think. Doesn't it?

This time, you don't tell me the answer. Maybe it is too much. Now you are looking at the ceiling, your eyes flitting back and forth as if there were a poem up there in ink. Read to me.

Out of nowhere you say: I think the saddest part of a novel is that you can't take it in all at once.

Is it?

Maybe that's why you painted, I say. To stand back. For the flush of feeling like that.

But you aren't listening.

It is not that I haven't had a full life, you say. You trail off. I can't tell if you're crying or if it's just your eyes. You close them.

Jane, don't go.

Your words are sparks in the night.

It hurts, you say then. It hurts.

What can I do but hold on to you? I do.

32

You remember—and this part's important, you say, because for so long, we weren't sure what would happen—Max getting into Brown. Yale. Swarthmore. It wasn't about the schools. It was about possibility. You remember, of course, he went across the world to Oxford.

You remember feeling proud of him—you still are. He is smart and focused. I can't take credit, you say. You don't have to.

You remember visiting Max in England, taking him out to tea, walking to the top of the dome, a bench in Kew Gardens where you read side by side. It is something you have always done, have always been able to. You remember his beard, long shoes, paying for things and putting the change in his pocket, his head going side to side at the Tate.

You remember it was easier when he was older—not because you were closer per se but because expectations were different. You didn't have to hold him to your chest, rock him to sleep, wipe his chin. He didn't have to let you.

You remember on Central Park West, the Afghani woman who sold the best bananas, yoga on Mondays, cider after the Thanksgiving parade, realizing that you'd owned a particular brown coat for thirty-some years.

And, in a way, you remember that after that time flies. Or it feels like that.

If a story is a question of release of information. Or relief of information. We lived. The days went.

You remember you were always my first reader and that the book you told me wasn't your favorite did the best. You remember the manuscript I never finished was the one that you never stopped hoping I'd return to. You remember coming with me on book tours except when I went to Germany because the kids at PS 84 had their annual art show celebration and you wanted to be there more. By that time, you had worked with them for well over a decade. You loved how they needed you. You aren't too proud to say it—or that it is about Max.

You remember the time you drew the two of us. White background. Flicky strokes of pen. We framed it in silver and put it over our bed. A famous art collector came for dinner one night and threatened to take it right off the wall and keep it for himself. He was holding a glass of red wine, and I thought—and I meant it—spill it everywhere except on that. The things you'd take in a fire and so on.

You remember the Modern Love I wrote about you getting sick and when Bernadette Peters read it out loud onstage at the Delacorte. You had your arm over my shoulders and held my hand in my lap. We walked home with Bernadette in the Park, in the dark. She said she'd been a fan of both of ours for many years. Not just as artists, but as a couple. And you said, It hasn't always been easy. And she said, No. Of course it hasn't.

You remember manicures (Elli's Salon), a waffle robe, candied kumquats, and polenta cake. You remember taking my mother to her PT appointments toward the end and how you held hands, her fingers like bird bones.

You remember one time asking her about her and Max, and she apologized for maybe overstepping and you just wept. No, you said. No.

You remember wondering when intelligence becomes wisdom and so on. There is a categorical and also indeterminable shift.

You remember when Max taught us to buy spices online and when he didn't come home for Thanksgiving (mostly).

You remember when my mother died and how you knew at the very moment. It felt as if something had fallen and smashed in another room you said. And then the phone rang. She was eighty-six and there were complications with pneumonia and how odd, you thought. There was never anything cold, not one single thing, within her. She lived well until the end. We hosted shiva and wished she could have helped us. She did everything with grace. You dab at your eyes. Your mother, you say.

You remember how Max didn't call you for weeks, as if it were your fault. As if he would have rather you went first. Not as if, you say. Because.

Stop.

You remember painting a mural for my mother at Sarah Lawrence. It was about women, specifically about mothers. The cashmere shawl was the background, of course. You asked David for his input. Oh, he said. It is impossible to be a mother in a lot of ways. I can only imagine. Blame feels beside the point. Even he had his gripes. Doesn't everyone?

You remember that Max went and saw it but he never told you that. I did. I wanted you to know.

You remember sharing a bag of cherries as we walked down Riverside Drive. You remember holding your palm out for my pits. You remember how you never wished we hadn't had Max, only that it had been easier. We could say that to each other. No one else.

You remember crocheting hats with flowers, meeting Bea and Collette and Leo Sinsky's partner (you became close after he passed) for independent films, marching in Washington with Faye Miller (she was married to one of my camp friends) and her three girls, and voting. And praying. And praying more around voting time.

You exhale loudly. At first, I lurch toward you. It is habit. Then I remember the meaning of breath. You are still alive. I exhale too. How many times have we sat here like this? How many exhales together? Apart? How many more?

You are propped up against the headboard. There is white everywhere—or it feels like that. Curtains open. Clean sheets. Bernie changed them this morning with you on top. She must have seven arms, I think. Wild strength. There is a throng of yellow dahlias on the windowsill, your favorite. Who brought them? I wonder. It wasn't me. It's winter.

Want me to read you something? I say. I touch your head. Warm. Too warm? Too cold? You nod.

I go in the other room only for a second. The adrenaline spikes when I don't have my eyes on you.

Mary Oliver. Today, I read you the one about the branches, the one about black oaks, the one about mysteries—and dancing. For a moment, I'm comforted. We live in cycles, not perpetuity. It takes a moment. Then all these hypotheticals, metaphors, fall flat.

Let's keep going, you say.

Okay. I sit up taller as if the memories are water. Don't drink lying down.

You remember years of trying to make your mother's hummus and finally discovering the trick: brine. You remember the doorman on Seventy-Second and Central Park West who had the best whistle you'd ever heard, and when he died of a heart attack and how you wished you'd recorded him. You remember so much of that. The stories that live only in us, within us, and how they die every day with us too.

You remember telemarketers calling and asking for Lulu. How could they know?

You remember that I dedicated every one of my books to you except the one I dedicated to the three of us.

You remember the sound of the keys in the door, the window unlocking, me printing out a draft.

You remember Max's first job at a gallery and how he talked to you about modernism at a café downtown. You remember his second and third jobs too. They called him the renegade, the prodigy. You remember Bea, Collette, reading about him in the paper for one sale or another. You can't remember which. There were so many, after a time. You remember him telling you how much he made in a year like he knew he was getting away with murder. He was.

You remember him never asking about your art really except about the money. You remember talking about it in therapy. You always came back to: you were just happy he was all right.

You remember the Halls of Gems and Minerals at the American Museum of Natural History, the chiropractor named Stephen on Eighty-Sixth whom you could have imagined as our son, yogurt sauce, Jing Fong's third floor, lights on Central Park West in the winter, when we went to the Biennial and bumped into Max. Hello, parents, he said.

You remember one day, meeting him in the Park. You were walking home from therapy and he had just been visiting with a client. You spent the whole afternoon at the Met. He knew everything. You listened and listened. You could have listened to him for years.

He knows that, I say.

You remember that you never felt entitled to be proud of him but that you were wildly impressed by him, his work ethic, his independence. He is a force in this world, isn't he? you say. Sometimes, you long to ask your mother if that was enough. As if only she could know. As if your mothering was entirely contingent on her mirroring it back to you. Yes or no.

You remember quitting coffee and when you realized it had been twenty-some years since your last cigarette and begging Max to quit. A do-as-I-say-not-as-I-used-to-do thing.

You remember holes in socks, packages with too much packaging tape, Vivaldi, a brand-new red wallet you dropped down the grates, losing your taste for cilantro, dinners with friends at their summer homes. You remember new moles, making a tiny tea set out of red clay, a button that wouldn't stay clasped, pain aux raisins.

You remember years and years of Paps, the yellow ceiling in the office, an awful picture of an orchid, framed in black, metal stirrups, paper gowns, and never not holding your breath. The word *remission* comes from the Latin to send back. Nothing more.

You remember therapy, a rosemary plant, carrying an umbrella in the sun. You remember counting your lucky stars. You remember—and it wasn't so long ago now—your Cooper Union mentees asking you about motherhood and art and you, shaking your head. It is the one thing I'm least sure of, you said. I'm not sure I can speak on it except to say, Ask for help from the people who love you.

You remember when our bathtub cracked and how sometimes, you still thought you could hear Max crying and it sent you reeling. Nearly thirty years later.

You remember holding my hand on Columbus and Seventy-Fifth, walking north on the east side of the street.

You remember one time, we went to Petrossian to celebrate. What? you ask. You don't remember. Me either.

You remember Donny Hathaway and dancing in socks. I was never a good dancer, but you were. You remember knocking over a vase of white tulips, cranberry seltzer, a purple scarf, and the Asian tourists who stood in line for a photo outside the Dakota.

You remember when we decided to redo the top two floors, the jackhammer inside instead of outside. You remember the day they took out the windows that faced the street and you asked them to wait a moment. It felt like taking an outdoor shower or swimming naked. The vulnerability. So much New York.

You remember your book club, the joy of laughing with them. But also when Tammy's son killed himself. They were so close, you say, different from you and Max; there is irony in there somewhere or maybe tragedy in real life. She came the next week. You all were reading *Heartburn*. You held hands as Bea read a section. Everyone's eyes were closed.

You remember Italian lessons with the son of an opera singer at their apartment on Fifth, going to Art Basel, wearing Irene Neuwirth's latest in exchange for one of your pieces. You remember blinding lights and being on a panel and signing autographs—it was so humid—and where was Max?

But okay.

Max came to most of my readings. But he never lingered.

Your words have loosened, pooled. Let's take a break, I say. You nod without moving. I go downstairs. Be right back! I come back, more tea, but you are asleep. Your chest rises and lowers still. I'll get myself a cup, I think. Or maybe I just want to wake you. But I look back. It is possible to be both here and everywhere. You, whispering to Max as he slept. You, getting into the bath. You, cracking an egg. You, smelling a red tulip with only half its petals in the Park. You, body stiff, your laughter like tap dancing against the gray as you wade into cold November water.

Don't go is what I want to say.

Remember when you were stronger, braver than me? Remember all that fighting you did? I never could have fought like that. You built an actual loft inside your studio. You tied my ties even when Max had us broken and I was so very wrong. You wore purple lipstick and a silver gown when you were honored. But the honor is everyone else's, you know. I know.

Don't go.

Remember all those nights we'd lie in bed? Are you awake? Are you awake? We'd turn on the lights in the kitchen and make toast with blackberry jam.

You remember when the Style section photographed our brownstone and the chrysoprase you wore around your neck. You remember the stylist who said she wanted to be you when she grew up. You remember making her tea and wishing she would throw her phone into the trash.

You remember when I was nominated for the award I'd always wanted. When I lost, we walked around the Village and stopped at a street corner where we'd fought so many years before. You remember when I won it two years later. We were in Norway for the first time.

You remember the meeting when our financial adviser told us we'd be more than fine. Even if you didn't ever sell another painting, I didn't sell another book.

You remember that was the year we got the house in Orient. You remember that the city never bored us but: something.

Suddenly, you sigh. You stop. Is it just me or is your voice changing by the moment? It feels wispier, drier, like something flaking off in pieces. An old letter. I make cups with my hands as if I might catch it, the words.

Soon, you fall asleep or something like it. I'm here, I tell you because they say to always offer. I'm right here.

It is dark outside. I can see only the outline of your face, or maybe it is from memory. I am next to you, feet under your bed, unsure if my eyes are open or closed, if I've remembered to breathe, to move, to eat. I ride on your words like a wake.

Jane? I whisper.

33

Jane, you remember summer skin, don't you? Wishing certain novels to go on forever? Max asleep in his crib on his belly, his hair matted to his head with sweat, my voice reading you Yeats on the sofa? Do you remember dreaming of a painting that you could never finish? It was white. I think I remember you saying that once.

What about the sound of a garbage truck? Do you remember watching a bubble become ice on sand? And our tradition of Black Forest cake on the first day of daylight savings? My first book of poetry? You always said it was your favorite because of that line about doves. You'd never read, you said years ago, anything so true and so dear.

Thank you.

Last week, I remember, you told me that you suddenly remembered the North Star—and waking up, wondering if you were still alive.

In the dark, just the two of us, I sing you a song that I hope you remember. It is the one that always got stuck in your head. Who was it? Bruce Springsteen? I can't remember. I just want you to have company. Something to carry with you. Something to carry you.

I stand up. My knees just about break. I open the window for a brief moment to let the air in. I think, You should have the salt breeze that you loved so well. When you feel it, a smile spreads over your face. Even I can see that. Even now. My heart lurches. For a moment, I forget the direction in which we were going. I forget what I was trying to say.

Don't get cold.

I hold your hand under the blanket and squeeze to remind you. To remind me. To ward off anything that tries to get between.

Jane, I hope you remember that you were never alone. Not when I was in the kitchen. Not when I went for a book, a walk. Not when I stood in the closet and held my own face, told my own self it was all right.

I hope you remember that before I left your side, I always checked your water, that you had a telephone nearby, and all the times I put my hand against your chest because it is this thing that you and I have done for years. There is a charge passed from me to you. There is not so much a beating now, but maybe footsteps when the lights are out.

Tiptoe. Thump thump.

I fall asleep on the floor next to you, my head on a blanket that smells like you.

When I wake up, my hand is in yours. You are squeezing it.

Abe? you say. There's more. This is it.

I want to ask you if you're talking about precision or time. Instead, I close my eyes. In this way, I let you take care of me.

You remember being here, in Orient. You remember, in winter, naked roads, spayed trees. You remember, in summer, strawberry pie and black sea bass sold on the side of the road. You remember rainbow beach umbrellas, cornfields, the lady with one goat who made cheese and sold it from her car. You remember learning to preserve and pickle. Blueberry-peach. String beans. You remember the pride of the pantry. You'd never had a pantry before.

You remember when we bought this house—how grand it seemed, and also forgotten, powdered with cracked windows, giant doors, mint shutters. You remember a tall bluff, like the Pacific Northwest, wind-whipped trees, salt like acetone, water on three sides.

You remember thinking, or maybe I do: Of all the places, this one. The gentle davening of gentle tides.

You remember finding a tomahawk in the backyard, lining an entire wall with sea glass, painting the foyer a color called black green.

You remember having pillows made from blankets we'd found in France, Mexican pottery in the kitchen, a drawer for our spices, warming hooks for our robes, feeling the weather in a way you just can't in the city—all the senses. You remember sweet peas, clouds, buds, thunder and rain.

You remember that was around the time, on East Eighty-Eighth Street, visiting an old friend, I was mugged in broad daylight. You remember they used a pipe on my knees. You remember I didn't care about the wallet, the cards, the money, only the notes from you, the Chinese fortunes, and the coffee card: one away from a free cappuccino, I'd said.

You remember it was around then, too, that the cancer came back. It was a shock; it was inevitable. You remember you'd just gotten your AARP card in the mail and how we joked about that. What choice did we have?

You remember Max sending flowers. When he came, he brought bags upon bags of food, but he didn't stay long. I don't blame him, you say. How could I blame him?

You remember sleeping till four in the afternoon, headaches, two rounds of chemo and a new pill that made you see everything more pink. You remember feeling that you couldn't fight in the same way anymore. You remember getting out of breath, just standing. You remember needing sunglasses until bed.

You remember, that time, it spread to your pelvis, the nodes, and a particular one near the base of your spine, and aorta. You knew because your right leg kept going numb. That is a thing that happens. Goddamn it.

You remember Dr. Isham and knitting him a scarf and a hat for his new baby not so he'd give you special treatment but because he stood like he was chilled.

I remember you making everyone kinder, softer, better. Always.

You remember how everything hurt. Your bones. Your belly. Your heart.

You remember remembering the things that kept you holding on. You had dry cleaning to pick up and the *New Yorker* subscription that needed renewing and a half a lemon, unwrapped, in the fridge. You remember wanting to learn how to do a diagonal basketweave stitch and make butternut squash ravioli from scratch. And Max.

You remember during treatment, everything a circle: the dreaming, the not dreaming, the walking, the not walking. Soft socks making soft sounds on the soft carpet, something always half-eaten and the wrong temperature on the nightstand. You remember everything felt halved.

You remember the time you met Bea in the Park—you had to take a cab—and she told you to make a little bit of art every single day—a purple squiggle, a black thumbprint, your name inside out and backward—and you did. And maybe that's why. She had become a professor whom students dedicated their life's work to. She is magnificent, isn't she? you say. You beam.

You remember when you went into remission but how you felt we'd aged anachronistically. Your insides were different. Mine, too, in a way. And something about time travel et cetera on the page.

You remember the relief and the terror of growing older: your skin changed first, bones second, teeth third. You remember clothes fitting differently not because you were thinner but because you were less. You remember every time David visited, no matter how young his boyfriends were, or maybe because of that, being alarmed by how old he appeared. And what that meant of us too. Time moves in one direction and isn't that really, really something.

You remember when sand started bothering your feet.

You remember sudden dangers in everything: car alarms, snow, stairs. You remember using more bandages, Dr. Isham telling you how you really needed to watch the thorns. You remember not watching the thorns and bringing him a thorny bouquet of flowers and smirking. He slathered you with ointment and laughed and he showed you photos of his kids on his phone. You asked him how his wife was doing with young ones, and genuinely wondering. Fine, he said. She's a trooper.

You remember a series of dreams: a car, a fireplace, a scruffy white dog who sat on your feet. You remember we discussed moving over chow mein from Shun Lee—and selling the brownstone, same day, full ask to a couple with three kids. They paid in cash.

You remember we moved in the spring. You remember butterflies from the porch, sun tea, your studio upstairs, besotted with light. You remember road and water and light like a photograph here, edited. You remember clouds that don't cloud the sky.

You remember joining the Y, a swim cap, salted pickled rye and French cheese, a tab at the local bookshop. We became board members of our little museum, joined the tiny yacht club in Orient so we could meet new friends for turkey sandwiches and vinho verde.

You remember that everything felt easier, sweeter, slower. We read Wendell Berry every morning. We wore hats to bed. We lived side by side, like two swings in the sunset. Kicking our legs, making everything move, together. The scene goes by.

I make us toast and tea. From downstairs, I call to you a dozen times. I'm coming right back, Jane! Just a minute, my love! Toast en route! Tea too!

Alas: your mouth is too dry for bread. The whole thing becomes paste, very white. Don't choke. Are you hungry? For heaven's sake, I think. I should have known.

You remember when you started giving your art away. You can't take it with you is something you've always said. So much was placed, sold, but people were always asking you for something small: any little doodle or inking. You always said yes.

You remember putting away certain pieces for Max.

You remember wearing sweaters most of the year.

It's a funny thing. Days cannot get longer except in the words. And yet.

I remember one day, on the porch, holding your hand, your unsick hand. I asked you where you wanted to go, what you wanted to do. You remember saying you just wanted to stay here for longer. I remember. You were healthy then. But still, Yes, I thought. I think.

Take a break. A breath. That feeling when you don't want a novel to end but this.

Every word must count.

34

You remember you knew when it came back the third time (bones and liver, lymphs in your neck). It was less than a year ago now. You remember it not so much as recognizing something as sensing something gone. A little bit of life, maybe. You were just getting into shibori again.

You remember we were growing four varieties of lettuce, pickling strawberries, radishes, lemons, cukes. We had given up caffeine, gotten into local politics, hosted poker on Thursdays; you'd mastered pasta. It felt like a golden era, coasting, didn't it? You remember it felt like you forgot to remember. You remembered only to forget. That's human nature, is what your therapist said. When things are working correctly.

It came in the night, or it came in the day. You can't remember. You remember one day bleeding into the next. Don't say *blood*.

You remember the feeling in your stomach, your shoulders, out of nowhere. Not pain exactly but not not-pain either. Like what?

Presence. An acorn, an orange segment, a thumbtack without the point. You knew what to expect.

You remember lying awake beside me, wishing for the universe to talk back. You remember that your mother slept on her roof in Baghdad's sweltering months. You remember tears filling your ears as you didn't sleep. You couldn't. How much time.

You remember it wasn't that you were afraid of me living without you. I would be okay. Or Max. He would, even more so. You just didn't want to leave this. You remember the longing was physical. You thought of your garden. It is a ridiculous cliché and yet.

You remember every time we'd go to the city for appointments, we'd make our way to the Park. Coffee, hot dogs, dog walkers, saxophone somewhere, a wagon full of kids and two teachers, reminding them to keep their hands to themselves.

Sometimes, as we sat, you leaned on me so hard that I wondered about my own strength.

You remember when we stopped going to appointments.

You remember wishing, sometimes, that Max would just show up.

You remember twice, always early in the morning, calling him and hanging up. There was something you wanted to tell him. Once, it was about your mother. A memory for him to carry with him. The other time, you're not sure. But you hung up.

There is nothing I could say, you say.

I'll tell him, I say. Anything you want.

You remember holding me in my sleep so tightly that I'd wake and ask if you were all right. You couldn't get the words out. You remember staying awake just to be here, watch the sky, the moon full again, waning again, full again. Again.

It is hard to breathe.

You remember sitting on our shower bench and wishing. Or maybe: even dying can feel like melodrama. And yet, in some ways, death is most anticlimactic of all. We just do.

For a moment, you stop remembering. I wonder if you want to take a break. But I do not suggest it. Instead, I put my hand on your cheek. I put your hand on mine.

What else? I hear myself saying. And again, I wonder who is holding up whom.

You remember being propped up, bathed, spoon-fed yogurt, tea through a straw. You remember remembering that it wasn't so long ago that you picked blueberries for hand pies, made the dough from scratch. You remember making sounds from the pain that you couldn't believe were yours. You'd look around. I'd tell you it was all right.

You remember our love like a river, a rock, a fountain, a rainbow. You remember it as an August evening, the holidays, the first spring day. You remember it as sparkle, or maybe I do. Why not? We had our bumps. You remember it wasn't always easy, but so often it was. How lucky are we? Sometimes, over the top is just enough.

You remember one night, you walked around the neighborhood till morning just to remember it. It was before Christmas. Everything was lit, including the sail loft on stilts by the sea. You were sick then, but you did it. I stood at the window and waited, held my breath, and when I saw you coming up the driveway, I ran so you might hold on to me. But I held on to you.

Jane, do you want me to take over?

35

You don't remember when you slipped into somewhere else. A place where I couldn't join you. A place away. You couldn't hear me or sense me. I'd come in and out of the room. I'd take your hand. Jane. Jane? Good morning.

I'd put my hand under your nose for your breath, which seemed not to belong to you but to a tiny, resting mouse.

You don't remember how your face went different then. Underwater, atmospheric. Like a pink cloud at dusk. Your eyes went rounder. As if they weren't connected to your heart but placed on top like a snowman's, two stones.

You don't remember staring as if you could see through the wall, down 25, the LIE, the FDR, and through the Park, where the sun was just setting. And how it looked, unbelievably to us both, as if the buildings themselves sustained the light.

You don't remember that on the days when I was most desperate, I'd bring the photo album onto your lap. Here we are at Yellowstone, with your night-blooming cereus, at the Zabelskis'. Your dress matched my tie. Here you are with Max. You can only see his back. Here you are, turning toward me just to smile before looking up at the canopy of elm trees in the Park's Mall, gleaning something useful, something staggering about shadow.

You don't remember when I'd beg you to eat.

You don't remember that I wiped yogurt from your chin, mucus from your nose, changed the bedpan. And you didn't turn away. You didn't look at me either. You just kept looking wherever you'd been. As if what was happening was fated, inescapable.

You don't remember when I begged you to prove me wrong that you were no longer mine. You don't remember how sometimes I squeezed your hand too tightly as if it might bring you out.

You don't remember when Max came and told me I was giving you too much medicine. You don't remember that I told him that he didn't have a say. Was he a doctor now too?

Enough.

You don't remember when I came back to you and apologized for him, for any part I had in all of it, any of it.

Instead, I remember you at twenty-three, eyes the color of autumn, a dimple spooning the side of your mouth. I remember you knew things I didn't, saw things I hadn't, and I could tell from your face. I remember wanting to be close to you as if you were the shore or a warm cat. I remember thinking that it was your strength, your ardor, that might offer a safety net for us both.

I remember you with blue paint on your pants, your mother's gold bangles on your arms, white sandals with two straps against your skin. I remember you swimming on your back, walking with your face up, reading, your hand making shade. I remember you painting, drawing, smudging. I remember you focused, with your lip curled. I remember you asleep, ink on the intimate side of your arm.

I remember you peeling a tangerine, walking toward me in sleet. I remember you filling a photo album, eating lentil soup with a small spoon.

I remember you soaping the sponge, using a straw. I remember you letting sand fall between your fingers. I remember you opening a door to a library. I remember you looking for a lamp switch and keeping your fingers to it even after the light was on.

I remember you walking fifteen steps ahead of me, and talking to me still. I remember how you'd hum a tune only you found true.

I remember you in ecstasy. I remember your doctor's visits. I try to forget them.

I remember that we got through the hardest things together. How it could have been otherwise. How we still found each other's bodies, capsized, underwater, but moving, for so so many years.

I remember how we used to sit on the benches outside Strawberry Fields, watch the dogs, scruffy, skinny, short, stocky, and remember. It wasn't so long ago now. Do you remember?

And, Jane, do you remember all those things you taught me? How to draw a rabbit, be patient, peel a grape with my teeth. Remember how you liked your tea? Remember how you liked your mornings? Remember how you used to love when I rubbed your back with the heels of my hands? Remember that Max was lucky to just be near you, okay? I want you to remember that.

For so long, the remembering kept you alive. You cannot turn back time on the page. That's what flashbacks are for. And we don't have the luxury of that. No matter how evocative the language, the life.

It is evening again today. And again. Tonight, I put my whole self on your whole heart. Cannot break you. No time for pronouns. Or to give breath. Warm body. Cannot be warmed.

But I can lie here. I can remember. I find the words to say that all this, language even, is finite. Breaths, body, steps too. My hand on your shoulder. Church bells. Songs. The ending point is distinct.

But love. Memories. A promise I whispered to you once. You were asleep.

I'll say it again. Nothing could stop it. Upend it. End it. Nothing. It goes on.

Okay, okay, I say out loud. It isn't a plea or a promise or a poem. The repetition, as you liked to say about art, is not for the sake of itself.

It might be a chorus. Repeat only for emphasis.

A story must only be as long as a piece of string.

The room is silent and the instinct remains.

The room is dead silent.

I listen. Hear it all. The breeze. My heart. The body's language goes on. And story.

Jane?

Love like driving with a nest of new doves on the hood.

The blanks are nestled in between everything. The non-sounds are deafening. Sometimes, the less sound, the more feeling. The more feeling, the more feeling.

The world flickers. The last sentence turns off everything. Ends on a moment. Stillness sets in. I count backward from a hundred. Forward to the end. If you are still counting, you are still breathing.

If you are still breathing, you are still listening. If you stop breathing: that's how you know.

The difference between stopping and ending is that one is intentional. Anything can be a beginning if you say it right. Any moment can be the end.

36

When Abe loses Jane, he comes to the Park alone. She isn't buried here, of course. She isn't actually everywhere. Still, he waits for her. The purple tulips twinkle in the sun. He lifts his face toward the sky. He wishes the weather would warm him. Or something. He eats half his strawberry frozen fruit—he's had only toast all day—but it's making him cold. Soon, a scruffy white dog with two sets of eyelashes comes and sits by him. He's not usually a dog person—Jane was—but Abe gives her the rest of his ice pop. He asks first. But then, wait. He hears the owner telling the dog to say thank you. His heart stops. You said her name was Jane? It can't be. The dog named Jane licks her lips; she leans into Abe. She is sitting on his feet, keeping him warmer. Her eyelashes are quivering in the wind. She is smiling, isn't she? Does she always do that? Either

way, Jane the dog is breathing, staying, smiling, taking in the day.
Jane used to do the very same. And when she leaves, and Abe is
alone again, he holds his own hand. It is sticky, and trembling.
He looks toward the sun and thanks someone. God? The leaves?
Jane?

37

JANE

On the day that Jane is first diagnosed—cervical cancer, late stage II—she walks to the Park. The office is on Sixty-Seventh and Madison and Jane goes one block west, two north, and enters between the green benches, burdensome stone walls, a broken flowerpot and a fan of discarded business cards, gray and wet, stuck to the pavement like skin.

How much of Jane's life, Jane wonders, has been spent entering and leaving this Park? Max in the stroller, hand in hand with Abe, alone, between runners and unhoused, green sandaled, bundled, elated, distraught, recently rushing south to north, to meet Bea for jam pastries, to tell her, because Bea has always understood, about how the art has made Jane feel whole again. After so long and so much doubt.

Today, Jane is wearing old brown leather boots and a cashmere scarf that Abe did not buy her. She bought it for herself. Still, she is cold and uncomfortable. The doctor's office must have been sixty degrees and she shivered for the entire appointment—no one to cover her. Even now, the chill won't quit. The day is raw. Jane is suddenly aware of the sky (darkening), the cyclists (speeding), and the cobblestones (so tricky). It wasn't this way before. Safety only flourishes in indifference, she thinks. And she is bleeding again. She can feel it.

At the office, Jane asked the doctor if it would have helped had she come in earlier.

How much earlier? the doctor asked.

A few months, Jane said. When I started feeling unwell.

The doctor shook his head.

Cancer started long before that, he said. Let's take it from here. Let's see how we go.

At first, Jane was in disbelief. As in, not that she didn't believe him. She did. She knew. But it's like trying to wrap string around snow. Nearly impossible to conceptualize oneself not living as one is. Jane can walk and talk and breathe and sneeze and make things with string still. And yet, there must have been some loose plastic rattling, she thinks, that she refused to get up and address all this time. One must suspend one's disbelief. One must believe in the possible even when it feels impossible.

Jane passes a man selling hot dogs, steaming and pungent. She heads quickly north and then west. She is not sure of where she is going; she only hopes not to bump into Abe, or Max with Abe's mother, on a little adventure after school.

Or Alice.

Jane has no idea what she'd tell any of them—where to even

begin? But she knows that she is not ready to say anything yet. She wants to wait, first, for something to settle in her body, some engine to shut off. She is ratcheted up. What if she waited for a good moment? A positive note? When might that be?

For a moment, Jane looks up to the sky as if for answers. There are none. Just black clouds, sick with weather. She walks slowly. She will not be rushed. She sets the pace now, she thinks. Time thickens. Coasting comes to a sudden halt.

For a moment, Jane stops. She leans against a tree, needs to catch her breath. It is like this more and more, lately: the air thins; Jane gasps. She used to be able to hold her breath longer than anyone. She'd search for shells on the sea floor for so long that Abe would wonder if she'd gotten lost. She'd come up with a fistful, panting, yards and yards down the beach—and make them into a collage of a school of fish and waves.

From the tree, Jane watches a mother and her son, maybe a bit older than Max, but with the same mop of hair, white-white teeth, and legs so long they seem to belong to a different animal: flamingo, gazelle. They are holding hands, mother and son, not quite skipping but not quite not. Every once in a while, they lock eyes to corroborate or conspire. The mother laughs and touches her heart now. The boy puts his head into his mother's belly.

Jane longs for such affection. It makes her own belly hurt.

So often Jane has wondered about being a different mother from the start. What if her mind and body hadn't betrayed her? What if she'd been able to come to the Park every sunset, Max swaddled to her chest, a big brown coat pulled all the way around them? Would that have changed things?

Do you feel that? she'd say of the sunset to her boy. Do you hear that? she'd say of the birds. She'd kiss his downy head, rock him to a song that only they could intuit.

They might have been head to belly now. And maybe she and Abe . . .

What then?

Jane thinks of her art. She can imagine a piece she hasn't yet made: a giant steel sculpture, flat, except for a swath of nearly imperceptible textured flowers on the front. You'd have to squint to see them, get close, and only then. And only in certain light. And only if you're lucky. Art gives only to those wide open.

It heartens her that Max seems so interested in art already: shapes and pencils and glue. If that is the only thing.

For a moment, Jane wonders how much art is left for her. How many long, hot showers? Crisp apples? Pots of tea? Will she ever fly to a place with blue-blue water again? Will she ever swim? Ride on inspiration like a buoyant wave? Will she ever be so lucky?

Will Max hug her? Will she ever let Abe?

The doctor could not say.

Perhaps, Jane thinks, if she'd been the kind of mother she'd hoped, she wouldn't be counting in this way. Perhaps disappointment is as insidious a chemical as the cancer cells themselves. It has poisoned them both. It strikes her then that perhaps she will not die from disappointment, a wound, a bus, her heart even. Her heart is a fist, full of disappointment.

The cancer grew, she thinks, when her studio door was shut.

Jane reaches into her bag for a tissue but there isn't one. Instead, she finds the almonds from Abe. She stuffs them into her mouth, one by one, then in one fell swoop. She chews hard and fast as if scrub-bing something clean in her head. She nearly chokes.

She wants to thank Abe, despite everything, but he isn't here.

Soon, there is a runner in his thirties, whizzing by.

For a moment, Jane tries to imagine Max at that age, years from now, not running and not alone but with his own son maybe, throwing a ball, sharing a pint of figs. Jane thinks, as she finds her way back to the Lower Loop: Max is sharing a picnic blanket with a wife and child. They are eating cheese and apples. There is a red kite and a soccer ball and a Frisbee nearby. They've just come from MoMA. Max has so much time to grow into that kind of person, doesn't he?

Please.

Long legs. White teeth.

How many more hours will Jane have with him? How many more slammed doors?

And Abe?

There will be good times, she thinks, closing her eyes, rubbing them with her thumb and forefinger. Jane is curled around Max on the floor. Their apartment is warm and safe, plenty of carpets, beef leftovers in the fridge, Jane's art on every surface, heavy or precar-ious, full of color, string or metal or clay; there is a plant, watered and well by the window in a terra-cotta pot. Abe is waiting for her in the living room, hands in his lap in the dark. He wants to help. He is such a brilliant writer. He has worked so hard. And for them too. He has put the wings on her back.

There has been so much good between them, Jane thinks. Jane doesn't have to remind herself of that or rouse it. She feels it like sun.

Jane has been far from perfect.

She is almost to the other side of the Park. For a moment, the clouds drop and there is a wild orange glow that opens up the fist in Jane's chest. She thinks of Abe. It is not forgiveness that she feels so much as surrender.

Was it the art that pulled Jane away or Jane herself? She was so desperate to find land again after Max. To heave onto shore, warm and solid. To get up, no belly over which to hoist. To make her way, strong legs, intact insides, big heart, heavy but hopeful, no wings. To come out alive.

Jane had to make something.

Without art, there is no daydream, forgiveness, trust. There is no ground, unwavering. There is no Abe even. Just sea. And Jane adrift, maybe even swallowed down.

It seemed like the only way to stay alive, to make things, didn't it? But what about now? The art cannot save Jane exactly. Though maybe Max's baby body could have. Or maybe more dinners with Abe. Or warm sheets, the three of them together, reading a book, making a fort, laughing laughing laughing.

Or maybe not.

When the lights go off, the sculptures are alone in the dark.

The art alone is life-giving in the moment but it never promised to give more life.

Whereas love.

Maybe Jane can save her life twice, she thinks. It is a messy business, illogical and bloody. Jane touches her heart. She isn't crying. She isn't laughing either. What she feels, perhaps, is life coursing through her still. It is like lightning, gasoline, prayer.

Jane is dizzy, breathless. She focuses on one foot in front of the other to keep from falling, and also running too fast. She longs to be with her family then—if not to tell them that she loves them,

then to just sit close, palpitations in her heart and fingers from hope
and anticipation and inspiration—and to draw for them a picture of
all the things they hold so dear. A picture of everything. All that
she can do.

Draw love.

ACKNOWLEDGMENTS

This book took a long time and there were many times it seemed it would not be a book at all. It absolutely would *not* exist without the following human beings I am so deeply lucky to love.

First and foremost, to Alex Forden: I would have given up. I don't have the words but you know them. For absolutely everything and more, thank you. I love you so.

To Stella Sands, who goes through every up and down, book-related and otherwise, with us: six indigo hearts forever. You are TBITWTDMTWNBTY. Love you love you love you. Thank you.

To Ula Jane: love is inspiration, motivation, and more—and heavens almighty, this love is the best. Thank you for being you, exactly. I love you without end.

To Shnoog, my Bea: ours is a love story too. I am so grateful for you and your safe space. Thank you. To my Ladybirds: you have kept me going, laughing, crying. You are inspirations, every one of you. Thank you. To Gaga, Grace Braaksma, for your incredible sunshine always. I couldn't have done it without you. Thank you.

To Crystal Meers, for the walks that were medicine and for your unwavering thoughtfulness. Thank you.

To Lois Markham, Bub, for your incredible eye and diligence. Thank you so very very very much.

To Lizzy Moore 1234: we both know this book would live in a drawer if not for your insight. I am so lucky to call you mine, all these years. Thank you. To Alex Gilvarry, for reading this book when it wasn't this book and believing in it despite itself. Thank you.

To Susie Merrell: for reading so many early drafts and keeping the faith. Thank you. To Sally Susman: for reminding me that I know things about writing, and for your cherished friendship. Thank you.

To Colum McCann: forever and always thank you thank you. To Margery Mandell: you are in these pages and will be in everything I write for the rest of time. Gosh, you did so much for so many of us. Thank you.

To the people who have made the work, the actual work, possible with a small child: my gratitude is immense. To Ana: you gave me a calm mind every time you were with Ula, which meant, in turn, I could write. Thank you. To Ms. Ann Marie, Ms. Krista, Ms. Megan, Ms. Renee, Ms. Stephanie: your care for Ula, the safety, the delight, gave us both wings. Thank you.

To Maya: how lucky I am to be with you. Thank you for being so wonderful, every single step. And to the super-duper crew at Dutton: John Parsley, Christine Ball, Ryan Richardson, and more. Thank you thank you thank you.

To the Central Park Conservancy: for what you do, all the

facts, the statistics, the stories, but also the tremendous beauty. Thank you.

Finally, to the magnificent and brilliant Julie Barer: you believed in me—ugh, it is so corny but *who cares*—when I did not believe in myself. That is the truest and I will never ever forget it. Thank you.

What a gift it is to write. But, oh, what a gift it is to write with fierce love at one's back. That is the greatest story of love I can imagine. Love as a force in the world from the first word to the very very last.

We did it. Thank you thank you thank you.

ABOUT THE AUTHOR

Jessica Soffer is the author *This Is a Love Story* and *Tomorrow There Will Be Apricots*. She grew up in New York City, attended Connecticut College, and earned her MFA at Hunter College. Her work has appeared in *Granta*, *The New York Times*, *Real Simple*, *Saveur*, *The Wall Street Journal*, *Vogue*, and on NPR's *Selected Shorts*. She teaches creative writing to small groups and in the corporate space and lives in Sag Harbor, New York, with her family.